Maggie Malone and the MOSTLY magical boots

Jenna McCarthy and Carolyn Evans

sourcebooks
jabberwocky

Published by Sourcebooks Jabberwocky, an imprint of Sourcebooks, Inc.
P.O. Box 4410, Naperville, Illinois 60567-4410
(630) 961-3900
Fax: (630) 961-2168
www.jabberwockykids.com

Library of Congress Cataloging-in-Publication Data is on file with the publisher.

Source of Production: Versa Press, East Peoria, IL
Date of Production: March 2014
Run Number: 5000907

Printed and bound in the United States of America
VP 10 9 8 7 6 5 4 3 2 1

We dedicate this book to our respective children. Raising you all is an out-of-this-world adventure, every single day. Never forget that you get to choose how big you want your lives to be.

Table of Contents

Jenna McCarthy and Carolyn Evans

Chapter 1

When I Get the Worst News of My Entire Life

"It's going to be fine," Stella tells me. "Really."

I try to nod my head up and down like I agree, but the tears pouring down my face are a pretty good sign that I *don't* agree. Like, at all.

"How…can…they…*do*…this…to…me?" I sob between huge, heaving breaths. A tangle of strawberry blond curls sticks to my wet cheeks. I am a total mess.

"Maggie, your dad didn't lose his job on purpose, you know," Stella says softly, removing a ringlet that's plastered to my neck.

I absolutely love Stella, but sometimes she acts like she knows everything. *About everything.* Like the time she insisted that her bowl of Lucky Charms had a green heart in it when everybody knows that the hearts only come in pink.

"Look! Look! I got a green heart in my Lucky Charms!" she shouted one morning after a sleepover at my house. "That's soooo lucky for me! I'm going to save it and wear it on a necklace!"

I tried explaining that her green heart was just a messed-up green clover, but she wouldn't listen. Some things you just have to let go. And I do, because we've been friends since before we were born (and our moms have been BFFs since forever) and she really is a great friend. Like, get this: when that green heart shriveled up to half its size but still had plenty of good luck left in it, she gave it to me—not Ginger Poole, not Alexis Parker—*me*.

"Of course I know he didn't *lose his job on purpose*," I practically shout at her. "But it still stinks. I've gone to Sacred Heart since kindergarten! How would you like to start a brand-new school in the middle of the year? And I don't know a single kid who goes to Stinkerton Middle School!" The name is actually

2

Randolph J. Pinkerton Middle School, or RJPMS or sometimes just Pinkerton for short. But everybody at Sacred Heart calls it Stinkerton.

"Wait, yes you do. Doesn't Izzy Zimmerman go to Stinkerton?" Stella asks, yanking around thirty tissues out of the box and handing them to me.

Stella and I are in Ranger Girls with Izzy Zimmerman—or at least we *were*, until Izzy got kicked out for stealing all the cookie money our troop raised. I went all over the neighborhood one day in the pouring rain wearing my too-tight ladybug rain boots to sell seventy-seven boxes of those suckers. Izzy only sold four lousy Snickerdoozles, all of them to her mom. At least I got a merit badge.

"Oh, sweet," I say sarcastically, wiping my face with a huge wad of tissues. "The one person I know at my new school is a criminal. This is going to be great. Just great."

"You know what? I just remembered I heard she got expelled," Stella says. "Apparently stealing cookie dough wasn't her only offense. Get it? Cookie *dough*?"

I know Stella is just trying to help, but I can't even manage a smile. I bury my head in my pillow and groan like I'm about to face the end of the world. Because in a way I am. The end of *my* world, at least.

"Let's see what Magic 8 Ball says!" Stella shouts, grabbing the worn black orb from my nightstand. The screen is pretty scratched up, and the inside usually gets stuck on "it is certain," so we like it better than the app on Stella's iTouch. That thing is always saying "ask again later." How annoying is *that*? If I'm asking right now, I'm pretty sure I need the answer, like, now.

Stella opens my closet door and pulls out the black magician cape I got the year we were twin vampire bats for Halloween. Stella always wears it when we consult the Great Eight.

"Come on, Stella, that cape is ridiculous," I say. I snatch the ball out of her hand and toss it—hard— toward the trash can next to my desk. Of course I miss by about half a mile. It's just that kind of day.

"There's no such thing as magic, anyway," I add.

"And that thing's just a dumb old toy. When we don't like the answer, we just ask it again until we get the one we want. Stupid pretend magic can't help me now. *Nothing* can help me now. My life is ruined."

"Hey, what about me?" Stella asks, her huge brown eyes filling with tears. Stella is the exact opposite of me, at least in the looks department. I've got what my mom calls a "buttermilk complexion" (I've never seen freckly buttermilk, but whatever), and Stella has skin the color of a perfectly toasted bagel. My head is covered with unruly reddish-blondish ringlets that tend to grow up and out before they grow down, which is why I only get my hair cut every few years. Right now, it's about halfway down my back when it's dry, and I can practically sit on it when it's wet. Stella's hair is so black it's almost *blue*, and it's raw-spaghetti-straight and cut into a super-neat bob. One time, we set her hair in my mom's tiny hot rollers and left them in all afternoon. When we took those curlers out, there wasn't even one tiny bend on her whole head. How can that happen?

It's got to be some sort of medical mystery, if you ask me.

"Did you ever think about how *my* life's going to change?" Stella demands. "Nothing is going to be the same anymore. Everybody at school knows us as Maggie-and-Stella. I bet there are people who have no idea which one of us is which! Sure, I know everybody at Sacred Heart—but I'm not going to have *my* best friend around either." A tear slips down Stella's face, and she quickly wipes it away.

"I'm sorry, Stella," I say, hugging her as hard as I can. "I know it stinks for you too. I just can't even believe this is happening. This is without a doubt the most horrible day of my whole entire life."

The most pathetic part is I have no idea how much worse my life is about to get.

Chapter 2

When History Strikes Me Down at Stinkerton

I am standing at the bottom of the gigantic set of stairs leading up to RJPMS. I feel like I'm inside a massive pinball machine, getting jostled by kids bumping into me from all sides. Sacred Heart had a whopping 242 students, and that was from kindergarten all the way through the twelfth grade. My new school (ugh, I can't stand saying that!) has that many kids in *one grade*. It's a zoo here. An absolute zoo. With no zookeeper in sight.

As much as I complained about having to wear a uniform at Sacred Heart, it sure made things a lot easier. I changed my clothes at least fifteen times this morning, finally settling on jeans and a plain gray sweater. My outfit may be drab, but at least it's not offensive or anything. You should see how some of these kids are dressed. I thought people only wore stuff like this in the movies or on that *Don't Wear That* show on TV. There's one girl in about five-inch high heels and a skirt shorter than some of my bathing suit bottoms, and a guy in a T-shirt so ripped up it looks like he got in a fight with a tiger. My mom would have a complete conniption.

I navigate my way through a sea of kids as I search for my locker, B163. I just pray that it's not a bottom locker. Bottom lockers are the worst because you have to crouch down to get in and out, and the person above you is always dropping stuff on your head. Also? That person always acts like they're doing you some big favor to let you in there for a whole second. The only thing worse than a bottom locker is a corner locker, because then you can't open your door until the person *next* to you closes theirs, and you're always late for class.

B160, B161, B162...

There it is. B163. Bottom row. All the way in the corner.

Why me? I'm a nice person. I hold doors open for old people and brake for squirrels on my bike.

The bell rings and there's this crazy burst of activity, but I can't get anywhere near my awful corner locker so I wait. Finally I see a little opening. I squat down and crawl around a dozen pairs of legs until I reach B163. The door is stuck shut because it's all dented and crushed in. It won't budge. I set my stack of books and my lunch bag next to me so I can pull on the rusty handle with both hands.

Squish.

Yeah, that would be the sound of my cream cheese and jelly sandwich meeting the sole of somebody's boot.

"Ewww, total grossness!" screams the mouth that's connected to the foot that is now wearing my lunch. I look up for a minute so she can apologize, seeing as she just trampled my sandwich and all. I quickly realize *that's* not going to happen.

"Are you okay?" I hear another girl ask, all

concerned. Well, at least someone around here has some manners.

"Um, yeah, I'm fine—" I start, but then I realize that the concerned girl is not talking to me.

"Thanks Brit, I *guess* so. Where did that even *come* from?" says sandwich-smasher. She starts hopping on her clean foot, kicking the other one and flinging globs of pink cream cheese all over the place. I'm still sitting there on the floor, stunned, when the second bell rings.

Perfect. I'm late to my first class on my first day at this miserable school. I scoop up all of my stuff and head to the office for a late slip, tossing my bag of mush into a trash can on the way.

When I open the door to room nineteen, every single face turns to stare at me. And not one of them is smiling or looks even the tiniest bit friendly.

"You're late," says the teacher. "Where's your slip?"

"Sorry," I respond, rushing to hand it to her. "It's right here."

"Is this your first day, Miss…" she glances at the slip in her hand, "Malone?"

I nod, wishing that a huge hole would open up in the floor and swallow me in one big gulp.

"Class, this is Margaret Malone," she announces. "She's new. Welcome, Margaret. Now please take a seat. We're on chapter seven."

Margaret? Really? That's my grandmother's name, not mine! Well, technically it's mine too, but the only time anybody ever calls me that is when I'm in Big Fat Trouble, and then it's more like Margaret-Flannery-Malone-You-Get-In-Here-This-Instant. Could this day get any worse?

I spend the next forty-seven minutes half listening to what the teacher, Mrs. Richter, is saying and half worrying about what I'm going to do at lunch. I purposely packed that sandwich so I could go find somewhere quiet to eat and *not* have to deal with the lunchroom scene. Now I'm going to have to do it, because I'm not one of those people who can skip lunch. When I don't eat every few hours, I get all dizzy and cranky, and my stomach makes these really embarrassing haunted-house sounds.

Finally the bell rings, and I'm the second person out the door. I race as fast as I can to my locker and crouch down to yank on the door. In seconds, I'm surrounded by legs. At least I made it here first.

I'm rummaging through my stuff when all of a sudden, out of nowhere—*CLONK!*—someone smacks me across the head with a baseball bat. Or maybe they dropped a sack of bricks or a piano on my head; it's sort of hard to tell. All I know is that I'm seeing stars. I slump down against my locker and reach up to touch my head where it's throbbing. The last thing I remember is seeing my hand covered in blood.

Chapter 3

When I Realize I
Am Totally Invisible

When I open my eyes, I am lying on a paper-covered mattress in a tiny room. I sit up and look in a medicine cabinet mirror next to me, which turns out to be not such a great idea.

CHIMICHANGA! I look like I'm on my way to a Mummy's Revenge Halloween party. My forehead is wrapped in a mile of white bandages, and there's crusty blood all around the edges. The part of my head on top where there's no bandage is even worse. It's a huge, frizzy pouf that looks like a family of rodents got in there and built a ginormous nest right on top of my head. And what on *earth* am I wearing? I stand up so I can see myself in full, and my head starts spinning. I'm wearing an enormous red sweatshirt with Rudolph (yeah, as in the red-nosed reindeer) on the front. It hangs all the way to my knees, and the sleeves are about ten inches too long.

A woman wearing a white coat with a pin on it that says NINJA NURSE walks in.

"What happened to me?" I ask her.

"History book," she says simply.

"A *book* did this to me?" I say. At least it wasn't a baseball bat.

"Yup," she replies. "Here's your sweater. Now back to class you go. I've got seven kids waiting in line for that cot you've got there." Then she bustles right out of the room.

I get my *second* late slip of the day and trudge out of the office, heading for my hateful locker. I get all of my books just as the bell rings. Doors fly open and kids stampede out into the hallways. *Where's that hole in the floor when you need it?* But a funny thing happens—and not funny in the *Crazy Home Videos*

TV show way. Nobody even seems to see me. It's like I'm completely invisible. There are groups of girls all giggling and whispering and bunches of boys slapping each other on the back and shouting at each other over the girls' heads, and not one person notices that I'm there. Which I guess is better than the alternative.

I look down at my schedule: Spanish. At Sacred Heart, you could choose your language, so I picked Latin. Well, my mom picked it because she said it would help me with my vocabulary (and don't tell her I said this, but it totally did). I can't even ask to go to the bathroom in Spanish!

I find the classroom and slide into an empty desk in the back. I'm arranging my stuff when a pretty girl appears beside my desk. She has honey-colored hair with just the right about of bend in it and is wearing a black T-shirt that says DRAMA QUEEN in sparkly pink letters across her chest. I smile meekly at her and go back to my organizing.

But she just stands there, her arms crossed.

I feel a not-so-gentle hand shove me on the

shoulder from behind. "You're in her seat," the voice says, in a *you're such a doofus* kind of way. "Go find another one."

Seriously?

Drama Queen takes a deep breath and looks around, like she's being overly patient with me since I've totally inconvenienced her. What else can I do? I gather up my things and slide out of the seat. She takes it without a word.

Yeah, you're welcome, I think, taking a seat as far away from her as I can.

Not even the Spanish teacher seems to notice my ridiculous outfit or my banged-up head. I don't get it. If I looked like this for a skinny second at Sacred Heart, everybody and their mother would be totally freaking out. What kind of school *is* this? And what sort of people act like it's normal when someone walks around looking like the main character in *Grandma Got Run Over by a Reindeer*?

I watch the clock all through Spanish class. Lunch is next. *Gulp.* My stomach is already rumbling, and I know I'm going to have to get some food in there or I'll pass out. Again. I don't think Ninja Nurse would be too happy to see me.

The bell rings, and I get swept along in the sea of bodies rushing toward the cafeteria. Everybody just slings their books and bags outside the lunchroom door, so I do the same. Then I take a tray and slide it along the metal rail. I stare at platter after platter of brown-and-green mush, trying to figure out what exactly they could have on them.

"Corned beef hash or meatloaf?" a lady in a hairnet growls at me. "What's it going to be? You're holding up the whole line."

"Oh, sorry! Neither, please," I answer, because they both look like canned cat food. "Just some corn and fruit cocktail, I guess." Yum. That should fill me right up.

Being pushed around in the lunch line is nothing compared to walking out into the big wide-open lunchroom. I've seen this scene in way too many movies, and I'm not about to go through the whole

17

"this seat's taken" routine. I hold my tray tightly—
please don't let me trip—and walk straight out the
double doors. There's a little patio out there, and
thankfully, it's totally empty. It's gray and wet outside,
and the cement bench feels like it's made of solid ice,
but at least there's nobody to ignore me out here.

I can't believe this is my new life. When I was a
little kid, I used to wish I were invisible. But now
that I am, I'd give anything just to have things the
way they were. I sure didn't appreciate what I had
when I had it. The worst part is tomorrow is my
birthday. Twelve! The big one-two. Who cares,
right? Birthdays used to be so cool. Turning ten was
huge, because of the double digits and also finally
getting to order the full-size spaghetti at Luigi's
instead of that skimpy kid's plate. And eleven was
awesome because I finally got to ride the Super
Screamer at Splashy's Water Park. But what do you
get when you turn twelve? Nothing, that's what.
It's still another whole year until I can see a PG-13
movie, and two more years until my mom will let

me babysit. Plus, I have to spend my actual birthday here, at Stinkerton.

I pick up a banged-up metal spork that looks like it's gotten stuck in the garbage disposal a few dozen times and shove a bite of cold, mushy corn into my mouth. It would be completely bland if the tears streaming down my face didn't give it a salty flavor. *Happy almost birthday, Maggie Malone. Welcome to your worst year ever.*

Chapter 4

When I Gag on Tiny Pig Parts

After lunch, I trudge to biology class.

"Find your partner and get your pigs out of the cooler," says the teacher, Mrs. Shankshaw. She's old and brittle and has the scrunchiest face you ever saw. It's all pinched like she's outside on a bright, sandy beach and forgot her sunglasses.

Wait, did she just say *get your pigs out of the cooler*?

Just then, a kid plops a tray down on the table right next to me. On that tray—ten inches away from me—is a pig, all right. A puny, gray, totally dead pig. I turn my head away and gag.

"Does everyone have a scalpel?" Mrs. Shankshaw

wants to know. I raise my hand to tell her that no, I don't have a scalpel—or a partner, or a stomach for dead pigs—but apparently I am invisible in here too.

"Okay, great then," she continues, oblivious to me. "Your first incision will be from the top of the throat to the bottom of the umbilicus. Don't cut too deep or you'll hit the internal organs." She sits down at her big desk and focuses on a stack of papers. I lower my hand and slump down in my chair.

Not getting noticed has one advantage: I have no partner, and no pig, and nobody even cares. I spend the hour holding my nose with one hand to escape the stench—there's a reason *dead pig* isn't a popular candle scent—and sketching with the other. I draw a cute little smiling pig with wings and a halo. Finally the bell rings, and we're released from the slaughterhouse.

I make it through world history without any drama. After the day I've had so far, I consider that a major win.

My last class of the day is art. Maybe my bad luck streak is about to end. I love everything about art. I love the way colored pencils smell right after you sharpen them, and I love trying to paint a perfect circle (ever since I heard that's the hardest thing in the art world to do, I practice all the time), and I really-super-love sketching. At Sacred Heart, I won the school-wide Whiz Kids contest three years in a row, and last year, my self-portrait made it all the way to the state competition level. I got beat by some kid who built this 3-D multimedia diorama of the human body. His dad is a famous surgeon, so we pretty much know who did *that* project.

The art room looks a lot like the science lab, with big square tables instead of desks. The tables are covered with buckets of mangled paint brushes and cups of murky water. But still, there's not a dead pig in sight, which is not something I ever thought I'd be particularly thankful for.

The art teacher, Mrs. Kibble, walks around the room putting paper plates globbed with tempera paints in the middle of each table. Then she walks around again and places a bowl of sad-looking fruit next to the paints.

"As you are painting today, try to remember what we've learned about perspective and depth," she tells us.

Sweet strawberry pie, finally a break! I take a dull, chewed-on pencil from a cup and start lightly sketching the rotting fruit. I don't want to brag, but my fruit bowl looks pretty darn good. My apples might be a little bit rounder than the ones in the bowl—thanks to all of that circle practice—but I'm really happy with the sketch. When I get to the painting part, my hideous day starts to melt away. I nail the shading on that bruised-up banana *perfectly*. I think this one might even deserve a frame.

I'm just about to raise my hand to show Mrs. Kibble my work when the girl across from me lets out the biggest sneeze you ever heard. There's no build-up or anything, just this gale-force, ear-splitting *achoooooooo* that sends me jumping out of my seat. Before I can recover from the shock, she lets loose with another gust. When she does, she knocks over two of the water cups between us. I watch helplessly as the murky liquid seeps across my perfect picture, smearing those circles into unrecognizable splotches of brown goo. I can't even cry. What would be the point? It's not like it would change anything.

I crumple up my soggy picture and wonder if this is just how it's going to be from now on. The final bell of the day rings, and I've learned exactly one thing today: this Stinkerton place officially *stinks*. Sort of like my life.

Chapter 5

When the Most Boring Birthday Present *Ever* Shows Up

I've never been so happy to go home in my whole entire life. I'm just not up for unwrapping my skull at the moment, so I squish and smash and shove and eventually I get my bike helmet to fit over my mummy head. I pedal as fast as I can all the way home, trying to get some distance between me and Stinktown, USA. I'm breathless when I finally reach my street and look up to see my neighbor, Mrs. G, right before I turn into my driveway. Her last name is Galifianakis. Can you say that? I can't either—that's why she's Mrs. G to me and my little brother Mickey. I guess she can't see my bandaged-up head under my bike helmet 'cause I'm pretty sure she'd be concerned. And this Rudolph sweater? Not to be mean, but she might have one similar. Mrs. G may not have great fashion sense, but she's a wizard in the kitchen and bakes the best sticky buns you ever tasted. I live for a good sticky bun. Sometimes she's waiting with a plate of them outside for me when I get home, but today she's just sweeping her steps. Figures.

I swing my right leg over my bike and hop off. When I do, I spot a brown box next to the front door. I sling my bike between the bushes and the front porch and get a little bit excited. Maybe it's an early birthday present from Granny Malone or Aunt Fiona. Hopefully Aunt Fiona. My Auntie Fi is a world traveler. My dad calls her a professional vagabond, and I don't exactly know what that means, but I do know that she sends me supercool presents from far, far away—which is exactly where I'd like to be right now. Last year, she sent me a fancy red silk kimono from Tokyo. I keep it in the box it came in and save it for sleepovers. When I wear it, my friends are all,

"Where'd you get *that*?" and I'm all, "Oh this? Let me see if I can remember…Oh yeah, it's from *Japan*!"

The box on the porch is wrapped in brown paper tied with a string and has tons of weird-looking stamps on it. It's *definitely* from Auntie Fi. Maybe this terrible, horrible day is going to have a surprise happy ending. Maybe Auntie Fi is sending me a plane ticket to join her in some distant land—even the dusty outback of Australia or some dilapidated village in Calcutta would be better than here.

I have, like, ten thousand chores I'm supposed to be doing the minute I get home, but considering the day I've had, I think my mom will understand if I try to squeeze a little something good into my afterschool wind-down.

I rip the brown paper off the box, imagining that inside there's a bottle of fancy perfume from Paris or maybe a set of those Russian nesting dolls. But when I lift the lid, all I find is a dirty, scuffed-up pair of old cowboy boots. In boring brown. *What?* I wasn't expecting any fancy wrapping paper or anything—Auntie Fi would never hurt a tree just so your present could look pretty. But still. Somebody's dirty old boots? And then I remember: I have a stinky, scuffed-up, super-not-fun life now. So it just makes sense.

I feel bad for not being more grateful for Auntie Fi's gift. It's hard to explain, but my aunt and I have this crazy connection. When we're together, she always knows what I'm thinking, even if it's about something *totally* random. And sometimes I find stuff she's given me in places I'm absolutely positive I didn't leave them. I'm not saying it's a haunting situation or anything, but there's definitely something different about Auntie Fi. The other weird thing is that we look nearly identical, which isn't that weird seeing as we're related and everything, but nobody else in the family looks one bit like us, with our wacky red ringlets and freckly, I mean *buttermilk*, complexions.

As the best gift-giver I know, I'm a little surprised that Auntie Fi thought I would love these boots, but times are tough and like my mom says, it's the thought that counts. I scoop up the paper and the box and tuck the boots under my arm. When I do, a rolled-up piece of paper falls out of one of the boots, along with a spider that scuttles away, probably off to spread some rare, incurable disease. I pick up the paper by a corner and give it a shake. It's a note from Auntie Fi. Those are always fun! I decide to read it in my room.

I close my door and flop down on my bed, unrolling the letter.

Dear Maggie,

Happy 12th birthday! I'm writing to you from a tent in South Africa, where I'm helping a Zulu tribe figure out a way to filter the water in their village. Can you imagine not having clean water to drink? Life is hard here, but it sure is beautiful too. I wish you could see it. I bet you will someday, if you decide you want to.

Listen, I know you're wondering why Auntie Fi

sent you some dirty old boots for your birthday. Your dad will tell you it's because I'm crazy, but the truth is they were mine when I was your age. Those boots are so special that I've carried them around the world with me twice, just waiting for your 12th birthday. Turning twelve is a really big deal. You're not who you used to be, but you're not who you're going to be yet either. You're in between, and it's kind of like you've got a toe in two worlds. It's a time when YOU get to decide how big you want your life to be from now on. Does that make any sense at all? Probably not now. But it will.

I know these boots don't look like much, but trust me when I tell you that things aren't always the way they seem. You'll see what I mean.

Gotta run—there's a troop of vervet monkeys tugging on my tent! Have fun with the MMBs, and tell Frank I said hi!

xoxo,
Auntie Fi

My dad said it would happen one day, and I guess he was right: Aunt Fiona has officially lost it. *What is she talking about, having toes in two worlds? And what could that have to do with these dingy boots? What's an MMB? And who the heck is Frank?* Auntie Fi's probably eaten too many wild berries or sipped too much wacky voodoo tea at those scary tribal ceremonies she's always talking about. I pick the boots up off the floor, and a big dirt clod falls off one and crumbles all over my zebra rug. *Special? These things? Not so much. Okay, maybe they'd be cute cleaned up with my jean skirt and a sparkly tank top. I wonder if they'll even fit.* After I tap them one last time over my trash can to get the last bit of dirt off, I walk over to my tall stand-up mirror and pull the boots on.

"Hey there, kid," says a strange man who is suddenly standing *right behind me.*

Chapter 6

When Frank Freaks Me Out

"Before you freak out, I'm Frank," the man says, holding up both hands. At least he doesn't have a weapon.

I scream like a banshee (actually I don't even know what a banshee is or if they even scream, but my mom says that all the time) and twist around, not sure if I should run or fight or just keep screaming. But when I do, the man is gone.

What the heck? I back toward my door, ducking to see if he's hiding under my bed or behind my curtains. Did I just imagine him? I'm almost to my door when I see him again, in the mirror. Now he's standing *right next to me!* I scramble up onto my bed, grab my dream catcher from its nail on the wall, and hold it up in front of me like a shield. Don't ask me why—it's all I can find. I squeeze my eyes shut and brace myself for whatever is about to happen. When nothing does, I gather up enough courage to open my eyes. When I do, he's gone again.

I race to my closet, swing open the door. Nothing. He's not under my bed or behind my polka-dot chair or my curtains either. He's gone. Which leaves me with only one of two possible explanations for the mystery man in my room: either I'm totally losing it, or I have a concussion and it's making me see things that aren't there. I *did* get bonked on the head pretty good today. I'm praying that's it.

You are totally safe and not at all crazy, I tell myself. I do another thorough scan of my room, but there's no weird man in here. Freaky.

Get it together, Malone, I tell myself. *Why don't you try to pick out an outfit for your birthday? That always cheers you up.* I pull my turquoise sparkly tank and my favorite jean skirt from my dresser. I'm holding the clothes up to try to see how they look when *the man pops up right behind me again.*

"We've got to stop meeting like this, Maggie Malone," he says to me.

I wheel around, snatching up my piggy bank that's chock-full of quarters, and cock it back ready to fire when I realize he's gone again. I lean into the mirror to see if my eyes are dilated—that's a sign of a concussion, you know, which would explain everything—and when I do, there he is again. Maybe crazy runs in the family! Maybe it's in my JEANS! I drop my jean skirt to the floor.

"You catching on yet?" the strange man asks, trying to pull his faded jeans up over his big belly. Yeah, that's not happening.

"Huh?" I say, because apparently now I'm talking to the peculiar man in the mirror.

I haul my five-pound piggy bank over my head and hurl it right at him, but it just lands on the floor and shatters into about a zillion pieces.

"Really, kid?" the man says, like *you really thought*

you'd clobber me with that? "Maybe you wanna take five or something," he says, shifting his weight from one boot to the other. "I'm Frank, *Frank the Genie?* Your Aunt Fiona was supposed to mention me in the letter she rolled up in those boots you're wearing. But of course she forgot to do that, didn't she? That's Fiona for you! These things never go like they're supposed to."

"Wait, how do you know my Auntie Fi?" I ask, swinging around to face him. But instead I'm looking at my coat rack, filled with hats and scarves and belts.

"Your aunt said you were some smart cookie, but you seem to be a little slow on the uptake here, pal. No offense, of course," Frank-the-genie says when I look back into the mirror.

He gives me a crooked smile and hikes his eyebrow up on the right side. I think it's the right side—it's hard to tell since I'm looking in a mirror. I decide to stay still this time and get a better look at this guy. He seems harmless enough. He's got a hound dog kind of face with tired-looking, droopy eyes like my Uncle

Doyle. He's wearing cowboy boots that look a lot like the ones Auntie Fi just sent me, and he's got a big tarnished silver belt buckle that says "Aerosmith" on it, whatever *that* means. Maybe he's an alien, not a genie, and that's the name of his spaceship. To top it all off, he's wearing this huge, worn-out cowboy hat with hot pink and green peacock feathers on the front.

"Genies aren't real," I tell him, putting my hands on my hips. "And if they were, I don't think they'd look like *you*. No offense." *Well, they wouldn't.*

"Of course genies are real, or else you'd be standing here yapping to yourself, and that would just be nuts," Frank says to me with a big laugh. "Oh, and no offense taken. But you shouldn't believe everything you see in the movies. I don't know a single genie who wears a turban or has a pierced ear. Just so you know." He pauses to check his watch and looks a little bit freaked out.

"Oh shoot, I'm running out of time," he continues. "Do you want to know about those boots you're wearing or not?"

Chapter 7

When I Find Out Magic Might Be Real

"What about these boots?" I ask Frank, looking down at my feet.

"Those boots you're wearing," he says "are *Mostly Magical Boots*."

"These boots are supposed to be magical?" I ask with disbelief. I mean, they're not even cute!

"They're *mostly* magical," Frank says. "And from the looks of that nasty head-wrap thing you've got on, you could use a little magic. Or at least, some help picking out hats."

"For your information, I was struck down by a gigantic textbook on my first day at my rotten new school,"

I explain. "I almost bled to death right there on the dirty floor." I add this last bit for effect and because, well, I *am* a teensy bit of an exaggerator.

Suddenly I remember that Stella is supposed to come over this afternoon. She could be here any minute, so I quickly lock my bedroom door. I wouldn't want her walking in on *this* conversation!

"You wouldn't be telling a tall tale, now would you, Miss Invisibility?" Frank-the-genie asks me. How does he know about *that*?

"Look, mister, I don't know who you are or who you *think* you are," I say, staring in the mirror. "Okay, you say you're Frank-the-genie, which, can I tell you? That sounds just plain crazy. Who goes around calling himself a *genie*? I've never seen you in my entire life or in my mirror ever before, but all of a sudden, you show up and act like you know me or something. For your information, there's a word for people who watch people when they don't know they're being watched, and it is definitely not genie. It's *stalker*!"

"Somebody's got her spirit back!" Frank says with a chuckle, adjusting his cowboy hat.

"That's a good sign," he continues. "Okay, Maggie Malone, let's take it from the top. Like I was saying, those boots you've got on there are called Mostly Magical Boots—MMBs for short. They come with magical powers…a very special kind of magic."

"What kind of magic?" I ask, getting excited, because who in their right mind (assuming I am, in fact, in my right mind) wouldn't be excited about possibly being able to wiggle her nose and turn her brother into a hamster or have her room all picked up?

"First things first," Frank says. "I show up when the boots show up, and only in the mirror. You can't look directly at me or you'll turn to stone," Frank-the-genie explains.

I shut my eyelids as tightly as I can. "Yikes! REALLY?" I stammer.

"No, not really, Maggie Malone," he says with a big belly laugh. "That one never gets old. I'll never forget the look on your Aunt Fiona's face when I gave her the old *turn to stone* scare. Ever seen Edvard Munch's *Scream* painting? She looked just like that. Fiona was the last one to wear the MMBs, you know. Got 'em the day before her twelfth birthday, just like you."

"*Really?*" I ask. "That's cool! But what—"

"Let me finish," he says, cutting me off. "Where was I again?" He starts turning his head to the side as if he's tuning in to some special genie frequency.

Just then, there's a loud knock on my bedroom door. I jump about six feet.

"Maggie!" Stella yells. "Open up, buttercup! I'm already three months older than you and I'm not getting any younger out here!" Stella knows where the hide-a-key to the front door is, but my mom doesn't like her to use it so that's usually a last resort. I guess she must have been out there knocking for a while.

I look at Frank in a panic.

"This is definitely not optimal," he says, rubbing his temples and shaking his head. "I guess it's time to see if you're as sharp as your old Auntie Fi says you are. Oh, and not a word about any of this to anyone, you hear?" Frank-the-genie says as he begins to fade away like a watery reflection in the mirror.

"Use this if you need me," he tells me, leaning down and sliding a little folding pocket mirror across the floor to me right before he disappears completely. It hits the leg of my tall mirror and is still spinning when Stella gets the door open with a paper clip.

Chapter 8

When Stella Almost Busts Me

"For the love of double-decker moon pies!" Stella shouts when she sees me. "What in the world happened to you?"

"Bottom locker," I tell her, stealing a glance in my mirror to make sure there's no genie there. I can't even believe I just did that.

"Ouch," Stella says, leaning in to inspect my gash. I must not look as freaked out as I feel, because Stella doesn't seem to notice anything but my head. "Was Pinkerton as bad as everyone says?"

"Worse," I tell her, still distracted by thoughts of Frank-the-genie. Did I dream that? I want to say something to Stella, but he *did* say not a word to anyone. Would that really matter if I imagined the whole thing in the first place?

"Want to talk about it?" Stella asks—referring to Pinkerton, of course.

"Honestly, I'd rather not," I tell her, shaking my head and trying to forget about Frank.

"It was pretty lame without you at Sacred Heart too," she says, noticing my bank all busted up all over the floor. "Hey, did you get in a fight with Mr. Piggy? Looks like he lost."

"Oh, yeah, I needed some spare change for the snack machines at school—can you believe they have Twinkies for sale in there?" I say, scooping up some broken pieces and trying to change the subject.

"Hey, what's with the cowboy boots?" Stella asks, coming over to inspect them.

Flying spider monkeys, I'm still wearing the Mostly Magical Boots!

"Oh, these old things?" I say, making my way to my closet. "My mom got them at a garage sale and I was just trying them on. They're really stinky, so you might want to stay back while I take them off." I slip the boots off and stuff them up into the way back of my closet and slam the door, wondering if my face is burning red. I *never* lie to Stella!

"Well, sorry about your day," she says. "But I have something that might make you feel better." She's holding both hands behind her back. I hold out my hands and close my eyes.

"Is it chocolate?" I ask.

"Nope," Stella says. "It's the new *Tween Scene* magazine!" Stella and I love *Tween Scene* almost as much as we love watching music videos on VTV. She got a subscription for her last birthday, and the day her issue comes in the mail is usually our favorite day of the whole month.

"And the best part is," Stella adds, waving the magazine around like a crazy person, "there's a whole huge section on Becca Starr!"

We flop down on my bed side by side and start flipping through the pages. "Becca Starr is the biggest rock star on the planet and she's only fourteen years old," moans Stella, flipping through about 2,395 images of Becca plastered across the pages. "That's just two years older than us! It's totally not fair. Look at her here all hugged up with Justin Crowe. How lucky can you get?"

"You can say that again," I say. *How does one person get everything—fame, fortune, Justin Crowe—and another person gets a gash the size of Texas on her head and a weird, disappearing cowboy-genie showing up in her bedroom?*

Which reminds me: Frank's pocket mirror. I'd forgotten all about it.

"I bet she's best buds with all the coolest kids in Hollywood," I say, standing up casually and reaching down for the mirror.

"No, more like all the coolest kids in the *entire universe*," Stella corrects me. "She's huge in Japan, you know." Stella points to a picture of Becca with at least four billion adoring Japanese fans surrounding her and making lowercase letter b's with their hands—the universal "I heart Becca Starr" sign.

I nod like I'm paying attention, but I'm sort of freaking out about the mirror. I turn it over in my hands. It's gold—and maybe even real gold since it came from a *real genie* probably—and covered with sparkly jewels and has initials right in the middle. My initials. MM. I open the mirror and let out a little gasp. It's *Frank's face* in the mirror looking back at me, not mine. I snap that thing shut immediately.

"Hey, what's that?" Stella asks, eyeing the mirror.

"Oh, it's nothing," I say, trying to slide it into my nightstand drawer. "Just a birthday present from my Auntie Fi."

"A birthday present from your Aunt Fi?" Stella shouts. "Those are the *best*. Let me see it!"

The thing about Stella is that there's no point arguing with her, so I don't. I hand her the mirror, wondering if Frank is going to strike me down with a lightning bolt or something. In my defense, I haven't said a word.

"Super cool," Stella says, flipping it over front to back and inspecting it closely before handing it back to me. Thankfully she's way more interested in *Tween Scene*.

"Look at Becca getting into that limo in seven-inch high heels," Stella says, pointing at a glossy picture.

I close my eyes and try to imagine living that life. Going to glamorous parties and signing autographs and never, ever, ever having to deal with dead pig parts.

"Becca Starr has got the life," I say, shaking my head. "She can buy whatever she wants whenever she wants from whatever store she wants. She probably has a whole house full of designer shoes and dresses and fake-fur coats."

"And accessories," Stella adds. "Don't forget the accessories. Sparkly headbands, gold bracelets, diamond rings, crazy hats, feather boas… She probably has a closet just for earrings." Stella leans back on my bed, picturing the piles of Becca's bounty.

"But only the clip-on kind," I say. "I read that her body is a 'no piercing zone.'"

"Oh, no, look at her here—those are definitely real holes," Stella says, pointing to a picture of Becca in a gold evening gown with big, sparkly earrings that hang almost all the way to her shoulders.

I decide to let that one go.

"Doesn't she always look so amazing?" I ask. "Can you imagine getting your hair fixed perfectly every day and having your makeup done by real professionals, not your mom or one of those ladies with the carts in the mall?"

"And staying in fancy hotels—the ones where they bring food *into your room* on a tray? 'Here you are, Miss Malone, hamburger and French fries with a side of jellybeans, minus the gross white ones, and a chocolate milk shake to drink.'" Stella stands, pushing a pretend tray across my bed before plopping back down against the mountain of stuffed animals on it.

"She probably has tutors that come to her so she doesn't have to worry about getting bonked on the head by books if she's got a bottom locker or accidentally bringing a Number One pencil to math class," I say.

"I bet she doesn't even have to do PE *or* a science

fair project," Stella adds. "How great would that be? I'd give anything to be her—even for just one day."

"Right?" I say in agreement, shaking my head at the unfairness of it all.

"I've got to go home now," Stella says, slapping the magazine shut. "My creepy cousins are coming over for dinner."

"The ones that bring their cats over on leashes?" I ask.

"Yep, those are the ones. See ya!" We high-five and she's out the door. I lock it behind her, open my closet, and pull the MMBs down from the shelf. Then I slip them on and flop down across my bed, waiting for something *magical* to happen.

Nothing.

Stella's *Tween Scene* magazine crinkles underneath me, and I pull it out. I flip through the pages, imagining what it would be like to be a world-famous rock star.

"Ugh," I moan, turning to my side and pulling my knees in close. "I want Becca Starr's life."

Chapter 9

When I Accidentally Say Exactly the Right Thing

What's that weird rumbling noise? I wonder, sitting up in bed. *And where did these hot pink satiny sheets come from? I don't remember my mom buying—*

I don't have time to finish my thought, because all of a sudden, there's a massive earthquake and everything on the bed—including me—goes flying and lands on the floor with a huge thud.

"Are you okay?" The door whips open and a pretty lady pokes her head in. "There was a tire in the road, and the bus driver had to swerve at the last second so he wouldn't hit it. Do you need help getting up? Are you hurt? Can I get you anything? Should I call a doctor?"

Nothing this strange lady is saying makes any sense at all to me. I must be having a dream. I shake my head back and forth, trying to wake myself up.

"Becca, are you okay?" the lady says, marching right over to me and shaking me by the shoulders. "Becca, *say something*. Please!"

Becca? Did she just call me *Becca*?

"Um, yeah, I think I'm fine," I say, grabbing onto the bed and pulling myself up.

"Are you sure?" the nice lady asks, sitting down on the bed next to me. She is wearing black jeans and a purple hoodie and has a clipboard stacked with papers on it in her lap. A tag clipped to a strap around her neck reads BECCA STARR STAFF. Beneath that it has the name Violet Kelly.

"Because if you are and since you're awake and all," she goes on, "maybe we should go over your schedule for today. We're almost at the arena anyway."

Either this is the most realistic dream I've ever had, or I'm actually *her*. I'm Becca Starr. But it can't be. It just can't.

"Yeah, right, my schedule, of course," I stammer, figuring I should go along with this craziness until I figure out what's going on. "Let's definitely go over that."

"Are you sure you're okay?" the Violet-person asks.

"Me? Oh, yes, totally fine. Really. Couldn't be better. Yup. I'm just dying to get a peek at that schedule is all."

"Okay, if you're sure…" she says, flipping over the first page on her clipboard. "Let's see. When we get to the Superdome, you'll go right into class so we can get that out of the way before hair and makeup."

She keeps talking, but I'm not really listening. So I *am* her, at least in this ridiculous dream. And I'm on a tour bus, apparently, on my way to an arena to do a show. Violet must be my assistant, or one of them. Maybe I have a whole bunch of assistants! *For the love of gooey green gumdrops, this cannot really be happening. Did she just say the Superdome?*

"How many people does the, uh, Superdome hold again?" I ask, trying to sound casual.

"Twenty thousand or so," Violet says. "You've only

done the 'dome, like, a billion times. Are you nervous today or something?"

"No, of course not!" I answer as fast as I can, nearly tripping over my words. "I just don't think I'm really awake yet."

"Well, it has been a crazy week, that's for sure," she agrees, saving me without even knowing it. "Six cities and two thousand miles in seven days might even be a record. Anyway, after hair and makeup, you have your photo shoot with Justin, next we'll do a quick sound check, and then you've got that commercial to shoot—the producer promised me it won't take too long since they've shot everything but your scene."

All I hear is blah, blah, blah, JUSTIN.

"Justin?" I ask. *She doesn't mean THE JUSTIN CROWE, does she?*

"Yes, Becca. Justin Crowe. The guy you're doing your next album with? Seriously, you're starting to freak me out a little."

"I think I need a glass of water or something," I tell her.

"Red!" she shouts, turning her head toward the door. "Becca needs water! Pronto!"

"You got it, Vi!" comes a voice back through the door. "Coming right up."

Before I can even count to seven, the door pops open a few inches and a hand appears holding a frosty bottle of water with a straw in it, just the way I like it.

A beverage put right in my hand the second I ask for it? I could get used to service like this, I think, grabbing the water and taking a huge gulp.

Chapter 10

When Frank Fills Me In

"You sure you're okay, Becca?" Violet asks.

"Sure, yup, totally," I tell her. "But maybe you could give me a second to, uh, freshen up a little?"

"No problem," she says, walking toward the bus-bedroom door. "Call me when you're ready." She shuts the door, and I scramble over to a mirror, not at all sure what to expect.

I still look like me—Maggie Malone! So how can I be *her*? What in the world is happening here? And I don't suppose there happens to be an earth-to-genie walkie-talkie on this thing. Wait, the mirror! Frank said I could find him there!

"Frank," I whisper, leaning in close to the mirror. "Frank! I need you, please. Pretty please with whipped cream on top! Frank, can you hear me?"

"Maggie!" bellows Frank, coming into focus behind me. He's wearing a black, furry bathrobe and has a towel wrapped turban-style on his head. You know, like a genie. I can't help it, I whip around again—but of course, he's not there.

"Or should I say *Miss Starr*," Frank-in-the-mirror says with a laugh.

"What…is…happening?" I ask in a panic.

"Yeah, well, we didn't really get to go over the *details* of those Mostly Magical Boots," Frank says with a sigh.

"You *think*?" I ask. "Maybe you could fill me in now. Wait, is that a *rubber duck* in your hand?"

"You caught me just getting out of the bath, what can I say?" Frank says. "But we don't really have time for stories, Maggie. The *mostly* magical part of the boots is that when you put them on and say the magic words, you get to step into somebody's life for a day."

"*What magic words?*" I ask. "You didn't tell me anything about magic words! What did I say? And how did I get here?"

"You wished for somebody else's life," Frank says simply. "Whenever you do that while you're wearing the MMBs, the next time you wake up, you're her. It's pretty simple."

"Well, that might have been some good information to give me up front!" I tell him. "So what do I do now?"

"Do?" Frank laughs. "You spend a day as your favorite rock star, that's what you *do*."

"But I don't know anything about being a rock star, Frank!" I wail.

"But you know *everything* about Becca Starr," Frank tells me. "And besides, the great thing about the MMBs is that this life you're living? It's like it's been yours all along."

"Huh?" I say, completely confused.

"It's complicated, kid," Frank says, "and we really don't have time for a history-of-magical-boots lesson. Just trust me—and yourself. You'll get the hang of it."

"Well, what if I don't like it and I want to go home?" I ask.

"What do you think this is, a taxi service?" Frank asks. "Once you're in the boots—and in the life—you're in, period. You wake up as that person and you go to bed as that person. When you wake up again, you'll be the one and only Maggie Malone."

"Okay, my mom is going to totally freak out if I just disappear for a whole day!" I whimper, starting to panic even more.

"Relax, Malone," Frank says. "Time stops when you're in the boots. Your mom will never even know you were gone."

"Promise?" I plead.

"Promise," Frank insists. "You've got this."

"Well, what if I need you?" I moan.

"Your pocket mirror comes with you," Frank says. "It's in your pocket right now. Get it? *Pocket* mirror? I love that one."

I reach into the pocket of my pajama bottoms, and sure enough, it's there. Frank is still holding his big belly and laughing when there's a knock on the door.

"You ready, Becca?" Violet asks right through it. "We're at the 'dome, and we're on a tight schedule, you know."

"Coming!" I shout as I watch Frank fade away before my eyes. I quickly pull on a T-shirt and pair of jeans I find folded on a shelf next to the bed and slip the mirror into my back pocket.

You've got this, I repeat to myself, opening the door. *Yeah, right.*

I follow Violet straight through the middle of this gigantic, fancy bus. I probably don't have to mention that it doesn't look like any bus *I've* ever seen. Hot pink velvet dotted with sparkly, silver stars covers the cushiony walls. There's a kitchen off to the right that looks like it's never been used and a long, white leather couch on the other side with a shiny metal table. To top it all off, the floor and ceiling are covered with tiny disco lights. I bet those lights change colors. I saw that once in a limousine when my aunt got married. Violet would know.

"Hey, Violet?" I call ahead.

"Becca, are you mad at me or something?" Violet asks. "You haven't called me by my whole name since the beginning of your first tour."

Forget the blinky lights—not important. *Be cool, Malone!*

"What? Oh, no! Sorry, um, Vi. I think I just need some food." I figure that's a harmless enough excuse for acting like a nut job. Everyone gets a little crazy when they're starving. And I am ravenous.

"Oh, you're hilarious this morning," Vi laughs. "You never eat breakfast! But if you're hungry, I guess there's time to grab a quick bite." She stops and looks at me square in the eye, and I have to resist the urge to look away. "You sure you didn't hit your head on the nightstand when you rolled out of bed?" she asks. I nod. She stares at me for another second before stepping aside and pressing her clipboard to her chest to let me off the bus. She leads me under a tent and into the biggest breakfast bonanza of my life.

Here's another thing about me: I live for breakfast. I could eat it for every single meal of every day. In fact, I probably average about nineteen breakfasts a week. And this place has about thirty times more food than any breakfast buffet I've ever seen. I think I am in heaven.

I pick up a plate and start piling it with bacon. Then I notice the sausage. Are you kidding me? Sausage and bacon on the same day? That doesn't happen in real life. I move on to the pastries— sticky buns (my favorite!), chocolate croissants, jelly doughnuts. And eggs—leaky ones, with the yellow ooze coming out on the sides—just the way I like them. When I get to the pancakes, there is no more space on my plate. How sad is that? I carefully lay a short stack across my meat and pour syrup over the whole mess. I firmly believe that just about anything tastes better with syrup on it. If you haven't tried it on pork chops, you're missing out.

"O-kay, Bec," Vi says, raising an eyebrow. "Going for the lumberjack breakfast today, are we?"

I just shrug.

Vi pulls a walkie-talkie from her hip. "Louisa?" she calls into it. "Becca is walking in five."

As in minutes? I look at my heaping plate that I can't possibly consume in that amount of time. I do the best I can to prioritize, stuffing in a couple good mouthfuls of the most fantastic, buttery pancakes I've ever tasted. I grab a bite of sausage and cram it in there too, even though I haven't swallowed the pancakes yet.

"All right then, let's go," Vi prods, snatching up my plate and handing it off to a guy in a white chef's hat. Torture! The best breakfast I never got to eat.

We walk to the far end of the tent where it's attached to a building. Violet flashes her badge, and a security guard pushes open a giant set of double doors. We wind our way down a crazy-long hallway filled with doors, then another, and then one more. Vi stops in front of a door that looks just like all the rest and swings it open.

I think I might faint.

Becca's entire band—including the kid who does flips across the stage at every concert *and* her three backup dancers who are also on that TV show *Dance Rock USA*, plus the drummer chick who has her own clothing line—are sitting around two long tables. They all look up. I smile and hold up my hand in a frozen wave like I'm pledging something really important.

"Hey Bec," says this whole room full of famous people. *To me.* I cannot make a sound. The last time I was totally speechless was when Ricky Garfinkle's shorts fell down in the lunch line and he was wearing underpants with rainbows and unicorns on them. I wish I could unsee that. I also hope I can keep it together in front of these super-cool teenage professionals. At Stinkerton, all I wanted was for someone to notice me. My mom says it all the time: be careful what you wish for.

Chapter 11

When I Get Caught Horsing Around

"Please grab a seat, Becca," Louisa says nicely. I am guessing she's the teacher or tutor or something like that. Vi hands me a stack of books and paper and leaves.

"Today we need to review chapters eleven through seventeen for your test next week," Louisa tells us. I flip through my book—that's, like, a hundred pages! I wonder how long "school" lasts and if there'll at least be a potty break. I'm guessing there's no recess around here.

"You're welcome to work alone or pair up and do some practice tests," Louisa adds. Wow, we get a choice? I like being treated like an adult!

I turn to the backup dancer sitting closest to me. Her

name is Macy McLean and she's fifteen; I know this because I'm a huge fan of *Dance Rock USA*. She's got at least thirteen piercings in each ear—all real, from the looks of it—and either her mom is way better than mine at putting on temporary tattoos or this kid who's not that much older than me is sporting *real* ink. Let's just say she doesn't exactly look like a bookworm. If I'm going to pair up with anybody and not get crushed like a bug, I'm thinking it's her.

"Want to be partners?" I ask.

"Sure," she says with a big smile. "Let's make each other a practice test." Then she winks at me.

Oh, I get it! We don't actually have to *do* this crazy math stuff. Phew! I mean, I get straight As at home and all, but this book is a few years ahead of me. I smile back at Macy and we each take out some paper.

I can't wait to see what Macy is going to do. Maybe she'll write a funny poem like Stella always does or make up a friendship quiz. I decide to draw her a picture, since that's my thing and I'm pretty good at drawing horses.

"You ready to switch?" Macy asks a few minutes later. I scribble "I (heart) horsing around!" at the top of my page, fold it in half, and slide it across the table to her. Then I open hers.

Macy did not write me a funny poem or make up a friendship quiz. She also didn't draw me a picture. No, Macy filled her page with about four hundred and fifty tiny, perfectly neat, totally impossible math equations. We each stare at our papers for a second and then at each other.

"Becca, what is this?" she whispers, looking worried.

"It's….well…it's a horse," I say. "I'm sorry, Macy. I just can't concentrate today. And this stuff is really hard."

"Why didn't you tell me you were having trouble?" she asks. "You know I'm always happy to help you with your schoolwork. I *am* a math tutor on the side, you know. And science and Latin, of course."

Well, knock me down with a squirrel sneeze! Apparently I was wrong about Macy not being the brightest bulb on the porch. And I guess when people treat you like an adult, you're supposed to *act* like an adult too. I'm going to have to work on that one.

Just then, Vi sweeps into the room.

"Sorry crew, we have to cut today's lesson short," she announces. "Becca needs to get into hair and makeup, and the rest of you have your workout in five."

We start packing up our stuff.

"Can I keep your horse?" Macy asks with a smile. "It's super cute. I might see if my tattoo guy can copy it!"

"All yours," I tell her, absolutely positive that if I turn on *Dance Rock USA* someday and see Macy McLean with a tattoo of *my* horse on her arm, my head will explode on the spot.

Chapter 12

When Things Get a Little Hairy

After the super-awkward horsing-around fiasco, I am ready to sit back, relax, and get pampered. Vi leads me through another series of hallways to a room full of mirrors with those big round lightbulbs going up the sides.

"Hey, Miss Thaaang!" shouts a spiky-haired dude in studded jean cutoffs, a white tank top, a fringed black leather vest, and combat boots. *Is he serious?* I wonder. "Give me the shake, girlfriend!" he shouts with a southern twang, extending a single finger toward me and planting his other hand on his hip.

Completely confused, I reach out and attempt to shake his long, outstretched finger.

"No, the shake! The way only the fabulous Becca Starr can do it. I want *the shake* before you get in my chair!"

Really? The shake. What would Becca do? I have no idea. I mean, I know everything about her, but I don't actually *know* her.

"Oh! You want *the shake!*" I say, deciding to give it one more guess. I throw my arms up over my head, start flashing major jazz hands, and wiggling my butt side to side really fast. I'm just getting into it, turning around in a circle, when Vi steps in.

"You know what, Chaz," she says, "Becca's not really feeling it this morning, okay? And we've got a lot of work to do here." Vi walks me over to Chaz's swivel chair. Chaz looks at me like I've lost my little rock star mind. If only he knew.

"Get you anything before we get started, love bug?" Chaz asks as he surveys my curls.

I'm about to say no thank you when I remember something. I'm a world-famous rock star! I read an article in *Tween Scene* about celebrities and the crazy things they ask for. One actor-guy only drinks from a specific brand of bendy straws, and another band has to have exactly one hundred white roses with all of the thorns cut off waiting in their dressing room when they get there. I sort of want to try that.

"Um, could I maybe have some, um...jellybeans?" I ask.

"Coming right up," Chaz says without any hesitation at all.

"But not any white or yellow," I say. Why not milk this a little bit? If I only get one day to be a rock star, I want to make it count!

"Or orange," I add. "Or blue. Actually, you know what? Could they just bring me the red and black ones?"

"No problem," Chaz says, reaching for the walkie-talkie on his hip.

This is crazy! Stars get whatever they want, no questions asked? I'd ask for a pony and a swimming pool with a high dive and an amusement park in my backyard!

"Anything else?" Chaz wants to know.

"Maybe a Coke? With a lime in it? No, wait.

Make that *four* limes. Well, four slices, not four whole limes!"

"Coke with four lime slices," Chaz repeats, his walkie-talkie poised in front of his lips. "Anything else?"

Could I ask for them to serve the Coke in a crystal goblet shaped like a shoe? Or have the whole thing delivered by a clown, or a lady in a goat costume? That would be *awesome*! But maybe a tiny bit unnecessary. I wouldn't want people thinking Becca had turned into a total diva on my account.

"I think that should do it," I tell Chaz.

"So you know what today is, right?" he says after placing my order. "That's probably why you're acting a little…funny. Girl, I get it. But we're gonna make this as painless as possible. Quick and easy, ready?" He reaches his hands up into my hair and yanks the bottom half right out.

"Holy smokes!" I scream. "Mother of a beetle's cousin, that hurt! Am I bleeding? Everything's going black! I'm going down!" I grip both sides of the chair, trying not to fall on my face for the second time today.

"What?!" Chaz says, all surprised. "Sweetie, we went with the glue-on hair extensions last time, remember? You said they were more comfortable for sleeping. Now look at these gorgeous new ones, made just for you!" Chaz holds up a mound of strawberry blond curls that look exactly like my own hair. "Since this is a big week, I'm going to put in the individual ones. It'll only take a couple of hours to do it."

"Wait, we're not going to straighten this mess?" I ask, hoping, wishing.

"Oh, right!" Chaz roars. "And disappoint all your little curly wig-wearing fans? Your curls are worth half the price of admission, sweet thang!" He tilts my head forward, bends down, and gets to work. My jellybeans and Coke arrive, and get this: it's a gigantic bowl of nothing but black and red beans, and my Coke has exactly four perfectly ripe slices of lime in it. It's hard to swallow with my chin tucked down to my neck, but somehow I manage.

I finally look up after, I don't know, maybe eleven

hundred hours and realize that I have approximately four times the number of crazy curls that I was born with and a monster crick in my neck. They *like* my curls? Huh. Well, it looks kind of good, I guess—in a world-famous rock star kind of way.

Chaz grabs my face in his hands, air-kisses me on each cheek, and tells me I look divine, then hands me over to Vi.

"Thanks, Chaz," I say. *For the torture treatment.*

Vi shuffles me over to the other end of the room where a table is laid out with enough makeup to fill up a department store. I start to relax. I mean, if I know anything at all, it's that this part is going to be *waaaay* more fun than the hair nightmare I just lived through.

Chapter 13

When an Amazon Woman Wants to Tattoo My *Face*

The tallest woman I've ever seen in my life, whose nametag says Lisbeth Kruger, comes over to me and gives me a quick once-over. I get the distinct feeling that she's not all that happy with what she sees. Without warning, she grabs my chin in her hand, gives me a weird little smile, and starts ripping my eyebrows out with pointy tweezers. One at a time. It feels like she's sticking scorching-hot needles into my face.

"Umm, Lisbeth?" I mutter, trying to blink back tears. "That really hurts."

"I know it's not your favorite," she says. "But we do what we have to do, right? Or are you finally ready to go with the tattooed brows? It really would be much easier—for all of us."

Get a tattoo? On my *face*? What planet are these people from?

"Yeah, that might be a good idea," I say. "Maybe we could schedule that for next week or something." I feel bad throwing Becca under the bus like that, but honestly. If I came home with a tattoo on my face, I am positive my parents would send me off to one of those boarding schools like my cousin Seamus went to after he got caught stealing Milk Duds from the 7-Eleven.

I sit in this makeup chair for what feels like a hundred million years and get smeared, smudged, and glossed within an inch of my life. I decide to keep my eyes closed and wait until Lisbeth is totally done to see my magical transformation. She spends at least a year applying eye shadow with the softest brush you ever felt. I wonder if it's made out of mink or something, but I decide that it's probably not because Becca is a huge animal-lover, like me. I would fall asleep sitting here if my mostly empty stomach wasn't rumbling louder than a chainsaw. I wonder if Lisbeth can hear it, but if she can, she is being very polite about it. After an eternity, she glues these fake lashes that look like sparkly spiders to my eyelids and announces that she's done. I open my eyes (I actually have to peel them apart since the spider-lashes weigh about seven pounds each) and I see…wait for it…*me*. Maybe a little shinier and sparklier, but it's still just me—with even bigger, curlier hair.

I can't believe Becca does this every single day, I think. I'm pretty sure that would drive me totally bonkers. Maybe being a rock star isn't as glamorous as I thought.

"You look fabulous, Bec," Vi says, helping me up from the chair. "Let's get you over to wardrobe ASAP or you'll be late for Justin."

Okay, maybe it's a little bit glamorous. Jeez Louise, who am I kidding? Wardrobe and Justin Crowe. Somebody pinch me. Wait, never mind. I've had enough pain for one day.

The wardrobe room is about the size of my

classroom at school—if you cleared away all the desks and lined the walls with rolling clothes racks. There must be thirty of them, all packed solid with the craziest, most beautiful clothes you can imagine. I walk around checking out the haul, afraid to touch anything. There's everything from sequin-covered miniskirts and long, ruffled jackets to this incredible pair of stretch-leather jeans that look like someone glued lace right over the top. One whole wall has racks stuffed with shoes from floor to ceiling. *All of this is for me. Well, for Becca technically. But today, she's me. Or I'm her. Whatever.*

"*Salut, ma cheri!*" a voice behind me booms. "*Ça va bien?*" I turn around and nearly fall over backward. Standing not three feet away from me is Toni Laroux, the famous fashion stylist from the TV show *Wear Ever.* I know Toni speaks English since I've never missed a single, solitary show, but maybe Becca is fluent in French on the sly and that's their little thing. Which would royally stink for me, seeing as aside from fries, my knowledge of French is, like, zero.

Toni leans in, squeezes my shoulders, and does the double-cheek kiss thing.

"Hi, Toni," I mumble. "Er, I mean, *saloomahshurry*." I try to say it just the way she did.

Toni collapses into a fit of giggles. "Oh, Becca," she gasps. "You *absolument* have not been listening to the French CDs I gave you, you naughty girl."

"I can order apple pie à la mode for dessert," I tell her. Well, it's true—and it's all I've got.

"This is a start," she laughs, shaking her perfectly blunt bob. *How many close calls can one girl survive, I ask you?*

Toni turns and pulls out—of all things—the leather-and-lace jeans. Talk about a step up from a reindeer sweatshirt! "These look like Justin Crowe style, no?" she asks. *As if I'd know!*

"I was thinking these with a simple T-shirt and piles of necklaces and maybe a gorgeous belt," she continues. "You like?"

"You're the boss, Toni," I tell her.

"Ah, *cheri*, you must be aware of the fact that

around here, the boss is *you*," she says, rifling through racks of necklaces and pulling out her favorites. She hands me the jeans, the T-shirt, and ten pounds of jewelry—including a pair of giant hoop earrings. *The clip-on kind. I knew it! I can't wait to tell Stella. Oh, shoot. I can't tell Stella. Rats!*

"*Allons-y!*" Toni says, waving her hands in crazy circles, obviously wanting me to do something—like get dressed. But where?

"Right here?" I ask, feeling my face turn bright red. Well honestly, I don't have a clue.

She points to a curtain in the corner, which I hadn't noticed before. "Vi said you were not yourself today," she says. "Don't tell anyone, but I think I like this Becca even better than the old one. She is very funny indeed."

At least I'm good for a laugh, I think, trotting off to the dressing area to slip into my rock-star gear. I let Becca's jeans drop to the floor, and when I do, my gold pocket mirror flips out of the back pocket and sails across the tile floor, spinning right in front of Toni. *Oh, nuts!* I've stripped down to my skivvies so I poke my head out of the opening in the curtain.

"Becca, love, what is this?" Toni asks, picking up my *genie information portal* like it's just some beautifully bedazzled compact, inspecting both sides.

"Oh, I *need* that!" I blurt out before I can think. *How could I be so careless? Toni's gonna faint on the spot when she looks into that mirror and sees Frank's leathery face staring back at her!* But there's no time. She opens the mirror and I squeeze my eyes shut, bracing myself for the screams of horror to follow.

Chapter 14

When I Survive Another Close Call

"Ah, voilà!" Toni says, smiling, pleased with her reflection.

Really? Voilà? Frank wasn't there? I really need more information on how all this works.

I throw the T-shirt over my head and lunge out of the dressing room. I almost slam one of Toni's French fingers inside the compact in my rush to snatch it back.

"Sorry, Toni!" I stammer, scampering back into the dressing room. "It's just that's a cherished family heirloom is all. It's really, really old—and fragile."

"Really, *cheri*?" Toni asks, questioning my claim. "It looks perfectly modern and positively chic, I think."

"Nope. Extremely old, from an ancient ancestor,"

I explain. "I'm pretty sure my great, great...great grandmother brought it over from her homeland on the *Titanic*...wait, it wasn't the *Titanic*...maybe it was the *Mayflower*...well anyway, it was way back in the days of yore." *What on earth am I talking about?*

"How fascinating!" Toni says without a hint of skepticism, like she believes me, but I'm not sure. "What is the meaning of the letters M and M in gorgeous jewels on the top? It is exquisite, *absolument*!"

"Oh!" I say. *This one's easy.* "Yeah, that's because it belonged to my Granny Malone. Her name was Margaret Malone too! I mean—*NOT TOO*—there was just her—she was the one and only Margaret Malone. Those are her initials." *Seriously, Malone? Why don't you just dig yourself a hole and jump into it?*

I am full-on freaking out at this point since I figure I'm cold busted. My excessive, over-the-top explanations are only making things worse. I pull the robe off the hook inside the dressing room and open the compact to consult Frank on exactly *how to* backpedal out of this tall tale I've spun. I open the mirror and there's Frank, shaking his head.

"Way to oversell it, Malone!" Frank says. "But don't fret, Frenchie there is none the wiser. I'm pretty sure she bought your *Titanic* story hook, line and sinker!"

"Cool," I answer back, not thinking, as I shut the compact.

"What is cool, Becca, my pet?" Toni asks. "You have caught a chill? I will have the heaters brought in *immédiatement*."

"That would be great, Toni," I say exhaling, completely relieved. "Thanks."

Crisis averted! Time to get into my rock-star duds. The leather jeans slide on like butter and fit like they were made by hand for my body. I squat down and stand up, and they don't wrinkle or pucker even one tiny bit. They almost look like they were painted on. My mom would have a full-blown heart attack if she saw me in them, so—as cool as it would be to have her see her own daughter being a famous rock star—it's probably a good thing she's not here. I add the belt and an army of necklaces, then pull back the curtain and shuffle out in my bare feet.

Toni is standing there holding a pair of silver ballet flats in one hand and a pair of platform wedge-heel boots in the other. "I think we will go with the flats for now, since you have a long day," she decides. "Plus we don't want Justin to feel shrimpy." It's all I can do not to throw my arms around her and hug all of the air right out of her lungs. I mean, I love clanking around in my mom's heels at home for fun, but this is different. The last thing I need is to be teetering around on six-inch heels and trying to look cool and then tripping on my face in front of none other than *the* Justin Crowe.

I slip into the ballet flats as Vi bursts back into the room. "Oh good, you're dressed," she says. "Justin's bus just got here. You ready?"

That's like asking an elephant if he's ready to go sky-diving, I think, but I can't exactly say that. Instead I nod my head yes and follow Vi out the door on spaghetti legs.

Chapter 15

When I Try Too Hard to Act Cool

I get the twitchy leg shakes whenever I'm nervous or excited. Like when I have to stand up in class and give a report or when I can't close my eyes the night before we leave for a super fun summer vacation. But this is different. Right now, I've got the twitchy leg shakes mixed with some major jumpy tummy—the kind that makes you feel like you're going to toss your cookies any second.

Maybe it's a good thing I don't have any cookies to toss—there wouldn't be time for that anyway. Vi walkie-talkies ahead to let Justin's crew and the photographer know that "Miss Starr is moving," and just before we arrive on set, another pair of double doors flies open like magic. I have to admit, it's awfully cool having someone announce your every move like it's actual news.

Right away, I see him. *Justin Crowe.* He doesn't have a real spotlight shining out of the top of his head, but he might as well. I don't know how to explain it, but he practically lights up the whole room. He's surrounded by a bunch of people huddled together wearing headsets. Until the big metal doors slam shut behind us, echoing a loud *boom* throughout the ginormous room. He turns toward us and breaks into the biggest, most beautiful smile I've ever seen, and I think I might just melt right into the cement floor. *Is this really happening? To me?* The closest I've ever gotten to anybody super famous was when I was four and my parents took me to see The Jiggles and I got my picture taken with the guy in the grape suit. I'm pretty sure that doesn't count anymore.

Justin keeps grinning—right at me—and holds up one finger, to say *just a sec.* That's cool, I think to myself. I can wait just a sec for Justin Crowe. As he turns back to the headset people, he does something that makes my head spin: he flashes me the *I heart Becca Starr* hand symbol, right off his left shoulder. *Seriously?* He hearts me! Justin Crowe hearts me! This is the single most superb day of my entire life. Wait, it's not technically *my* life, I remind myself. *But it is today, and it's totally, amazingly, ridiculously awesome.*

Justin's crew scatters, and he comes running over to me, scooping me off my feet and spinning me around. *Spinning. Me. Around.* Is there anything better than being spun around by Justin Crowe? I can say, for sure, the answer to that question is no. No, there is nothing better than that.

"Becky!" Justin says. *Becky? Either he doesn't actually know my name or we are total BFFs.* "What's up? I've missed you!"

"Uh…yeah! I know!" I stammer. "I've missed you too!? It's been, like…how long *has* it been?"

"A whole month since our duet at the VTV Music Awards," he says. "Can you believe it? And you've been around the world and back since then! Hey, we really missed you at the *Vanity Square* party last week."

I nod like a cartoon bobble head, terrified to say the wrong thing. Or anything at all. *Get with the program, Malone. You're supposed to be a rock star. You'd better start acting like a rock star.*

"Dude, I hear that scene was totally bangin', for real!" I say.

"What did you just say?" Justin asks, looking at me sort of funny.

"What?" I say, cocking my head to the side and giving it another try. "I'm just busting a rhyme, double time, dog!" I get my shoulders into it a little bit to boost the confident rock star effect, but I'm crossing my fingers hoping that sounded a little better.

He stares at me for a beat and a half and then busts out laughing. "Oh, I get it!" he laughs, shaking his head. "You're being that wannabe rock star kid backstage at Madison Quad that time, right? He was all *I'm talking to rock stars so I'm going to talk just like a rock star.* Like we talk like that! People kill me."

"I know, right?" I say, feeling like the world's biggest dork. "People are ridiculous sometimes."

Like, especially me—right now. I'm totally blowing it. But what do I do? Justin actually seems pretty...normal. Maybe I should try being a normal person too. That I know how to do.

"Tell me what's up with you," I say, because it's always nice to ask people about themselves.

"Same stuff, different day," Justin says, pulling up a folding chair for me and sitting backward in another. "On the road, on the bus, in the chair, sit around and wait. Of course, I love the fans and the performing and all that just like you do, but the whole thing can get exhausting. And lonely."

Rock stars get lonely? But there are all these people around all the time! I guess there's not a lot of hanging around, though. I think about all the time I spend with Stella at home. I sure would miss her if I lived on the road.

"Are you sleeping any better lately?" Justin asks.

"Umm...I rolled out of bed this morning—right

onto the floor!" I say, hoping this is something that might actually happen to a rock star.

"That's classic!" Justin laughs. "You always crack me up."

Right then, my stomach rips out an embarrassing, monster rumble.

"Dude! It sounds like a bowling alley in there!" Justin laughs again. "Have you eaten lunch yet?" I thought I loved him before, but I *really* love him now.

"I'd kill for a cheeseburger," I admit.

"Me too," he says and calls across to a guy talking to the photographer. "Hey, Butch! Can we get a couple of cheeseburgers over here, pickles on the side? Thanks, man. You're the best." He turns back to me with that smile again. "Pickles on the side for my high-maintenance friend." Becca and I both love our pickles *on the side*. Talk about a lucky coincidence!

Vi hears this and quickly jumps in. "Actually, Butch, Becca will have a peanut butter protein shake. Tell Chef it's for her—extra creamy. Thanks!" She comes over to Justin and me. "Bec, you know you can't have solid food once you're in full makeup!"

Rats! Make that double rats with stinky rotten goat cheese on top! No burger and I happen to be allergic to peanuts. I won't be able to sing a note once my throat closes up, and all the makeup in the world won't be able to hide the head-to-toe hives I'll break into if Mr. Peanut even looks at these perfectly polished lips.

"Oh, yeah. Sorry, Vi!" I say. "But about that shake… Can we hold the nuts today? I'm sort of in a chocolate mood. Maybe I could just have a plain milk shake—with extra protein, of course."

"Sure, not a problem," Vi says. "And then we've got to wrap up this catch-up session. The guys are starting to load in the gear, and we've got some amazing pictures to take."

Out of nowhere, a team of hair and makeup artists appears and starts in again with the glosses and powders and sprays. I slump back in my chair. Didn't we just do this?

Chapter 16

When I Meet the Meanest Dude in Show Business

After seventeen costume changes, eleven lip gloss reapplications, and at least a zillion blinding flashes in my face, the photographer—only the uber-famous Zane Black, the guy who shoots for all the big, glossy fashion magazines—declares that he's got what he needs. *Not a minute too soon, buddy*, I think. My face aches from smiling.

"So guess what, B?" Justin asks as the crew packs up their gear. "I get to stay for your show tonight! I was supposed to have to take off, like, now—but I convinced my manager to make a little magic with the schedule. I'll be up in the box cheering for you. I'll be the one holding up the biggest 'b,' so look for me."

He gives me The Smile and a huge hug, and I think my heart actually stops beating. "Break a leg, Becky," he adds, and I smile weakly. I know that means "good luck" but right now I'm hoping that *I don't actually break an actual leg.*

"Sound check in five!" shouts one of the headphone guys. "Rory, get Becca mike'd up."

"On it," says Rory. He strolls over to me, and before I can even say hello, he twists me around roughly so that my back is to him. I don't even have time to think before he yanks the back of my shirt up really high. *What in the name of Ursula's ugly uncle is he doing?* I grab the front of my shirt to keep it from riding up too. I feel a cold hard box being pressed against my back and then clipped to the top of my leather pants. Rory yanks down hard on the box, pulling the back of my pants down with it. Hello, if he makes me flash some cheek I'm seriously going to lose it here!

"That staying?" he growls.

"Yup! Not going anywhere!" I insist, pulling my pants back to my hips.

Rory shoves an earpiece into my ear and plugs in the wire. "Okay, let's do a line check," he says, twisting me back around, and not very gently, I might add. "Give me a test."

Um, what's the capital of North Dakota? Can you name all seven dwarves? What's fourteen times fourteen?

I clear my throat. "Testing, one, two, three..." I say, but nobody besides Rory can hear it, because the most horrible screech you've ever heard in your whole life—the kind that makes you cover your ears and double over—fills up the entire 'dome and bounces off the ceiling and walls like we're inside a giant popcorn popper.

"Jeez, Curtis, would you level that already?" shouts Rory—right into my ear, which is still echoing from the screech.

"Sorry, Rory," Curtis calls back. "Okay, try it again."

"Hey, Becca, maybe you could just say *check-check* like we always do," Rory says in a very unpleasant tone. He is not happy with me right now, that's for sure. Maybe his boxers are stuck up his butt or something. I decide to call him Gory Rory—in my head, of course.

"Now?" I ask, my ears still pounding.

"No, darling, a week from now," Rory says all sarcastically. "Yes, *now*! What do you think this is? A picnic in the stinking park?"

The other thing about me? I don't like it when people are rude to me. Like, I can't stand it. *At all.* My eyes start to fill with tears, and all I can think of is the sparkly-spider lashes and the dozens of layers of makeup and powder beneath them and the melting-clown mess I'm going to be if I even think about blinking. Why did I ever think I wanted to be a rock star? Maybe because I had no idea what it was all about. I wish I were somewhere else right now. Anywhere else. Even worse-than-awful Stinkerton.

Get it together, Malone. This is it. You're doing great, don't mess it all up now. You can do this. You will *do this. You don't have a choice.*

I square my shoulders. "Check-check," I croak. It

comes out like a froggy whisper, but at least there's no screech.

"*What on earth is going on up there?*" Rory roars again, this time even louder. "You bozos want to give me any juice, or do you want me to try to guess what she's gonna sound like tonight? Unbelievable." He mutters the *unbelievable* part under his breath, and I decide that his boxers are not only up his butt but they must be crawling with fire ants. I know it's not a nice thing to say, but I sort of hope they are. I mean, I truly, honestly can't stand this guy. This is actually a good thing, because now I'm not so much upset as I am mad. And nobody better mess with Maggie Malone when she's mad.

"We got it fixed, Rory," Curtis shouts. "Bad connection. Try it again—it should be good now."

"It better be," grumbles Rory.

"Check-check," I say, loud and clear. The sound of my voice fills the arena, and I get chills down my own spine.

"Beautiful," Rory says. "All right, give me a line.

And before you can ask what I mean like you've never done this before, I am asking you to *sing something*, princess. Anything, I don't care."

That I can do. I mean, I know every word to every Becca Starr song ever recorded, and I don't know about onstage at the Superdome, but at home in my shower, I'm not half bad. *You're a rock star now, so act like one. Don't hold back! Show them what you've got.*

"Way back when, before I knew," I belt out, loud and proud. I close my eyes and pretend it's just me, Maggie Malone, singing into my bottle of conditioner. Not to brag or anything, but I think I sound pretty good. I'm about to really get into it when Rory shuts me down.

"That's fine," Rory says, cutting me off. He doesn't smile or anything—I don't know if he's even capable of smiling—but at least he doesn't look like he's going to bite my head off anymore. Mickey might like it if I came home headless, but my parents would bust a serious gut.

The rest of Becca's—I mean *my*—band gets the

same lovely Rory treatment, one by one. When he's satisfied, he stalks off the stage without even a "see ya." *That's right, take a hike, Gory Rory.*

"We put up with him because he's the best," says a voice behind me. I turn around, super happy to see Vi.

"I guess," I say. "But does he have to be such a jerk?"

Vi just shrugs, and I decide right then and there that when I'm a world-famous rock star, I will have a very strict No Jerks policy. If you want to work for Maggie Malone, you'd better be nice. End of story.

"Hey Bec, I have some bad news," Vi says, steering me back down the hallway. Man, am I beat. I look at my watch and thankfully it's still pretty early. I'm definitely going to need a little nap if I'm going to be expected to perform an actual rock concert tonight.

"What's up?" I ask Vi, picturing myself sliding into that delicious satin bed.

"Your mom called," Vi says, not looking at me. "She can't make the show tonight. She said to tell you she's really, really sorry but her fund-raiser co-chair got sick and she has to run the whole auction tonight by herself and she knows that this happened last time and the time before that too but there's nothing she can do and she promises she'll make it up to you." Vi spits this last bit out in one rush of a breath, and even I can tell she's trying to cover for Becca's mom. It's no biggie to me, of course, but I feel super sad for Becca. Her own mom doesn't come to her shows?

I think about my mom. She's never missed a single soccer game or school play or even a silly field trip. Never, not even once. I decide to do something really nice for her when I get home, like make her breakfast in bed or pick up all the disgusting dog poop in the backyard without even being asked. I follow Vi back to the bus, thinking how weird it is to feel sorry for Becca Starr.

Chapter 17

When I Speak Japanese

I barely have one foot on the bus when Vi stops me.

"Hey, Bec," she says. "Where're you going?"

"Yeah, I'm kind of beat," I explain. "I was just going to take a quick power nap before the show."

"You're funny," Vi says. "Seriously, if you need the potty, go ahead, but we've got to get to the soundstage for your commercial shoot in less than thirty. Hair and makeup will meet us there."

Those guys again?

"I guess I'm good," I say, jumping back down off the bus.

"Great, 'cause your car is already here," Vi says, looking at her clipboard and speaking into her walkie-talkie. "Moving!"

We walk around the back of the bus where my "car" is parked. And it's definitely no car—it's a super-stretch, supremely stylin' limousine. *Yeah baby! That's what I'm talking about.*

I pick up my step, trying not to break into a sprint toward the limo. I'm reaching for the handle when a dude in a black suit stops me. "Allow me, Miss Starr," he says, all serious. How could I forget? A rock star doesn't open her own car door!

I slide across buttery leather seats and immediately take my shoes off so I can feel the plush carpet under my feet. There are mile-long black couches running down both sides of this thing. I'm not even kidding; I bet I could fit my whole Ranger Girls troop in here. There's the longest sunroof I've ever seen over my head, so I start fiddling with the buttons until I find the right one to open it. Vi is talking on her phone, of course.

"Tell them we have no comment," she says, sounding pretty irritated. We buckle our seat belts, and the limo starts moving.

Vi is chatting away, and I'm staring up at the sky flying past, and all of a sudden, I can't stand it. I know I shouldn't unbuckle but I just can't resist. I stand up right through the middle of the sunroof and open my arms wide, feeling the wind whip through my hair. *Heaven!* I think to myself. *I'd do this every single day of my life if I was Becca Starr.*

Right then, two hands grab me around my waist and pull me back inside the limo lickety-split.

"*What are you DOING, Becca?*" Vi says, trying not to raise her voice. "Chaz is going to have a panic attack when he sees what you just did to your hair!"

"I'm sorry," I say, feeling my curls—they are a little twisted up. "I just wanted to…" My eyes start filling with tears.

"No, you know what?" she says, getting herself back together. "*I'm sorry.* I'm just a little stressed—that phone call—never mind, it doesn't matter. They're going to have massive fans blowing straight at you for this commercial anyway, I'm sure."

"They are?" I say, confused.

"Remember?" Vi asks. "The Japanese car commercial? I showed you the storyboards last week. It's the one where you're in the convertible."

Before I can ask any more questions, the limo stops in front of this humongous metal building in the middle of nowhere. Vi hops out, and I have no choice but to follow her. *This is where we're filming a real commercial? Looks more like an abandoned paper plate factory or something.* We walk inside, and it's like stepping into another world. We're in the middle of some big city at night with tall buildings and twinkling lights, a starlit sky, and a full moon overhead. I'm not sure you'd actually be able to see the stars in a big city like this, but it looks really good.

There are at least a hundred people rushing around with headsets on. One of them rushes up to Vi and bows, like he just finished his second grade Thanksgiving play. Then Vi bows right back at him. Next thing I know, I'm bombarded by all those people in headsets bowing at me. Just in time, I remember what my Aunt Fi told me about the bowing custom in Japan—it's a respect thing—so for once in this crazy rock star life, I know what to do. I bow at everyone and they all bow back. It's hard to keep a straight face.

Vi shuffles me through hair and makeup. Chaz only has a mini freak-out when he sees my windblown hair and gets it back into place pretty quickly.

There's a red convertible parked in the middle of the fake city street. The guy in charge comes over to Vi, motions toward the car, and says something in Japanese. It's kind of hilarious when he says the thing in Japanese because he gets this super excited look on his face. Vi nods and comes over to me.

"Okay, so here's the deal," she explains. "You're gonna get in the car, they're gonna get the fans blowing, paparazzi are going to swarm the car flashing bulbs, and you're going to say, *KONO IWA*! You know, with lots of feeling and excitement."

"Wait, do they know I'm not old enough to actually drive a car?" I ask, because I'm just twelve, and Becca's only fourteen!

"Yeah, they don't care," Vi says. "Repeat after me, *KONO IWA!*"

"KONO IWA," I echo back.

"Again," Vi says.

"KONO IWA," I say again. "Wait, what does that even *mean?*"

"What?" Vi says, looking up from her clipboard. "Oh, I don't know. I can find out, if you'd like."

"Well, don't you think we should know what I'm saying?" I ask. "I mean, what if they've got me saying *I LOVE HULA-HOOPING POLKA-DOTTED PANDAS* or something?"

"Listen, Bec," Vi comes in close, whispering into my ear. "They're paying you two million dollars to say two words—that's a million dollars a word. I think it's something like 'this car is awesome!' but I'll find out if you want me to."

"Yes, please," I say with a smile. It just seems like the responsible thing to do. And just as I start to feel the tiniest bit thirsty, somebody puts a cool soda in my hand.

Vi comes back from talking to the man in charge. "It means THIS ROCKS! Okay, are we all good?"

"All good!" I say and step into the car. They start up the music and the fans and the photographers get into position around the car. Vi points to me when it's time for me to do my thing.

"*KONO IWA!*" I say with as much feeling as I can muster in a foreign language I don't speak. The bowing man says something to Vi.

"Again, Bec!" Vi says from the side of the set. "With a little less excitement—more rock star attitude, please!"

I squint my eyes and turn my head a little to the side and say, "*KONO IWA.*"

The guy in charge is waving his hands, trying to explain to Vi what he wants. "That's better, Bec!" Vi yells, "But they want a little more everyday American teenager vibe."

I say *THIS ROCKS!* in Japanese at least sixty different ways and finally get it right.

We walk out of the warehouse and I can't stop saying it: "*KONO IWA!*"

"You love doing commercials, don't you, Bec?" Vi asks, putting an arm around me.

"Yeah, that was really fun!" I say.

"You know what else is really fun?" she asks me, sliding into the limo. "You did such a great job, they just *gave you that car*!"

"But I can't even *drive*!" I remind her.

"Yeah, like I said," Vi reminds me, "they don't care!" And we laugh together—until Vi gets another call, of course.

Chapter 18

When I'm Attacked
by a Dinosaur

We make it back to the bus in record time.

"Okay, Bec, you've got thirty minutes of downtime to chill," Vi says. "I'll be back with your dinner." I nod, and she closes the door to my bus-bedroom.

I unload the necklaces and bracelets lining my neck and arms, peel off the sticky leather jeans, and pull on some stretchy leggings, a hoodie, and Becca's bunny slippers. I have a pair almost exactly like them at home, and I'd wear them to school if my mom would let me. They're *that* comfy.

I'm about to curl up with a magazine when there's a knock at my door.

"Come in!" I shout. Vi nudges the door open. She's got her cell phone in one hand and she's covering the mouthpiece with the other.

"So sorry to bother you, Bec, but I've got Jonie Lake on the line," Vi says. *Jonie Lake?* Sister of a striped stegosaurus! Jonie Lake is the infamous, thousand-year-old entertainment journalist who gets her kicks ripping celebrities apart in her gossip column for *Starz* magazine. She's had so much plastic surgery she looks like a cross between the Joker from Batman and one of those creepy dolls whose eyes are supposed to close when you lay her down but they get stuck open all the time. Talk about scary with a capital S.

"What does she want?" I ask nervously.

"What she always wants," Vi says. "A comment on her absurd, made-up story. This time, she's going to be writing about how all of your Becca Starr merchandise is manufactured by underpaid children in Chinese sweatshops." Vi sighs and shakes her head. "No comment, I assume?"

"But...but...why wouldn't I comment?" I stammer.

"That's a horrible thing to print!" Then I have a terrifying thought.

"It's not *true*, is it?" I ask.

"Oh Becca, of *course* it's not true," Vi assures me. "Nothing that vile woman prints is true! You know that."

"Then…shouldn't I defend myself?" I ask.

"You certainly *can*," Vi says. "You just usually don't want to deal with it."

"Well, I feel like dealing with it today," I tell her. "I'll take the call."

Vi lifts both eyebrows but says nothing as she hands me the phone. I take a deep breath before speaking into it.

"This is Becca Starr," I say with confidence I definitely don't feel. "May I help you?"

"Jonie Lake here," she growls. "So, you got kids in China, working their little fingers raw for peanuts so you can make millions selling piece-of-junk dolls that don't even look like you, if you ask me. Any comment?"

"First of all," I say slowly, "I'd like to know where you got this information." It's not just a stall tactic.

In my journalism class at Sacred Heart, you weren't allowed to make any sort of claim without being able to back it up. That's pretty basic stuff, in fact.

"Can't reveal my sources, sorry," Jonie snarls. "You got a comment? I'm on a deadline here."

"My comment is that it is absolutely not true, not a single word of it," I say. "All of my products are made right here in the United States. And for your information, I don't make millions off those dolls. In fact, I don't make a penny. I donate every single cent I make on my merchandise to the Pack It Up Foundation. You are welcome to confirm that with them."

I *so* nailed that! Stella and I have watched the Becca Starr documentary at least a dozen times, so I've actually *seen* her manufacturing plant. It's in somewhere like Detroit or Pittsburgh or one of those other cities where they make a bunch of stuff. I can't remember exactly, but I'm positive it's in the United States because they made a big deal about it in the movie about how hardly anybody makes anything in the United States anymore, which is sad. Then later in the movie, there's this whole scene about Becca's work with Pack It Up. Every year, she gives them money to buy backpacks and fill them with school supplies for kids who can't afford to buy them. Becca even helps them pack those bags herself. I'd never even thought about not having enough money to buy a *pencil* before I saw that. It's a tearjerker of a scene, and after we saw it the first time, Stella and I both took our entire allowance and stuck it in an envelope and mailed it right off to them, along with my favorite Crazy Kitten pencil case packed with as many supplies as we could stuff in there.

"Well, that's not what *my* source said, so I guess you don't really have anything to add," Jonie grumbles. And then there's a click.

Is this some kind of joke? She was asking me about *me*! And I told her the truth and she didn't even care. And now she's going to print her evil article full of lies, and there's nothing I can do about it? It's so totally not fair.

This is almost *exactly* like that time at Sacred Heart

when somebody started a rumor that Sally Keester had six toes on her left foot. Nobody even knew how the rumor started, but it sure did spread like wildfire. As if it wasn't bad enough having to go through life with a last name that's another word for backside, that poor girl walked to school in the snow wearing *sandals* all winter, just so people could count her frozen toes for themselves. (There were only ten. And she asked me to count them, for your information.) Even after Sally nearly got frostbite, kids still said she had one little piggy tucked underneath the others. Some of those kids still call her Six Toe Sally to this day. Why are some people mean for no good reason? It should be against the law.

I look at Vi helplessly and hand her the phone. A tear slips out of the corner of my eye. Vi sits down next to me.

"Sweetie, this is all part of being a star, you know that," she says, hugging me. "People are going to say what they're going to say and think what they're going to think, and all you can do is keep being you. You know as well as I do that this will only make headlines until she makes up something even worse about somebody else. Until then, all you can do is ignore it. Besides, who cares what a bunch of strangers think? Those of us who know and love you are the only ones who matter, anyway. Right?"

I nod and look down at my lap. Vi stands and slips quietly out of the room. Who knew being a rock star would be such a roller-coaster ride?

Chapter 19

When I First Hear the Scary Sounds of Stardom

I try to take my mind off the Jonie Lake disaster by thinking about food. I am so hungry I could eat a hot dog, which may not sound like much, but I haven't eaten a hot dog in four years. That was when I nearly choked to death on one at the Sacred Heart Harvest Carnival. Tiffany Treadmore said that's what I got for trying to eat on the Whirly Bird, but I think she was just mad because some of my ketchup flew onto her Rocking Rolls T-shirt when that Bird started Whirling.

Knock, knock.

"Come on in," I call.

"You ready for dinner?" Vi asks, peeking her head back in.

"Is water wet?" I ask.

Violet laughs. "I'm glad to see you're feeling better and that you didn't let that Jonie Lake thing get you too down. We need you to be on your game tonight and not be worrying about *that* crusty old toad."

Vi's right, there's nothing I can do. I'm not wasting another ounce of brain space on dinosaur-face. Right now, I'm thinking about dinner—as in real, solid food that I get to *eat*. Pretty please with pineapple on top, let it be something good.

I follow Vi out to the living room of the bus to find a silver domed plate waiting for me. I slide into my spot at the table and lift the lid. *Yes!* I'm staring at a plateful of spaghetti with meatballs the size of my head. I dig right in because you never know how long you've got to chow down around here.

"As soon as you're finished eating, we'll get you in for your final hair and makeup touch-ups and then we'll do this deal," Vi says. "You've got about twenty minutes or so."

And then she leaves.

Have you ever eaten a whole meal at a table all by yourself? It's weird, let me tell you. At home, dinner is loud and fun and even when Mickey is getting yelled at for making farting sounds with his armpit or trying to slide bites of food to our dog Willy, everyone's usually laughing and happy. But I have nobody to talk to, not even Vi, who is probably off doing something Very Important for me. Is this what my life is going to be like when I'm back home, as me, at Stinkerton? I don't want to be the Girl Who Eats Alone forever. I shudder and try to shove that thought out of my brain.

When every last morsel of food is gone, I wipe my mouth and lean back. As much as I want to lick the plate, I don't. Even without my mom here to tell me not to, I know that would be really bad manners. I wonder if she'd be proud of me. The sun's starting to go down, and back at home, that's when I usually do my homework while my mom starts dinner. She doesn't need to help me much with it anymore, but I still do it in the kitchen because I like having some company. I'm really starting to miss her. I wonder if Becca misses *her* mom all the time…or if she's just used to it by now.

Vi rushes back onto the bus. "Okay, superstar. Security says seats are already starting to fill so we need to get moving. We don't want a repeat of what happened in London last year, do we?"

I have no idea what happened in London last year, but Vi's raised eyebrow is enough to tell me it was not fun. I shake my head no.

After *another* round of hair and makeup, Vi scoots me over to wardrobe for my first costume. I go straight into the dressing room since I know what to do this time. I'm blabbering to Toni from behind the curtain about how gorgeous the tiny sequins are on my perfectly fitted, silver slip dress when I notice a rumbling above my head, like the whole arena is moaning or something.

"Umm, Toni?" I ask through the curtain. "What's that sound? Do they have messed-up plumbing in this place or something? It sounds like the roof's about to cave in."

"Ah, *cheri*, that is the sound of your adoring fans anxiously awaiting your arrival, of course!" Toni says. "They seem extra excited tonight, yes?"

I get a lump in my throat as fear shoots through my body like a lightning bolt. I'd sort of forgotten about the whole *twenty thousand people* I'd be singing in front of. I feel a little dizzy as I emerge from the dressing room.

"*Magnifique!*" Toni says, throwing her arms in the air like a gymnast who just nailed a perfect landing. I give her a huge hug because, well, I really need a hug.

Vi steps in. "The warm-up band is clearing the last of their gear now," she tells me. "You're on in five. All set? You look great!"

I sort of nod. *You didn't like being invisible? Not a problem, Malone.*

"Miss Starr is walking," Vi announces into her

walkie-talkie and starts moving for the door. I wonder if it would look suspicious if I asked her to come back and help me unglue my feet from the floor.

Chapter 20

When I Come *This* Close to Losing It

"You coming?" Vi asks, turning around. "You look a little pale," she says, handing me water with a straw. "Hydrate! And here's your set list. I know you like to hold it in your hand before you go on."

I take a look and I know all of the songs. Every one, completely by heart, which is a relief, but how will I *sound?* I mean, Rory didn't exactly give me time to get my groove on during the sound check. *Just pretend you're alone, in the shower, singing your heart out like you always do.*

Vi gives my arm a nice tug, and I manage to unstick my feet. She's leading me through the hallway maze when some headphone guy pops out of a door and gets me mike'd up while we're walking. It's still not a super-fun experience, but I'm not about to complain. At least it's not Gory Rory.

The nervousness that started in my toes has spread all over my body, and I can feel my ears getting hot. That's not good. The last time that happened was when I was in the second grade Christmas pageant. I had a pretty minor role—I was the innkeeper, for Pete's sake—and all I had to say was, "I am sorry. There is no room for you in the inn." But by the time Joseph and the Virgin Mary (who was riding on Willis Freedman's back since he was the donkey) made it next to me at center stage, all I could hear was the blood pumping inside my thick skull.

"Uhh…uhh…" I said and looked at Mrs. Finklestein, who looked at me like, *Say it! Say it!* But I couldn't. I was frozen like a stone troll in *The Hobbit*. With my mouth hanging open. The only reason I know that I looked like a baby bird waiting for his mom to feed him a worm is because every student was

132

given a DVD copy of the play as a keepsake. And for months, every time Willis Freedman saw me in the hall, he'd drop his jaw and laugh. *Jerk.*

So right about now, I'm wondering *why, of all the lives on the planet that I could have chosen to step into, why, oh why, did I choose one where I would most definitely have to perform in front of people?* And not in front of the whole school, but in front of the equivalent of the whole county. The closer I get to backstage, the louder the blood pumps in my ears. How am I going to do this? I decide I need a mini genie conference, so I have no choice. I give the desperate peepee plea.

"Vi," I say, trying not to let my voice quiver. "I know this is a terrible time, but I've got to hit the bathroom before I go on."

"*WHAT?*" she answers, shuffling papers and grabbing her walkie-talkie. "Well, better now than in the middle of the show. *BUT HURRY.*"

I skedaddle into a big, empty backstage bathroom, into a stall and whip my pocket mirror out of the little tote I'm carrying that will be taken back to wardrobe as soon as I hit the stage. I told Toni it was my good luck charm and that I felt like my great, great, *great* granny Malone was somehow with me onstage if I could keep it with me until I go on. I think she got a tear in her eye. She also promised to take it back to the bus for me. She's so taken with the whole tale I've spun, I just know she's gonna ask to hear more from the real Becca Starr. Oh well. Can't be helped. I open the compact, but only see my own reflection in the glass.

"Frank! Frank!" I say in a whisper that quickly turns to a yell. "Where in the world are you? I'm dying here!"

Finally, Frank shows up, and I hear Hawaiian music in the background.

"What's up, Magpie?" Frank says, sipping something from a coconut. He's clearly someplace tropical. "You having fun?"

"Um, no! No, I'm not!" I say, a little irritated because he's just so relaxed. "Where the heck are you, anyway?"

"Macau," Frank says. "Do you know where that is, Maggie Malone?"

"Uh, no, and I'm not in the mood for a geography quiz, Frank. I'm scared stiff! I'm losing my marbles here, and was supposed to be onstage five minutes ago!"

"Uh huh," Frank says, taking a long pull on his coconut drink.

"I think I'm ready to go back home now," I finally say. "Wait, I don't think I'm ready, I *know* I'm ready. I did this, okay? I got to live Becca's life and it was great and all of that—well, mostly great, anyway. But all good things have to end, so let's get me back to 337 Willow Avenue. Please and thank you." I squeeze my eyes shut because I figure Frank might not want me to see what happens when he beams me back home.

"I can't do that, kid," Frank explains. "And anyway, you're just now getting to the best part. You see, each life you step into will involve a certain task, a challenge, if you will. And I hope you will. Because if you stare that challenge right in the eyeballs, you've got it licked for life. Not many people get that opportunity, you know."

"Ugh!" I say, irritated. "*Really?*"

"Yes, really, Maggie Malone. Now get out there and look your fear in the face. And remember, it's as if this life was always yours. Now go live it!" Frank says and leans back onto a lounge chair, tipping his cowboy hat over his face.

I guess we're all done here.

"Becca?" I hear Vi's voice say. "WHAT is going on? WHO were you just talking to?"

I hadn't heard her come in. *YIKES. Think fast, Malone!*

"Um…" I say, sliding the compact back into the tote and opening the stall door. "Yeah. I figured I'd run through a few of my positive affirmations while I peed. Deekap ChoCho told me I should do that before I perform. Well, he didn't say that part about peeing *while* I say my affirmations, but…"

Vi takes me gently by the arm and guides me out of the bathroom, saying, "*You*, my dear, are a piece of work today."

My little talk with Frank didn't do much to calm my nerves. It feels like every cell in my body is on high alert when Vi helps me up onto a small, square platform under the stage.

"All right, Bec. Give 'em a good show. And remember: have fun!" Vi says, adjusting a few stray curls and stepping back off the platform. She flashes me a big grin and the "b" sign. I give her a shaky smile and a thumbs-up in return.

Have fun? That's a tall order. I'm just looking to survive.

Chapter 21

When I Take the Stage

My knees are wobbling uncontrollably as I hear a loud boom like fireworks, and then the platform starts rising. *Get a grip, Malone. Ready or not, here you go!*

I rise up to stage level in a sea of fog. As it clears, I realize I am standing face-to-face with a bajillion girls who look *just like me*. And man, are they going CRAZY. I'm talking full-on, hog wild, cuckoo-ca-choo crazy, worse than the time my four-year-old cousin Cameron ate that jumbo Fun Dip, three sticks and all. They're screaming, jumping, and crying (why are they crying?!) and I haven't even opened my mouth yet. Becca Starr gets all of this just for showing up? Crazy!

Their high-pitched wailing pierces my ears. At least I can hear something over the blood pounding in there. I hear "'Dance Like You Mean It' in 3, 2, 1!" inside my earpiece. I step off the platform as the guitar player gives me a nod, like *start singing*. I can feel my lower jaw starting to go slack. My chin hits the mike with a loud thud. The band looks at each other, confused, and starts to repeat the intro. *Get it together, Maggie. You're not in the second grade anymore. Look your fear in the face!* I look up and realize that because of the blinding stage lights, I can only see the first three rows of fans. They seem to really dig whatever I do, so I decide to *just* focus on them.

"Are you guys ready to dance?" I ask the first three rows, but the whole dome erupts in a booming "*YEAH!*" I really should've expected that kind of volume, but I've never had 20,000 people answer a question before, so I jump about three feet in the air. The band plays louder, and I know it's time to do this thing. The first bit of the song is kind of a rap. Stella and I used to sing it every day when we rode our bikes to school together. Anyway, I know it by heart so I go for it.

"*So you THINK you can dance, you can really, really dance?*" I start rapping and dancing with the backup dancers like I've done this routine, like a million times, because the truth is, Stella and I *have* performed it in my bedroom at least a million times. Maybe more.

The song goes pretty well, but there isn't really much singing involved. The next song is still a pump-you-up, get-those-wigs-a-wagging kind of song— "Party Like a Rock Star." I have to say, it's not my favorite, but I know it because they play it on 95.9 The Whiz all the stinking time. That one's super loud with a ripping guitar, so you can barely even hear me singing. As I wrap it up, I see Toni at side stage waving at me like *come on, let's go!* I run off the stage, and the backup dancers take center stage to entertain the crowd while I…yeah, I don't know what I'm supposed to be doing back here.

I follow Toni down six metal stairs and when I get to the bottom, at least four sets of hands start ripping my clothes off, yelling at me—and each other. They pull my slip dress right up and over my head so I'm like, *hello*, practically NAKED in the middle of all these people, but no one seems to care. Did I mention I'm a teensie bit modest?

"Arm, Becca! *ARM!*" a frantic-looking lady towering over me shouts for me to slide into a long-sleeved lace top, which is kind of hard, considering my arms are drenched with sweat from the lights and the dancing.

"Oh, sorry!" I say, starting to comprehend what we're doing here.

Then another woman at my feet yells, "Left foot—NOW!"

These people are animals. It's freaking me out how they're pulling and pushing me—I think one of them scratched me on the back. I haven't had so many people screaming at me since the sack race on field day last year when I fell down and couldn't get back on my feet until after Annie Spelzer had crossed the finish line. Being yelled at didn't help then, and it's not helping today.

"Becca! Please focus! You act like you've never

done this before!" the giant woman says, whipping me around, putting a belt on my waist.

"Easy there, tiger!" I say, grabbing the ends of the belt and buckling it myself. Vi appears out of nowhere, grabs my arm, and hustles me back up the stairs. Holy smokes. *How many more costume changes do I have to endure?*

The next song is a ballad, "I Still Believe." That means it's just me and my guitar player at the front of the stage. No fun backup dancers to distract from my less than perfect dance moves. No backup singers to fill in if I croak out the wrong note. I know five people just dressed me, so why do I feel completely naked?

I focus on my first three rows of expectant fans looking up at me as I approach the stool at the front of the stage. The guitar player runs through the beginning bit. I take a deep breath and start to sing. *BUT NO ONE CAN HEAR ME.* I look around. My curly-haired twins look confused. *I'm confused.* I smile a half smile and spot mean Rory on the side stage with his face as red as a ripe tomato, so furious he looks like he's going to explode. Technical difficulties. The cheers in the audience turn to a low hum, and I make a vow right on the spot that if this microphone starts working, I will never hide my gum wrappers between the couch cushions or call my brother Icky Mickey ever again. I tap on the mike and a loud *boom, boom, boom* fills the arena. And then everything goes quiet.

I look over at Rory and he's waving his big arm, like *AGAIN!*

"Let's try that again," I say quietly, almost to myself. But they hear me this time, and the arena explodes once again with screaming, jumping, cheering fans.

The band kicks up and I start to sing, "*Way back when, before I knew, some fairy tales just don't come true…*"

And here's the freakiest part: I sound exactly like her. Becca Starr's velvety voice booms out of my lungs like it's always been there, waiting to be heard. My heart feels like it's going to explode with happiness. I am a real-life rock star and my fans love me. I close my eyes and belt out the words, and I'm pretty sure every person in the arena is singing along with me. Me! *Remember this moment forever*, I beg my brain, pretty sure that won't be a problem.

Chapter 22

When I Do Something Really Nuts

I don't mean to sound full of myself or anything, but the next song comes and I am *on fire* on the stage. I don't miss a single beat, and when the backup dancers join me, I fall right in line. I am a real-life, full-fledged, bona fide rock star. Mostly Magical Boots? Try *Totally* Magical Boots. I could do this all day, every day.

Eventually I wrap up the show with Becca's first-ever hit song, "Breaking Hearts," and when I do, I swear to you, the entire audience is a sea of b's. *We heart you, Becca Starr! We heart you with all 20,000 of our hearts!* It's the craziest thing I have ever seen in my life.

After my final bow, I step forward to the edge of the stage. I'm past the blinding row of lights so I can see that practically every person in the whole crowd—mostly girls around my age and younger—is reaching for me and screaming. I try to touch as many of those hands as I can, and when I do, each one of those girls screams even louder and looks like she's going to lose her mind or faint right there on the spot. I hope somebody on my team knows CPR.

Out of the corner of my eye, I see Rory giving me the *wrap it up* signal. He wants me to leave the stage? But *why?* This is the best part—like saving the frosted part of your cupcake for last! I decide to ignore him and head over to the left side stage and give them a little Becca love. The whole left side of the arena goes wild as I pace back and forth, high-fiving every hand in my path. It wouldn't be right to leave the right side hanging, would it? I skip across the stage and start blowing kisses that way.

I look up and see Justin smiling down at me, and I blow him a big kiss. Then I look over and think I can actually see steam coming out of Rory's ears. Ugggh! Okay, I guess it's got to end sometime.

"Good night, everybody! I LOVE YOU, NEW YORK!" I shout (I've always wanted to say that!) and run off the stage, right over to Vi.

"Great show, Becca!" she says, giving me a huge hug. "But we're in Houston."

"Whoops! Sorry!" I say. "It just sort of slipped out."

"No biggie," Vi says. "I'll deal with that tomorrow. You ready to get comfy?"

I am *so* ready to get comfy. I can practically feel those furry slippers hugging my feet already.

"Starr," I hear a voice behind me yell, just as Vi and I link arms and start to make our way toward the backstage exit.

I turn around and see Rory's mean old face. He's giving me the iciest stare I've ever seen.

"Yeah?" I call back, planting my hands on my hips.

"Pull that little routine again and you can find another sound engineer," he says. He bends back over on the floor and starts ripping tape off some of the wires behind stage. He's clearly done with me, but I am *so* not done with him. I walk over and stand directly over him.

"Rory, can I talk to you for a second?" I ask his back.

"What do you need *now*?" he barks at me without even turning around.

"It's just, well, I just," I stutter. Man, this is not easy. I take a breath. "I really don't like the way you talk to me."

Rory stops what he's doing and stands up really slowly. He turns to face me, glaring.

"Oh, really?" he hisses sarcastically. "And what are you going to do about it, little miss superstar?"

"I'm going to fire you," I say before I can stop myself. Holy fish sticks, I cannot believe I just said that. Me! Maggie Malone. I just *fired* Becca Starr's big-time sound guy.

"You can't fire me, you little brat," Rory spits.

"Actually, yes, she can," says Vi, who has snuck up behind us. "Becca's the boss." She puts her arm around me.

"You'll both be sorry," he shouts, dropping all of his gear and storming off the stage.

"I doubt it," I say to Vi with a little giggle.

"Well, he sure had that coming," she says. "And good for you, Becca. That was very brave. You've wanted to fire him forever. I was wondering if you'd ever get up the nerve to actually do it. So, *now* are you ready to get comfy?"

I nod. I can't wait to chill on the bus and watch some TV and have a little snack. That is, if I don't pass out first from being more tired than I was after riding every ride twice at Disneyland.

"Okay," Vi says. "Go get changed then. I'll meet you back here in five."

"Huh?" I say.

"Your meet-and-greets are waiting. And then you've got autographs. We won't run out of pens like last time," Vi assures me.

Meet and greets? Autographs? Are you kidding me? *A rock star's work is never done.* But that's okay, 'cause I am on top of the world right now. I totally rocked the house—I mean *the Superdome!* And now I get to feel the love all up close and personal. This has got to be what it's all about.

Chapter 23

When I Meet My Fans Up Close

I swing back through wardrobe to slip out of my last sweaty, sparkly outfit. Toni hands me a soft, colorful T-shirt dress, a cozy red cardigan (because it's actually freezing in this place when you're not racing back and forth across a stage), and a pair of cushiony flats.

I skip around the corner with these big security guys surrounding me on all sides. As I get close to the room where I'll be signing autographs, I can hear the chanting. "Bec-ca! Bec-ca! Bec-ca!" How awesome is that? I have to say, I'm kind of getting used to the *beyond bonkers fan-love* these people have for me—I mean Becca. I wonder if I would ever get tired of it. Probably not.

I take a deep breath and smile. When the security dudes open the door for me, the chanting turns to high-pitched, burst-your-eardrums screaming. Yeah, I might be able to do without *that* part. Whoa.

My fans, mostly moms and daughters, are gated off with a red velvet rope, and they are going completely crazy. The girls are screaming and crying and jumping up and down. A few of the moms are too. Some of the moms are holding their daughters back as they reach out to touch me when I walk by. One lady apparently let go of her little gremlin because all of a sudden, I feel this yank in the back of my head.

Sister of a twisted sock monkey! Somebody just pulled my hair out! Just a little bit, but what in the world? Are these fans totally nuts?

Vi rushes over to me. She is not happy. She yells something I can't hear at the security guys.

"I'm so, so sorry, sweetie!" she says. "They're just so obsessed with your hair. I promise it won't happen again."

"What? Why would they do that? They want a

souvenir *of me*? Ewww!" I yell so Vi can hear me over the screaming.

"I know, I know," she says, encouraging me. "This is not your favorite part, but remember, the fans are why you get to be the world-famous Becca Starr, right?"

I nod in agreement, rubbing the back of my head.

Vi walks me into another gated-off section with special red carpet and fancy, satin curtains around it. I plop down on the little couch, take a few big swigs of water, and catch my breath.

"Do you need a minute or are you good?" Vi asks.

"I'm good," I say, because by now I know I'm supposed to say that, even if I'm not.

I had no idea what a "meet and greet" was when Vi first said it, but it doesn't take me long to figure it out. Of all of the millions of kids who want a piece of Becca, a special handful get to spend a whole two minutes in her—I mean my—company.

Vi brings in my first meet-and-greet, a mother/daughter duo. The mom sits down next to me, smiling like the cat that caught the mouse. The little girl stands smack in front of me. She seems really nervous and for some reason, she's not saying a thing.

"Becca, this is Harmony Lynn and her mom Shayna Lynn," Vi tells me. "They drove all the way from Abilene to see you tonight."

"Harmony Lynn! You stand straight up, girl, and do it just like we practiced!" Shayna Lynn is barking like a dog and poor Harmony Lynn, who must be about six years old, looks terrified.

Do *what*? I wonder. Then Harmony Lynn starts to sing in a sweet, raspy little voice that I can barely hear over the crowd.

"*If this is the road, then where do I go? Nothing's for real, when it's all for show…*"

"That's enough!" the mom yells, turning to me. "She doesn't do that next part too good yet. But what do you think? We think she's got what it takes to make it big in the singing world. That's why we named her Harmony. We knew the second she popped out she was gonna be a star. Just like you, Becca. Do *you* think she's got what it takes? Do you? Do you?"

"Well, I…I think she's great!" I stammer, not knowing what else to say and looking over at Vi.

"And here's her picture from the Abilene Teeny Queen Pageant," Shayna Lynn says, shoving a wrinkled newspaper clipping in my face.

Vi picks up on what's happening and slips her phone into her pocket.

"Okay, ladies, a quick picture and then we've got to keep things moving," Vi announces.

"Our number's on the back of that clip, Becca! Let us know what you can do for Harmony Lynn here!" Shayna Lynn yells as she is ushered out.

Was that an *audition*? Super-duper weird. But if I've learned anything today, it's that things can always get weirder.

Chapter 24

When I Put a Woobie in My Mouth

"Okay, Bec, next we have Angel and her mom Betty-Jo," Vi says, giving me the heads-up as Angel and her mom come in. "You'll remember them from the Dallas show?"

The little girl grabs a bottle of water from my side table like she owns the place and plops down way too close to me.

"So here's how I see it, Becca," Angel starts, smacking her chewing gum and breathing a burst of sickeningly sweet berry right into my face. She can't be more than eight years old, even though she's carrying a grown-up purse and is wearing high-heeled sandals. "Your third costume change is getting really tired looking. You need to get something new there, and I suggest a bright blue. That's really good for TV too, you know. And that backup dancer girl? The one with the nose ring and the spiky hair? She has *got* to go."

"Oh…well, I—" I begin, but Angel is not finished.

"And you totally didn't do that flip over thingy with the boy dancers during 'Saturday Night Par-tay' like you did in Topeka," Angel continues. "Big mistake. Overall, I'd give tonight, like, a six."

I sit there with my mouth kind of hanging open. Who does this girl think she is? Some kind of big-time Becca Starr expert? To think Becca has to put up with rude kids like this every day! Wow. I'd like to tell this little monster where to shove her stinky mouthful of Dubble Bubble. But I don't.

"Al-righty then, Angel! And what an angel you are. Thanks for the feedback and we'll see you in Austin," Vi says, rolling her eyes in my direction and sending them on their way.

"What's Angel's deal?" I lean in to ask Vi.

"Oh, you can't possibly have forgotten about your

traveling fan club, could you?" Vi laughs. "Angel is the kid whose dad started Little Kibble Kitten Chow. Her parents homeschool her so she never has to miss a concert. You know, they ride around in that bus that looks just like yours, and they put your picture right next to Angel's on the side of it? It's totally creepy. And obnoxious, right?"

"Umm, yeah, a little bit!" I say, thinking how I definitely could not handle these people on a daily basis.

Next comes a sweet little girl, maybe about five years old, dragging a dirty blanket behind her. She's sucking her thumb along with a corner of the blanket and snuggles in next to me. Her dad stands off to the side.

"What's *your* name, sweetie?" I ask. She's totally cute.

"Bailey," she answers, looking up at me with big brown eyes.

See? This is what all of these "meet and greets" should be like, I think to myself.

Her dad steps in to make Bailey's request for her.

"Bailey would like to get a picture of you with her woobie, if that's okay," he asks, very respectfully.

"Sure!" I say. Because how sweet is that?

The little girl hands me her blanket and I have to tell you, the smell almost knocks me over. It's sticky and crusty at the same time. Blech! I hold it out to the side and smile with her for the picture, but Bailey looks down, like she's going to cry.

"Umm," her dad says hesitantly. "She'd like it if you would put a little bit of it in your mouth. Like she does—just the tip. If you don't mind!"

Surely, he's joking, I think. *But no.*

Bailey looks up at me, all hopeful with those big brown Bambi eyes. She is smiling and trying not to cry at the same time.

Oh, for the love of stinky baby blankets! "Okay, Dad, are you ready?" I yell. I take the disgusting woobie, and for one half of one second, I stick that thing in the corner of my open mouth and smile. I almost gag, but Bailey is grinning ear to ear.

"Wait, I'm not sure my flash went off…" the dad is saying, fiddling with his camera, as Vi ushers them out through the gate.

Where's the germ juice? I need a breath mint! Is this what Becca has to deal with every night? What's all that security for anyway?

I meet a ton more kids and some of them are totally normal and don't tell me what I did wrong or ask me to chew their gum, which is a relief. I sign autographs until I can't feel my hand anymore. A lot of the fans even seem like girls I'd be friends with back home at first. Except when I talk to them, they start shaking and crying. And every single one asks me to sign my autograph to "my BFF" and tells me how much she loves me. How weird is that? They don't *love me*! I mean Becca. They don't even *know her*!

It's after midnight when the whole crazy backstage thing is finally over. I limp back to the bus with Vi. I've never stayed up this late at my own sleepover party or even 'til the ball drops on New Year's Eve.

"Great show tonight," Vi says. "You were on fire! I don't think I've ever seen you so…"

But I'm sound asleep before she can even finish her sentence.

Chapter 25

When I Realize
It Really Happened

The pounding sound keeps getting louder. I can't figure out what it is. The warm-up band banging out some crazy drumbeat? Two million feet attached to a million stomping fans? Maybe it's the roadies loading the gear onto the bus. Whatever it is, I wish it would stop. My head is throbbing and my eyelids feel like someone superglued them shut. It's probably the sparkly-spider lashes all stuck together. Did I even wash my face before I fell into bed last night? I honestly can't remember.

"Margaret Flannery Malone, for the love of lasagna, *open this door!*" shouts a voice from very far away. "I've been calling you all morning. Is your phone off the hook or something? Ummm, HAPPY BIRTHDAY! Hey, are you still *sleeping*? It's almost nine o'clock! I brought doughnuts—with rainbow sprinkles! Open up already!!!"

I sit up in bed and pry my eyelids open. There's my polka-dot chair in the corner, and my zebra striped rug and the purple vanity table that I helped my mom paint. I swing my feet around and they land on the floor with a loud *plop* that startles me. Why am I wearing a dirty, scuffed-up old pair of—

The MMBs.

The whole day—all of it—comes rushing back to me in a flash. The bus, falling out of bed, Vi and her clipboard, the breakfast tent, Chaz and the hair extensions, Lisbeth and her tweezers, mean old Gory Rory, the Superdome, the fans, hanging out with Justin Crowe... *It was real. I was her and it was real and now it's over.* I jump off the bed and race over to my mirror. I don't look any different. *Am* I different? I'm not sure yet.

"Hang on, Stella," I shout, pulling off the boots and shoving them back into my closet, up on the highest shelf I can reach. I unlock my door, and Stella practically knocks me over in her rush to get in.

"Honestly, Maggie, are you sick or something?" Stella wants to know, pushing my stuffed animals aside so she can plop down on my still-warm bed. She has her laptop with her and she fires it up. I slide in right next to her.

"I mean, *HAPPY TWELFTH BIRTHDAY!*" Stella announces all official-like with big *ta-da* hands. She puts the plate of doughnuts in my lap and starts clicking away at her keyboard. "Anyway, check this out: Becca and Justin are *boyfriend and girlfriend.*"

"Um, I don't think they are—" I start to say, but Stella interrupts me.

"They are too, it's all over the web," she points to the supposedly true news story that has a picture of Becca and Justin hugging.

"I think they're just good friends," I say. "I wouldn't believe everything you read."

"You got a better source?" Stella asks.

"Well, no, but—" I stammer.

"And get this," she says, all excited. "Check out this picture of Becca yelling at some poor guy that works for her. She must have a real temper. Or maybe she's becoming one of those total divas. It happens in Hollywood all the time, you know."

I look at the picture. It's Becca looking steamed all right. And the guy she's steamed at? None other than mean old Gory Rory.

"Well, that's because—" I stop myself just in time. "I mean, that guy is probably some big jerk, and she's yelling at him because she's sick of him being totally rude to her all the time. Or something."

"It says here that she *fired* him!" Stella gasps. "What did I tell you? Diva!"

"You never know—" I say, but Stella interrupts me again.

"Look at *this*," she says, scrolling down the page. "Here she is lounging on the beach in Mexico. Life is so totally not fair. I mean, she gets to lie around all day and sing for a couple of hours at night. Tough life. Where do I sign up?"

"I bet it's not as glamorous as you—er, *we*—think," I say. "I mean, she probably has to be on the road a lot, driving from show to show and all, and think about what goes into a concert! The lights and the equipment and the microphones... There's so much that can go wrong, it must be really stressful. I'll bet even all that fussing over your hair and makeup gets old after a while..." I decide I'd better stop talking before I blow my own cover.

"If it makes you feel better to pretend Becca Starr has this really awful, miserable life, knock yourself out," Stella says, snapping her computer shut. "I'm pretty sure her life is perfect."

"Like my mom always says," I tell Stella, "you don't know what you don't know until you spend a day in someone else's shoes."

And boy, do I know.

Chapter 26

When It's Back
to (Stinky) Reality

My alarm startles me awake to the sound of disc jockeys laughing way too hard, bantering back and forth about something that makes no sense to me. I'm still pretty tired from my birthday weekend extravaganza.

I didn't want a birthday party this year, so on Saturday night, my parents took the whole family, plus Stella of course, to the Ichihana. My brother Mickey and I love that restaurant because the chef wears this ridiculously tall white hat, chops the food up right there in front of you, and plays tricks on the kid having the birthday. This chef was pretty impressive and caught, like, three shrimp tails in his lofty hat. And a raw egg that didn't even break. Then he tossed a delicious shrimp bite right into my mouth.

After dinner, Stella and I put our drink umbrellas behind our ears and danced in our seats when they beat the drum and sang the birthday song to me. It was a great night and after dinner, we had a sleepover at my house and stayed up way past our bedtimes making up dance routines and doing our toenails and watching *Frenemies* reruns. I went to bed around eight o'clock last night but I still feel like I could sleep for another year. Which would be awesome, because then I could snooze right through the rest of sixth grade at Stinkerton.

But I know that's not an option, just like I know my mom will go batty if I'm not up and dressed when she calls me for breakfast, so I blink hard and try to stretch myself awake.

Finally I shuffle across my room to the blue sparkly tank top, black cardigan, and jeans I laid out the night before. Dread fills up my now twelve-year-old body. All the excitement of being Becca Starr, a super-fun birthday weekend, and now I'm right back in the same spot, getting ready for another agonizing day at my monster of a stinking school. When I was Becca Starr, if I was confused or angry or scared, all I had to do was pull out my MM pocket mirror and get some good genie advice from Frank. I could use a little of that right now.

I get dressed and sit down at my desk. Then I pull the pocket mirror from the way back of my desk drawer and open it up.

"Good morning, Maggie!" Frank says from inside the mirror. *He's here! SWEET!* "Ready for another adventure already?"

"Um, not really," I stammer, because I remember I wasn't supposed to bother Frank until I was ready to take the MMBs for another spin. "I just wanted, you know, to say hey. And so…hey."

I realize my voice sounds pretty shaky on that second *hey* because Frank asks, "You okay, kid?"

"Uh, yeah, not exactly," I say, slumping down in my chair.

"Do me a favor," Frank says. "Go back and read

that letter from your Aunt Fiona again, the one that came with the boots. You'll understand what you have to do. The choice is yours. Now I gotta go. There's a kid in Taipei trying to strap a pair of jetpacks onto the back of his MMBs. Shame the boots don't come with a healthy dose of common sense."

"What?" I ask again, completely confused.

"You get to decide, kid," Frank says, starting to fade away.

"Wait! Decide what? *Choose WHAT?*" I ask, pulling the mirror closer, but Frank is fading fast.

"See you next go-round, Maggie Malone!" he says as his reflection turns to mine.

Flaming fiddlesticks! Does he have to play the mysterious disappearing genie card EVERY time?

I stash the mirror back in the far corner of my desk drawer and go to my super-secret box under my bed where I keep my diary, every birthday card I've gotten since I was a baby, and now, Auntie Fi's letter. I scan the letter, trying to figure out what Frank wants me to remember from it. What exactly am I supposed to decide?

I read: "Trust me when I tell you that things aren't always the way they seem." Well, that certainly turned out to be true. I mean, the life of a rock star sure isn't what I thought it would be. But what does that have to do with me, now, today?

And then I read: "You get to decide how big you want your life to be from now on."

How *big* I want my life to be? I hadn't really noticed that part of the letter before. What does that mean, anyway? *Not helpful, Frank.* What good is having your own genie if he disappears right when you need him the most?

Chapter 27

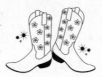

When My Life Circles the Toilet Bowl

I brush my teeth and figure it's time to do battle with my unruly ringlets. But instead, I decide to just wet my hands, scrunch my curls, and let a few fall toward my face, the way Chaz did when I was Becca, which is exactly what Auntie Fi does, now that I think about it. These curls aren't so bad, really—I think maybe I just need to stop getting in fights with them.

I grab my lunch bag and smear some butter on an already toasted English muffin. My mom has everything laid out for me—even OJ in my favorite tiny, blue juice glass. I look at the clock on the microwave and realize that my mini-Frank conference has almost made me late.

I yell into my mom's steamy bathroom where she's showering, "Bye, mom, I love you!"

"Love you more!" she calls back. "Have a great day!"

"I will!" I say, because that's what I always say. But I have a sinking feeling my day is going to be about as great as trick-or-treating in the rain. On crutches. With your dentist.

Stella and I figured out that if we meet at exactly 7:36 a.m. on the corner of Spruce and Maple, we have enough time to ride together for three blocks before she turns left toward Sacred Heart and I hang a right for Stinkerton. We brake on the corner before heading off in our different directions.

"Good luck at Stink Town," Stella says with a half-smile and a thumbs-up.

"Hey, Stella, I was thinking," I say, a little hesitantly, scarfing the last of my muffin and washing it down with some fairly fresh water from my squirt bottle.

"Yeah?" she answers, adjusting her bike helmet.

"Since I'm going to be going to Stinkerton, like, probably forever, maybe we should start calling it Pinkerton," I say. "I don't know, I just think it might help."

"Totally," Stella agrees. "It can't hurt." Then she gives me a big, goofy overbite grin.

"Do I have poppy seeds in my teeth?" she asks. "My mom ran out of cinnamon raisin bagels and gave us the poppy seed ones. Am I good?"

"All good!" I confirm. "See you this afternoon!" And we wheel off in our different directions.

It's kind of crazy how Pinkerton is almost exactly as close to my house as Sacred Heart. I'm glad I don't have to cross a major four-lane or anything—not that my mom would let me do that on my bike. I pull up in front of the school and slide into the spot on the end. I like the end spot the best. It gives you a little elbow room, unlike my locker. As I'm twisting my lock, I notice a girl who's probably in my same grade locking her bike up on the opposite end. She looks up at me but quickly turns away. I figure I've got three minutes to get into my locker and to class so I skedaddle as fast as I can.

I make my way through the crowd to my locker and duck down, holding one hand over my head for protection, just in case. I keep my lunch bag in the other hand, which makes it a little hard to unlock my locker. But you really can't be too careful around this place. When I stand up, I'm nose to nose with a blond-haired, blue-eyed girl—the same one who stomped my sandwich on Friday.

"Excuse me," I say, trying to step around her.

"No prob," she says, moving out of my way. She actually smiles when she says it, but I'm sure it's really one of those nasty "I'll get you later" sort of smiles. I tuck my chin to my chest and rush off, making a mental note to stay as far away from her as I can.

I have a great morning, in the sense that I'm not late to a single class, nothing falls on me and slices any body parts open, and I don't trip and crack my front tooth or anything. It's pretty sad that this is what having a great morning means to me now, but it is what it is. I'm trying to ignore the growling in my stomach, because I'd rather not think about the lonely lunch hour that starts in one minute.

Man, that minute went fast. The bell rings, and the entire school rushes toward the cafeteria. I grab my sandwich from my locker and dart into the bathroom. I decided earlier that I was going to eat in a bathroom stall. It's totally gross, I know, but at least it's warm in here.

I listen as girls come in and out, giggling and chatting. They don't sound so horrible from in here, but I'm sure that's just because I can't see them ignoring me. Finally there's a quiet spell, so I wrap up my lunch trash and tiptoe out of my stall. When I round the bend toward the sinks, I catch a glimpse of the mirror and let out a scream.

"How's it going, kid?" says Frank. *Frank-the-genie is here, at Stinkerton, in the girls' bathroom mirror. As my mom would say, jumping Jehoshaphat! I have no idea what that means, but I like the sound of it.*

"What are you doing here, Frank?" I hissper. I

made that word up. It's like a hiss and a whisper combined. I bend down to see if there are any feet in any stalls.

"It sort of seemed like you could use a little help," Frank says.

"I'm doing fine," I tell him, pointing at my head. "Look? See? No blood!"

"Did you reread your aunt's letter?" he asks.

"Of course I did," I tell him, a little bit insulted. I'm about to tell him that he doesn't know a thing about me if he even has to ask me that, but right then two girls walk into the bathroom and make a beeline for the two sinks next to me.

My heart is pounding in my ears just like it did when I was onstage as Becca Starr. I lock eyes with Frank in the mirror and send him a silent message: *HELP ME, FRANK. HELP ME NOW!*

"Relax, Malone," Frank says. "They can't see me. Or hear me. But if you talk to me, they'll hear *that*, so try to be cool."

Try to be cool, he says. That Frank is hilarious.

"Hey, did you finish your pig dissection diagram?" one girl asks the other.

"Ugh, I did," her friend answers. "Thank goodness *that's* over! Can you say dis-gus-ting?"

I'm trying to look very busy washing my hands when I hear Frank's voice.

"You know you can chime in there any time, right?" Frank says. I glance up at him but say nothing. "Oh, I get it. You're waiting for *them* to talk to *you*! Well, that's a great plan…if you want things to stay exactly the way they are. When your aunt said that part about deciding how big you want your life to be, she wasn't talking about whose shoes you were going to step into next. She was talking about *you*. Think about it. How big do you want your life to be, Maggie?"

I just don't know what to do. I open my mouth to say something just as the girls finish up at the sinks and bustle out of the bathroom.

"Maybe next time," Frank says. His face fades just as the end-of-lunch bell rings.

Chapter 28

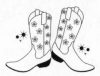

When I Figure Out How to Turn Things Around

I shuffle into the freezing-cold biology lab. There's a table in the back where nobody is sitting yet, and I start to make a beeline for it. Then I hear Frank's voice in my head. (At least I *think* it's in my head. It could be coming through the loudspeakers, for all I know. I'm not sure about a lot of things these days.)

When your aunt said that part about deciding how big you want your life to be, she wasn't talking about whose shoes you were going to step into next. She was talking about you.

I really, super-want my life to be good. I want to make new friends. I want to like it here at Stink— *Pink*erton. I want to *not* be invisible anymore. *What* *would Becca Starr do?* I ask myself. *Piece of cake: she'd sit wherever she darn well pleased. Why shouldn't she? And why shouldn't I?*

"Is this seat taken?" I ask a girl who's sitting by herself, writing something in a spiral notebook.

"Nope, it's all yours," she answers, hardly looking up.

"Thanks," I say, sliding into the seat next to her. She goes right on writing.

Well, this is going well. People here at Pinkerton just must not be very friendly. I mean, why doesn't she…

Just then, the sandwich-stepping girl breezes in and sits down right across from me. She's got that same little smile on her face, the one that makes me want to run right back to my bathroom stall. But I can't do that. I *won't* do that. I'm not exactly sure how big I want my life to be, but I'm pretty positive I want it to be bigger than a bathroom stall.

You've been on a stage singing for thousands of total strangers, I remind myself. *You have your own genie. You're funny and intelligent and kind and, don't forget, you've lived the life of an actual rock star. Start acting like it.*

"I'm Maggie," I announce, just like that, my voice shaking a tiny bit. "I'm new."

"Alicia," the sandwich-stepper says, holding out her hand to introduce herself. I shake it, and it's actually a nice, solid handshake. My dad always says you have to watch out for limp-fish handshakers. If we're going on handshakes alone, Alicia might just be okay. Maybe that's even a genuine smile after all. "Nice to meet you."

"Nice to see you too," I say, because my mom says it's smarter to say nice to "see you" instead of "meet you" in case you met that person before and don't remember. It's a cover-your-behind move. Thankfully, Alicia doesn't remember the reindeer-rocking, mummy girl from last week. I decide to just go with it.

"That's Crystal," she says, pointing to the girl next to me. "She's cool and the smartest girl in the sixth grade. Maybe the whole school. You must be pretty smart yourself to snag a seat next to her!"

Crystal looks up and smiles, then goes back to her notebook.

Alicia slides her biology book to the side. Underneath it is a folder with a picture of Becca Starr on the front.

"Hey, you like Becca Starr?" I ask.

"Are you *kidding* me?" Alicia laughs. "Who doesn't like Becca Starr? She's totally amazing. Have you ever been to one of her shows?"

"Yeah, well, no, well, actually—" I stutter. I'm trying to figure out how I can possibly answer this question honestly when a pretty girl with honey-colored hair slides up behind Alicia and clears her throat. I do a double take. She's not wearing the same T-shirt, but I'd know that DRAMA QUEEN face anywhere. It's the girl who apparently owned the seat I was sitting in that first day in Spanish class. Looks like she owns the one Alicia is in now too, even though the one right next to it is wide open.

"What's up, Lucy?" Alicia says, all cool-like.

"That's my seat," Lucy huffs.

Alicia pretends to look around her.

"I don't see a name tag or anything, and I'm sitting in it now, so I guess you'll have to find somewhere else to park it," Alicia says with a shrug. For a minute, I think Lucy might push her out of the chair or start stomping her feet like a buffalo, but finally she lets out a big, noisy *arrrgh* and storms off in a huff.

"That's Lucy St. Claire," Alicia leans in toward me and whispers. "Otherwise known as Lucifer. She's the *worst*—thinks she owns the school just because her grandfather bought new bleachers back in like nineteen-something. Anyway, don't let her push you around, okay?"

I nod and smile.

"Anyway, Becca is coming to town next month, and I'm going to the show with some friends," Alicia goes on. "Do you want to come with us?"

"Can you teach a rock to stay?" I answer before I can stop myself. That's a Maggie-and-Stella joke, and for a second, I wish I could take it back, in case Alicia thinks I'm a big dork now.

Alicia laughs. "Good one! Okay, I'll email you all

of the details. Here, write down your email address." She pushes her Becca Starr folder toward me and I jot it down.

"Um, there's just one thing," I say, sliding the folder back toward Alicia. "My best friend from my old school? She's like the biggest Becca Starr fan on the planet. Maybe in the universe. Would it be okay if she came too?"

I hold my breath. As much as I want to make new friends, Stella comes first. She'd be crushed if we didn't go to that show together, and besides, I'd never throw her under the bus like that or just ditch her for some new friends. We have history—and you can't jeopardize *that*.

"The more the merrier," Alicia whispers as Mrs. Shankshaw shuffles in the door.

"Today we are going to be comparing and contrasting plant and animal cells," Mrs. Shankshaw says. She opens a cabinet door and starts plopping microscopes randomly on tables. "You know the process. Grab a partner and find an open microscope."

"Want to be partners?" Alicia asks.

I nod, and we stand up to make our way to a nearby open microscope. As we do, I notice a girl just standing in the doorway. I realize she's the girl from the bike rack this morning.

"Um, excuse me—" she says, holding a late slip out to Mrs. Shankshaw as she walks by. Mrs. Shankshaw promptly ignores her—probably because she doesn't even see her.

"Hang on a second," I say to Alicia, walking over to the girl, who I notice has a Band-Aid across her nose. I have a feeling I know what's going on.

"Are you new here?" I ask her.

She nods her head. The poor thing looks as if she's about to break down bawling. I've sure been in *those* shoes.

"Bottom locker?" I ask, pointing at her nose.

She nods again.

"I'm Maggie," I tell her. "Maggie Malone. What's your name?"

"Elizabeth O'Connor," she says in a mouse voice.

"Well, welcome to Randolph J. Pinkerton Middle School, Elizabeth O'Connor," I tell her, linking my arm through hers.

"Is it as bad here as everyone says?" she whispers as we make our way through the room.

"Not if you don't want it to be," I tell her.

I give her my biggest smile, and her face lights up. When it does, I realize I don't just want my life to be big. I want it to be huge.

Maggie Malone's Totally Fab Vocab

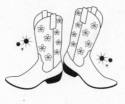

Just like I love to try out new lives, I also love to try out new words! Here's a list of some sort-of-fancy words I used in this book that you might not have known before. I included a synonym for each, but you could probably figure out what they mean from the way I used them in the story. Now that you know these words, don't be afraid to use them. Being smart is totally cool.

1. absurd: crazy
2. advantage: benefit
3. alternative: possible choice
4. ancient: old
5. appreciate: enjoy

6. approach: draw near

7. attempt: try

8. aware: conscious

9. bland: tasteless

10. bombarded: attacked

11. brittle: weak

12. budge: move

13. buffet: food bar

14. casual: offhand

15. challenge: test

16. character: role

17. comprehend: understand

18. confirm: insist

19. conniption: fit

20. consume: eat

21. crew: team

22. crumple: scrunch

23. declare: announce

24. desperate: urgent

25. distant: faraway

26. drab: boring

27. effect: impact

28. emerge: come out

29. excessive: exaggerated

30. exquisite: beautiful

31. extend: offer

32. fantastic: delicious

33. fret: worry

34. gale: windstorm

35. gash: cut

36. genuine: real

37. gigantic: huge

38. haul: loot

39. insist: demand

40. instant: on-the-spot

41. introduce: acquaint

42. incision: cut

43. incurable: fatal

44. jeopardize: risk losing

45. jostle: shake up

46. limp: hobble

47. lofty: tall

48. mane: hair
49. merit: excellence
50. minus: without
51. motionless: still
52. navigate: steer
53. oblivious: unaware
54. option: alternative
55. optimal: best
56. pathetic: pitiful
57. pause: stop
58. peculiar: odd
59. process: procedure
60. professionals: experts
61. puny: small
62. ravenous: starving
63. recover: bounce back
64. request: inquiry
65. resist: combat
66. rodent: rat
67. scorching: burning
68. skepticism: disbelief

69. sole: bottom of a shoe
70. solitary: alone
71. stall: delay
72. stench: bad smell
73. superb: best
74. surround: enclose
75. survive: continue to live
76. swivel: spin
77. task: assignment
78. temporary: not permanent
79. umbilicus: navel
80. unruly: wild

Take a sneak peek
at the next

Maggie
Malone

adventure!

Maggie Malone
Gets the Royal Treatment

Coming November 2014

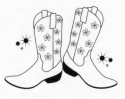

Everyday is Freaky Friday for Maggie Malone and her Mostly Magical Boots. Whenever she slips on the MMBs, Maggie gets to be whoever she wants for a whole day. And whose life could be more fun to try on than the glamorous Princess Wilhelmina of Wincastle's? Even better—Wilhelmina is a bridesmaid in the Royal Wedding of the Century!

But little does she know that even pampered princesses have whopper-sized problems—and hers is an evil archenemy named Penelope. Will she survive Penelope's tricks or will the whole wedding turn into a royal disaster?

When Stella Gives Me a Royally Good Idea

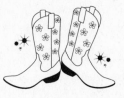

"So how are things over at Stink—at Pinkerton?" Stella asks.

See, before I went to Pinkerton, Stella and I—and everyone at Sacred Heart and pretty much all over the rest of the world as far as I can tell—called my new school Stinkerton. But I decided if I was going to be stuck at this place, I was going to have to give it a chance. And as soon as I made that decision, things really did seem to get better.

"Actually, things are getting royally ridiculous over there," I tell her.

"Oh yeah?" Stella says, looking up from her laptop. "Tell me more!"

We are flopped out on my zebra rug, scanning the Celebrity Times homepage, which is our favorite thing in the world to do, besides ride our bikes to Dippin' Donuts and chow down on crullers the size of our heads.

"Well, there's this big deal about the Pinkerton Ball and Royal Court Assembly and everybody is going totally nutso about the whole thing," I explain. "It's pretty ridiculous if you ask me."

"A Royal Court Assembly?" Stella laughs. "That's hilarious! What does that even *mean*?"

"Well, the 6th and 7th grades each pick three Princess Apprentices—stop laughing!—who kind of serve the 8th grade Pinkerton Princess when she's elected. Like, you get to carry her books and order her lunch and stuff. Seriously, Stella. It's not *that* funny."

Stella is rolling back and forth on my zebra rug, bent legs stomping and making sounds like a spastic hyena. I do love her, but she really can take things a teensy bit too far sometimes.

"I'm sorry, Maggie... I just... I can't... Princess... Apprentices..." she spits between spasms. "Princess Apprentices!"

"It's not *that* bad," I say, feeling my cheeks beginning to burn. "It's actually a real honor to be picked to be an apprentice. And last year, the 8th grade Pinkerton Princess was crowned Marshmallow Festival Queen for the whole county."

"Marshmallow Festival Queen? Seriously, Maggie," Stella says, sitting up. "You're starting to scare me with all this fake, made up royal talk. You want to talk about princesses? Check *this* out."

Stella slides her laptop my way and points to the Celebrity Times home page.

"Now *here's* a real princess." Stella angles the laptop so we can both get a look at Princess Mimi, the one and only Princess Wilhelmina of Wincastle. She's holding a ribbon next to a beautiful black stallion, probably after one of those big fancy horse shows she's always doing.

Stella and I have been kind of obsessed with Princess

Mimi ever since we were eight and *Tween Scene* magazine did a big cover story on her. Mimi had just turned ten at the time and I guess over in Wincastle, that's a major big deal. They had this week-long party for her with about thirteen different cakes, each one the size of a kitchen table. They showed her being escorted into one of the parties by an army of soldiers all dressed in red, and of course she was wearing a real diamond tiara which Stella and I agreed was the coolest thing ever. It's sort of embarrassing to admit, but until I read that article I didn't even realize that princesses were *real*. Seriously. I mean I knew they had princesses in the olden days, but I kind of thought they died out like dinosaurs or something and that they were mostly made-up for fairy tales and movies. I certainly didn't think there were princesses *my age* out there in the world right this very minute being all royal and everything.

But since I figured that out, Stella and I have spent a lot of time imagining what Princess Mimi's life might be like. We decided she probably sleeps in her tiara and has a solid gold hairbrush and monogrammed toilet paper. (We also designed our own personalized TP, just in case we found out we were princesses. Mine was going to be pink leopard print and have MM on every square; Stella picked turquoise circles with one big aquamarine S in the middle. I tried to argue that turquoise and aquamarine are pretty much the same thing and didn't she want a little *contrast*, but when Stella gets her mind set on something there's no use even trying to change it.)

"Jeez," Stella says, skimming the story. "Could Princess Mimi's life *get* any better? She's fourteen and owns an entire *country*. Not to mention a yacht and a plane and a stable full of horses. *And* she's on the cover of a zillion magazines every single month. Can you imagine being called Your Royal Highness, like, for real? 'Oh, did somebody call Her Royal Highness? Yup, that's me, right here!' *Seriously*."

"*And* she has front row seats at all the fashion shows and gets driven around in a limo," I add, forgetting all about pretend Princess Apprentices for a minute. We flip through a slideshow with pictures of Princess

Mimi lounging on the back of a ship, loaded up with shopping bags and riding a horse that looks exactly like Black Beauty from the movie. "I'll bet she never has to do chores or make her own bed," Stella says with a sigh. "She probably even has a Royal Tooth Brusher to do that for her."

"She's big-time into volunteering, too," I say, because my mom says it's more important to focus on what people do rather than what they have.

"I'm just saying the girl's pretty much got it made. I'd love to have her life."

"Who wouldn't?" I ask.

"Well, at least you've got that Princess Apprentice thing going on at school," Stella says. "I'm sure it's pretty much the same thing."

"Very funny," I say, giving her a sideways shove that sends her rolling around the floor again—the girl seriously cracks herself up—but I'm hardly paying attention anymore. *Or,* I think to myself, *I could slip into my trusty MMBs and become actual royalty—the one and only Princess Wilhelmina of Wincastle—for a whole entire day.*

Acknowledgments

You know how you can build a much better fort or club-house with a bunch of your friends than you could ever build all by yourself? Well, the book you're holding is a lot like that. With that in mind, we would like to thank our brilliant, beautiful, intrepid agent Michelle Wolfson, whose passion, tenacity, and humor truly know no limits. Next, we would like to acknowledge our exceptional editor Aubrey Poole, whose keen eye and bottomless enthusiasm for this project made it better in every way. And finally, we offer our humble gratitude to our friend Jerry Jenkins, who got elected to the unpaid position of generous mentor and never once complained or asked for a raise. We are eternally grateful to you all.

About the Authors

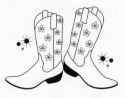

Jenna McCarthy is a writer, speaker and aspiring drummer who has wanted magical boots since she learned to walk. She lives with her husband, daughters, cats, and dogs in sunny Southern California.

As a writer and lover of international travel, Carolyn Evans has shucked pearls in Australia and biked the foothills of the Himalayas. Now she's happy at home with her husband and kids living by a river in South Carolina, dreaming up grand adventures for Maggie Malone.

The Cupcake Club

A treasure trove of delicious treats—the Cupcake Club will satisfy any sweet tooth! Catch up on the first five books in this popular new series by New York Times bestselling author Sheryl Berk and her cupcake-loving daughter, Carrie. Each book features yummy original recipes from the story and fun extras to enjoy!

Dear Brio Girl,

Ever heard the saying, "garbage in/garbage out"? The bottom line is: Whatever we put in our minds, will eventually come out in our actions. It's an important truth to *know*, but a difficult truth to *learn*.

The BRIO gang is worried about Tyler. When he left for California, he knew what he believed and why. But after spending some time with his cousin, Chaz, Tyler returns to Copper Ridge a different person . . . and with a secret.

Maybe you've fought a similar battle—what not to let inside your mind. And maybe you, too, are hiding a secret you desperately hope is never revealed. You're not alone. Tyler understands. But more importantly . . . God understands and offers help, healing and hope.

Your Friend,

Susie Shellenberger, BRIO Editor
www.briomag.com

BRIO GIRLS

from Focus on the Family®
and
Bethany House Publishers

1. *Stuck in the Sky*
2. *Fast Forward to Normal*
3. *Opportunity Knocks Twice*
4. *Double Exposure*
5. *Good-Bye to All That*
6. *Grasping at Moonbeams*
7. *Croutons for Breakfast*
8. *No Lifeguard on Duty*

brio girls

REAL Faith MEETS REAL Life

Jacie Hannah Solana Becca

No Lifeguard on Duty

Created + Written by
LISSA HALLS JOHNSON

BETHANYHOUSE
MINNEAPOLIS, MINNESOTA

Focus on the Family books are available at special quantity discounts when purchased in bulk by corporations, organizations, churches, or groups. Special imprints, messages, and excerpts can be produced to meet your needs. For more information, contact: Resource Sales Group, Focus on the Family, 8605 Explorer Drive, Colorado Springs, CO 80920; phone (800) 932-9123.

A Focus on the Family book.
Published by Bethany House Publishers
A Ministry of Bethany Fellowship International
11400 Hampshire Avenue South
Bloomington, Minnesota 55438
www.bethanyhouse.com

Printed in the United States of America by
Bethany Press International, Bloomington, Minnesota 55438

Library of Congress Cataloging-in-Publication Data
Johnson, Lissa Halls, 1955-
    No lifeguard on duty / created [and] written by Lissa Halls Johnson.
        p.   cm. — (Brio girls)
    "A Focus on the Family book."
    Summary: Two weeks of surfing in California expose Tyler to new friends, new music, and new influences that distance him from the Brio girls, Allen, and his commitment to God.
    ISBN 1-58997-081-0
    [1. Christian life—Fiction. 2. Interpersonal relations—Fiction.
3. Surfing—Fiction. 4. California—Fiction.] I. Title. II. Series.
    PZ7.J63253No   2003
    [Fic]—dc21   2002012874

LISSA HALLS JOHNSON is on staff at Focus on the Family where she writes some books, edits others and torments her co-workers with outrageous questions, flying toys, and generally being a nuisance. When she's not held captive by her gray cubicle, she's hanging out in the mountains she adores, usually hiking with her dog Kyna. Previously a member of the ADVENTURES IN ODYSSEY creative team, she's completely surprised that she's the author of fifteen novels for teens and the young reader.

chapter

Of all the places Tyler could imagine spending Saturday morning, the senior citizens' sing-along at the Community Center would have been about last on his list. He leaned closer to Becca and whispered, "Uh, listen. It's a beautiful day. Why don't we just wait outside till it's time to—"

"*Tyler*," Becca said. "You just don't want to spend time with anybody older than 50, that's all."

"Fifty, Becca?" Tyler said. "I don't think there's anybody in there under a hundred. And besides, it has nothing to do with their ages. I like old folks just fine. Shoot, my grandparents are old folks. It's, uh— the music."

The sound of a cheap organ swelled out from behind a door near where Tyler, Becca, Hannah, and Nate stood in one of the hallways of the Community Center. Because the chords were all wrong, it took Tyler a minute to figure out the song: "Take Me Out to the Ballgame."

"Come on," Nate said. "You have to love this song. I mean, this is Americana. Kind of a national anthem. And I especially love the rumba beat."

"Yeah, this song is great—when we drive up to Denver to watch the Rockies play. But on a summer morning in Copper Ridge, I think I'd rather hear a little Jars of Clay, you know?"

"Oh, Tyler," Becca said, stroking his cheek. "Did we upset your delicate musical balance? I'm so sorry. But you know what? This has nothing to do with music, and everything to do with supporting Mrs. Peterson. Now . . ." And she quickly went from stroking to pinching Tyler's cheek—hard—and grabbed Nate's with the other hand. "I want you boys to march right behind me into this room and smile at Mrs. Peterson and then sit and sing. You hear me?"

"I'm sorry, Becca," Richard said, walking up. "You can only have one beau. Take your pick; either one is fine."

"Run, Richard, quick!" Tyler called. "Before it's too late. She's about to make us go in there!"

Richard smiled and opened the door; the tones of the organ and a couple dozen quavery, 70-something voices swept over them:

Buy me some peanuts and Cracker Jack,
I don't care . . .

"I should probably mention," Richard said, "before you say anything else, that Mrs. Peterson is my great-aunt. And I'm down here because she asked me to come help her with the refreshments."

His great-aunt? Rumba Rhoda was Richard's great-aunt?

Nate found his voice first. "Refreshments? Well, then . . ."

The four of them filed in as the singers brought the song to a close. Mrs. Peterson, seated at the organ, glanced up and smiled brightly. "Oh, Richard, honey!" she called, waving. "Bring your friends and come in! We could use some more voices!"

"Now you've done it, Richard honey," Tyler muttered. "Tell her no thanks—we'd love to, but we've got to go over to the animal shelter and help clean the earwax out of a few Rottweilers and pit bulls."

"Hush!" Becca whispered. "They're not deaf!"

"Are you sure?" Tyler asked. "Did you listen to the singing?"

"Yes—they're over 70 years old and they *still* sing better than you do."

"Mr. Williams, Mr. Nelson, could you scoot over there and make some room for these young people?" The organist directed the men in the back row with her free hand as she launched into the first line of the next song on the keyboard with the other. Obligingly, the two elderly men shuffled down a few seats.

Tyler slowed, then stopped. "I don't think I know these songs," he said. "I don't think I know anything that was a hit before Columbus discovered the New World."

"Stop it!" Becca hissed, leaning close to be heard over the quavery voices and the bouncy organ. "She'll start singing some hymns pretty soon; you'll know those."

Richard didn't sit. "You guys hold down the fort here," he said. "I'll go get the coffee started."

"Need some help?" Tyler asked. "I hate to miss the singing, but—"

Richard gave him a light push on the chest. "Sit." He turned and moved off toward the kitchen.

No sooner had the four of them sat than Jacie and Hannah came in. "Hi, girls!" Mrs. Peterson said, waving. "So glad you came! My, there's so much youth in the room today! Please, sit, and we'll sing 'Down By the Riverside.'"

"I'd *rather* sing down by the riverside, or up by Pikes Peak, or pretty much anywhere but here," Tyler muttered.

The chords swelled, then Mrs. Peterson swung her hand in the air for attention and launched into the verse, with her "choir" at least a half-beat behind her.

Gonna lay down my burdens,
Down by the riverside,
Down by the riverside . . .

"Isn't she great?" Hannah whispered, leaning across Jacie's lap toward the boys.

"Uh, which part?" Tyler asked. "Is it her dynamite keyboard work, or those screamin' vocals? You know, the Spice Girls disbanded. Maybe she should—"

"*Shhh!*" Jacie was giving him a look, and it wasn't one of undying affection. "You. Sit. Sing. And singing is all I want to hear out of you till she's done. You got it?"

Tyler looked at Nate. Nate looked at Tyler. Simultaneously, they turned toward Jacie and saluted. And then sat. And sang.

Gonna lay down my sword and shield,
Down by the riverside . . .

● ● ●

"Regular café mocha," Tyler said.

"What is it with you and café mocha lately?" Nate asked. "That's all you've been ordering all summer. You know what it is? It's hot chocolate with a little coffee thrown in to make you feel grown up."

The six of them were crowded onto their regular sofas at Copperchino's. Tyler was the last to place his order, and he watched the new waitress—he couldn't remember her name, but she was cute—walk away. "I don't need artificial stimulants to make me feel grown-up, Nate; it comes naturally. Sorry about your situation."

"My situation is—" Nate stopped, listening intently. The muzak playing through Copperchino's sound system had shifted from some silly symphonic version of a Beach Boys song to something with a lot of percussion, vaguely South American-sounding. "Isn't that Richard's great-aunt?" he said, grinning.

Jacie rolled her eyes.

Tyler laughed. "I couldn't believe it. Where'd she get that organ? That thing must be valuable. I bet it's a hundred years old. They don't make those anymore. I mean—why would they? Who would buy one?"

"Okay, easy on Mrs. Peterson," Jacie said in a low voice.

"Mrs. Who?" Solana said, sauntering in and sliding onto the sofa.

"Mrs. Peterson, down at the Community Center," Nate said. "We were over there this morning, supposedly to help Becca get the tables set for breakfast, and then we got roped into singing along with Mrs. Peterson while she auditioned the Medicare crowd for—gosh, I hate to think what she was auditioning them for. I hope there aren't any harps involved."

"Anyway," Tyler said, "she played this organ that had one of those automatic percussion beats, you know? Only it was stuck in some kind of Latin rumba thing—BOOM, ticka shick, ticka BOOM ticka SHICK-a shicka, BOOM, ticka shick—you know. So everything she played, even 'Home on the Range,' sounded like Fred Astaire and Ginger Rogers ought to be dancing to it in gaucho outfits." He launched into: "Home . . . *ticka shick, ticka* . . ."

Nate joined him.

". . . home on the range . . . *ticka shick, ticka BOOM ticka shicka shicka* . . ."

"You know, guys," Becca said, laughing in spite of herself, "Richard might just walk in here any minute and have to beat you both up."

"I don't know," Tyler said, "I think he'd have to agree. He might not want to, but—I mean, when she launched into 'The Old Rugged Cross' with that crazy beat, I was biting my tongue, and my lips, and my hand, and my toes—anything to keep from laughing."

"And it wasn't just the music!" Nate said. "It was—okay, I don't want to be unkind or anything here—"

"You don't?" Jacie said. "You're doing a pretty good imitation of it, then."

"But—didn't she look like Yoda?"

All of them except Jacie and Hannah burst out laughing.

"I know who you mean now!" Solana said, making them laugh even harder. "I know exactly who you mean! She's Richard's aunt? She *does* look like Yoda!"

"In 'Ball Game Take Me Out to,' join me now you will," Tyler said in a Yoda voice.

"Really!" Nate said. "Her hair's blue instead of green, but it kind of wrinkles across her skull just like Yoda's head with little stray hairs sticking out, and her ears—"

"Okay!" Jacie said. "All right! I'm not interested in your opinion of her ears!"

"You guys are being really mean," Hannah said.

Solana shook her head. "Hey, it's not mean to just point out the truth. I mean, she's got the stoop, the hunched back—"

"She's got one thing Yoda doesn't have, though," Becca said, wiping her eyes.

"I don't want to know," Jacie said.

"I do!" Nate said. "What?"

Becca could barely get it out. "Armflaps," she said, and shoved her fist to her mouth.

"Armflaps?" Hannah said, confused.

"Don't encourage them, Hannah," Jacie said.

Becca raised one arm and shook it. "You know—those things that hang down from the bottom of your upper arm and jiggle and flap all around. She's got major ones—I'm sorry, Jacie, but it's true! How could you *not* notice?"

"There's a difference between noticing and being cruel enough to joke about it," Jacie said.

Becca continued as if she hadn't heard. "When she started waving her arms around to conduct her choir, those things were waving so much I thought she was going to fly!"

"Raptured!" Nate yelled, and he and Tyler and Solana and Becca lost it completely.

When they finally got themselves back under control, Tyler noticed that Jacie was scowling at him in particular. "What?" he said. "I wasn't the only one laughing."

"You were the one who started it," she said. "Talking about her music."

"Well—come on, Jacie," Tyler said. "Her music was—it was—I mean, I can't even describe it. 'Out of it' doesn't even come close. It wasn't just that the songs were old—I like a lot of old songs. She was—they were—hopeless. How does she expect—"

"You could do better, you think?" Jacie asked.

Tyler paused, surprised. "Well—yeah. Don't you?"

Jacie took a sip of her coffee. "Tyler, you're a good song leader. But don't you think it's just remotely possible that Mrs. Peterson is doing what she's doing simply because God wants her to? Because she's the right person for it?"

"The older people seemed to enjoy it," Hannah added. "You have to admit."

"Let me tell you something about Mrs. Peterson," Jacie said. "She's very sweet. She would love all of you dearly if you let her get to know you. And I hope you do, too. Because then you'll realize that she's also a little fragile. Her health isn't all that great, and she's awfully lonely. She's been a widow for years and years. She *lives* for those Tuesdays and Saturdays at the Community Center, when she can—"

"Hey—look, I'm sure all that's true. So what? I'm not talking about her as a person. She's Richard's aunt," Tyler said. "I'm sure she loves him and he loves her and everything's all rosy and sweet with hearts and flowers circling around in the air over her head and everything. And she probably deserves to sit right up there on the platform with Billy Graham, but that's not what I was talking about. I just think—okay, times change. Music changes with the times. Either you keep up with it, or you get left behind."

"I wouldn't exactly say she's been left behind," Becca said. "Or at least if she has, all the rest of the old folks there today got left behind with her. You mentioned Jars of Clay—do you really think you could bring your guitar in there and swing into a couple of Christian rock songs and have them singing along with you? Maybe 'Take Me Out to the Ball Game' *is* a little more up their alley."

"She's a saint, Tyler," Hannah said. "Really. A saint. I mean it. I think that her spiritual maturity puts the rest of us to shame. Think about it— she's 75 years old and she still goes down there twice a week to lead those sing-alongs, and then sticks around afterward to lead a Bible study. How many of us will be doing that when we're old and tired?"

"Okay," Tyler said. "Whatever."

"No, not *whatever*," Jacie said. "She's a dear, sweet woman who lives to serve Christ. Period. Do you really think her choice of songs, or the way she plays the organ, is more important than that? We should all take lessons from her."

"Not music lessons, I hope," Nate said under his breath, and he and Tyler tried to suppress snorts of laughter.

Jacie shook her head. "You guys are hopeless. And I'm not joking. Okay, change of subject before I start throwing things. Who's up for doing something tonight? Anything. Movie, just hanging out at some-body's house . . ."

"I'm in," Nate said.

Becca smiled at him. "Me too."

"Me three," Solana said. "Tyler?"

"Uh—" Shoot. He should have known this was coming and figured out a graceful way out ahead of time. "Can't."

"Can't—what?" Solana asked. "What do you mean *can't*? You work-ing or something? Hot date?" She smiled. "Who with?"

"No, no hot date—I just, uh, told J.P. I'd do something with him tonight."

A look of distaste washed across Jacie's face, but she said, "Well, bring him along. After all, it's our last Saturday night with you for a couple of weeks."

"No, we, uh—"

"Or maybe we should just all tag along with you instead, if you've already got plans—"

"No!" Sheesh. Would that ever be a bad idea. "I've got some things I want to talk to him about. You know. Important stuff. So—maybe it would be better to do that without—you know."

"Some things you want to *talk* to him about . . . what kind of . . . oh," she said, raising her eyebrows and drawing out the *oh* as if she suddenly understood. "Oh, yeah. You mean . . . ?" She looked at Tyler for confirmation.

"Well, yeah," he said, only half understanding. "So it'd be better if we didn't have an audience . . ."

Becca nodded. "Wow. *Really* important stuff. Well—okay. Hope that goes well. I'll be praying for you."

He looked around the table. Jacie smiled; Hannah gave him a thumbs-up. "I'll be praying too," she said.

They think I mean I'm trying to witness to him tonight, Tyler thought. He gulped his lukewarm café mocha. *And I guess I made them think that—or at least made it sound like that. Bad idea. But—what choice do I have?* He nodded back at Becca and smiled a little. But it felt like a sick and awkward smile to him, and he wondered if they could all tell.

chapter 2

J.P. yanked on Tyler's sleeve. "Come on, man. Movie's over. Let's depart."

"In a minute." Tyler watched the credits roll across the screen. Not that he was really that interested in who did the casting, and who played the part of the convenience store clerk. All he wanted was a few minutes to think through what he'd just seen.

And hoo boy. Had he just seen something.

The River Runs Downhill. The movie was said to be on the short list for an Academy Award for best picture, but critics were already starting to complain that, even though it deserved the Oscar, it wouldn't get it, because the Academy was "too conservative to give the award to a director bold enough to take chances." And this director had definitely taken some major chances.

The movie had set some personal records for Tyler, although he wasn't sure how he felt about that—not too good at the moment. Most profanity he'd ever heard in a movie. Most skin he'd ever seen in a movie, male and female both. Yes, the movie had definitely set new standards for—something. Tyler wasn't sure what.

J.P. yanked again. "Come *on*. You don't care about this stuff. And I sure don't. So let's get outta here." J.P. stood up.

Tyler followed slowly. He wasn't really sure why he'd wanted to see this movie. To see what all the fuss was about, he guessed. He'd read the reviews, heard his basketball friends talking about it. And, yeah, he had to admit—he knew it was going to be racy and exciting. And it *had* been racy. But exciting? It had been more depressing than anything else, really. It had—

J.P. grabbed his arm and pulled him toward the exit. "You know, they close these places eventually. If I wait for you, we might get locked in for the night."

They were at the Carmike 15 theater at the big Chapel Hills Mall in Colorado Springs. The movie hadn't been playing in Copper Ridge—no surprise there. The theaters in towns like Copper Ridge tended to be pretty conservative and not book the really controversial movies. At first Tyler had been glad that they would have to go all the way to Colorado Springs to see the movie—less chance of being seen. But then J.P. said, "Okay, let's get a Coke at the concession stand and then hang out in the mall."

Tyler pulled back.

"*What?*" J.P. said, getting angry now.

"Our car's out back," Tyler said. "If we go through the mall, then we have to go the long way around. Let's just go out the back way and get the car, then we can stop for a Coke at Sonic."

J.P. looked at him for a few seconds in the dim light of the theater hallway. "Boy, I'm glad I brought you along tonight. Mr. Excitement. Life-of-the-Party Jennings. Tyler, uh—out *there*—" He pointed toward the theater lobby and the mall beyond. "Out there is life." He threw an arm around Tyler's shoulders. "Young people our own age. People who enjoy having a little fun, and maybe—who knows?—even some attractive young ladies. One for me and, yes, Tyler, perhaps even one for you, although tonight it sounds like you need one who's about 80 years old." He steered Tyler toward the lobby. "So let's—"

Tyler pulled away. He'd just seen Amanda Johnson and Sue Ellen McCusker standing by the concession stand. Amanda was a good friend of Solana's. The last thing he needed was J.P. telling them they'd just seen *The River Runs Downhill*, and then Amanda telling Solana . . . "Hey," he said. "Didn't you say Buzz and Andrew and Jarvis were all just hanging out at Jarvis's house tonight?"

"Yeah. So?"

"So, you know those guys. They're all sittin' there lookin' at each other, seein' who can burp the loudest, because none of 'em has the brains to figure out anything to do."

"So what? That's their problem."

"Come on, J.P. We've got your dad's Prowler, it's Saturday night, and we're young and insane. Let's go get the other three and cruise Copper Ridge. I'll buy you a Coke at what's-its-face, that place you like on the way out of town, the one with the mean old lady you always give a hard time." He dragged J.P. toward the back exit to the parking lot.

"Cruise Copper Ridge," J.P. muttered as he allowed himself to be dragged along. "Tyler, do I know you?"

● ● ●

In the car, slurping his Dr Pepper, Tyler reviewed all the reasons he'd given himself for thinking it would be okay to go see *The River Runs Downhill*. For one, it's not like he was some spiritual baby. He was mature enough. There's no way he would lose his faith in God over a movie. Wasn't a movie just an artistic artifact, like a painting or a sculpture? You study it, you think about the technique, you enjoy the craftsmanship. And, he had to admit, there had been plenty of craftsmanship in that movie to enjoy. That was probably the best movie he'd seen in years—maybe ever—in terms of script, acting, directing, music . . . they'd done a *great* job with it. Great.

But—what a hopeless story! And you definitely got the impression that the reason the story lacked hope was because the writers and director had no message of hope to give.

It had been the story of a man—played by William Weston, one of Tyler's favorite actors—searching for meaning in life, for satisfaction. He tries everything—drugs, sex, money, fame, power—and finds nothing that satisfies anywhere. He had even quoted the Bible occasionally in the movie, but always the same passage, from Ecclesiastes: "Meaningless! Meaningless! . . . Utterly meaningless! Everything is meaningless."

The director had tried, Tyler thought, to give the movie a feeling of victory at the end—when, after realizing that there was no satisfaction to be had anywhere in life, the man had refused to live life on those terms and had instead sunk into a catatonic state and been placed in a mental hospital! *That* was the positive message at the end. Life on my terms or else I check out.

"Yeah, I see what you mean," J.P. said, driving. "This is a lot more fun than spending the evening with a couple of cute Colorado Springs chicks."

Well, there might be one way to redeem the evening. After all, weren't the Brios expecting him to use this as a witnessing opportunity? "So what did you think of the movie?" Tyler asked.

J.P. shrugged. "It was okay. Wasn't really as good as I thought it would be; everybody was making such a big deal out of it on TV and in the papers and everything."

"Didn't it seem kind of . . . hopeless?"

"No. Hopeless is a guy who gets a chance to meet some cute girls and instead decides he wants to get three retarded bozos and cruise some little town he spends his whole life in anyway. Now that's hopeless."

"You know what I mean. The guy was surrounded by meaninglessness, so he went looking for something that had meaning in life, and he ended up a vegetable. In the end, nothing meant anything."

"Yeah, okay. But what did you think of that one chick that wanted to marry him, that dancer? Remember when she danced for him on the beach?"

"Yeah," Tyler said, "I remember the scene. Believe me, I'll remember it for a long time. But do you hear what I'm saying? I mean, I think that was a real tragedy! Life is not hopeless!"

"Not for you, maybe, but look at him. Why would he turn into a cabbage if there was anything in life worth having—to him, I mean? And you got to admit, he tried everything. Including a lot of stuff even I don't want to try."

"But that's just the point. He didn't try everything. All he had to do was turn his life over to God—"

"Hey—he did that, remember? He went to seminary and everything."

"Yeah, but that was just another scene written by somebody who didn't know anything about God! So how was he supposed to show how God can fill the empty places in our lives?" Tyler suddenly remembered something Allen Olson, his former youth pastor, often said. "It's like we all have this God-shaped vacuum in our lives," he told J.P. "There's only one thing that can fill it. The guy in the movie tried to fill it with money, with drugs, with—"

"Hey, Tyler, you gave me this God-shaped vacuum speech before. Twice. Listen, when we get back to town, why should we just drive up and down Main and hang out in the Copperchino's parking lot? It's summer. Let's forget the clowns, get a couple of six-packs, pick up some girls, and go up to—"

"You're changing the subject, J.P.," Tyler said. They were almost back to Copper Ridge; if he was going to make any headway in this conversation, he had to make it now.

"Yeah, I'm changing the subject. Consider it changed. That wasn't a

God movie, Tyler. Maybe you didn't notice, but that wasn't a movie most church people would have been real comfortable in." Tyler winced. "So why try to start a lot of God talk about it? Take it for what it was. It was a good movie, it had some scenes in it I'll be running through my mind as I lie in bed for many months yet, and it gave me the chance to spend a wonderful evening with party-hearty Tyler Jennings, so what more could I ask? End of movie discussion. Okay, we're almost at Jarvis's house. Are we gonna cruise with the clowns, or you want to get some chicks and roll up to the reservoir?"

● ● ●

In the end, Tyler talked J.P. into forgetting the six-packs and the reservoir. Unfortunately, they also had to forget the Prowler, for the very practical reason that it has just two bucket seats, no backseat. They traded it for J.P.'s mom's car—a P.T. Cruiser. Odd, Tyler realized as they pulled away from Jarvis's house with Jarvis, Andrew, and Buzz in the backseat. These were about the last four guys he would have expected to be hanging out with on a Saturday night. J.P. had been his friend for a long time, but they were rock-climbing and mountain-biking and bas-ketball buddies, not Saturday night buddies. Andrew was on the basket-ball team, but the other two were virtually strangers to Tyler, even though they were part of J.P.'s weekend crowd.

No sooner had they pulled onto Main than J.P. slapped the wheel and hooted. "Our lucky night, my friend! Look who's coming out of Albertson's—your lovely Jessica Abbott, and for me, the outstanding Andrea Green." He zipped into the grocery store parking lot, and a few minutes later, after a lot of half-hearted protests and laughter from the girls, J.P. and Tyler were in the backseat with Jessica and Andrea on their laps, while the other three crowded into the front, with Andrew thrilled to be driving the Cruiser down Main on a Saturday night, where everyone could see him.

Jessica's perfume washed over him, and her face smiling at him from just a few inches away reminded him that he still thought she was an absolutely beautiful girl. *What a strange night*, Tyler thought. *First the movie, and now here I am cruising down Main with Jessica on my lap and a carful of borderline characters, for all the world to see. I am going to hear about this.* He would hear about it, in particular, from Solana, Jacie, and Becca. Jessica was an old girlfriend who had moved back to town last fall, nearly causing a major rift between Tyler and the Brios when he'd started spending most of his time with her. He still dated her occasionally, although the heavy romance they'd all expected—all except Jessica, apparently—had never quite developed. She was rich, she was popular, she was sweet . . . and she was very hot.

"So tell me," she said in that throaty, intimate voice she had. "Why is it we've hardly seen each other this summer?"

"Good question," he said, realizing he'd have enjoyed spending time with her almost more than he cared to admit. "I had that missions trip to South America. I guess that was it."

"Oh, yeah," she said, looking interested. "I'd like to hear about that. Maybe we could get together next week and you can tell me about it."

"Okay, let's—no, wait. Not for a couple of weeks. I leave Monday morning for my cousin's out in California."

"Yeah," J.P. said, "my buddy Tyler takes a surfin' safari every endless summer." He broke into a cracked, off-key falsetto rendition of "Surfer Girl." "Come on, *everybody* sing!"

Laughing, Andrea stuck her hand over his mouth. "Is that what that was? Singing?"

"Two weeks?" Jessica gave a little pout. "So I won't see you till you get back?" She smiled a little smile. "Maybe you can call me—if there's ever a time when you're not surrounded by surfer girls."

"I won't notice the girls," Tyler said, breaking into a grin. "I'll be too busy."

"Oh, really?" She winked. "You'll notice and you'll let me know what they're wearing so that I can be the first girl in Colorado to wear it, too."

"Hey, forget surfer girls," J.P. yelled. "You should have seen some of the babes in the movie me and Tyler saw tonight."

Great, Tyler thought.

"Really?" Andrea said, with a mock-disapproving look. "What was it? *Locker Room Hidden Camera?*"

"Listen," Tyler said, "it was no—"

"Worse than that—*The River Runs Downhill,*" J.P. said, loudly enough Tyler figured everybody on the sidewalks could hear him, and maybe those in the restaurants and coffee shops too. "Saw it down in the Springs at the Carmike 15. Good thing my friend Ty and me have both reached the proud age of seventeen, because they *were* carding people, so take notice, all you underage people who were thinking of seeing it."

Jessica studied Tyler's face. What was that expression she was giving him? "Wow," she said. "I didn't think you would want to see a movie like that."

"Was it really as bad as everybody says?" Jarvis piped up from the front. "A lot of people say it was pushing the R rating."

Tyler said, "It really wasn't—"

"I think those people were right," J.P. laughed. "Some of those people had their clothes off more than they had them on! Unfortunately, that went for the guys too. And there was this one guy, this Vietnam vet, I don't think he could say anything unless every other word had four letters. I think the speakers were beginning to melt down by the end of the movie. It was cool. Right, Ty?"

"It was a pretty dark movie," Tyler said, trying to think of some way to get the discussion off the movie. "Depressing. Kind of slow-moving in places. It was well-made and everything, but I don't think I would recommend it. Anybody seen the new Schwarzenegger movie? I think it opened last—"

"How about William Weston?" Andrea asked. "Was he—you know. Did he take off—"

"Only about a hundred times!" J.P. said. "Listen, whatever you want to know about William Weston's physiology, you will find out in this movie. First he . . ."

And the discussion forged on. But Tyler turned his head and watched the crowd milling around on the sidewalk. As much as he enjoyed Jessica's presence, as beautiful as he thought she was right this minute, he wished he were somewhere else right now. He could tell that she was watching him, studying his face, trying to figure out why he was tuning out, but he couldn't look back at her because he knew he couldn't hide the look of unease and worry on his face. The whole evening had been a bad idea. If he could just figure out some way to get J.P. to drop him off at home, Jessica or no Jessica.

chapter 3

Church felt a little strange to Tyler the next morning. It was very unsettling, sitting waiting for the service to begin, holding his Bible in his lap, and remembering the movie the night before. Especially some of those scenes that kept running through his mind . . .

He knew he should read a chapter or two of his Bible, or pray, or something to get himself focused on God so that he could be in the right attitude for worship when the service began. But somehow—he just didn't feel like it. Something felt wrong. He was almost relieved when the worship team swept onto the stage and the music director raised his hands, indicating that it was time for everyone to stand. Maybe he'd feel better once things got rolling.

As he stood, he was surprised to see Jacie slip in beside him. He turned to greet her, but she wasn't looking at him. She pressed a note into his hand. "What's this?" he whispered, but she wouldn't answer.

She just stared straight ahead, her jaw set. He knew that look well. She was ticked.

What was this all about? He stared at her for a moment or two, ignoring the worship song starting all around him, and then looked down at the note in his hand. He unfolded it.

> *Alyeria right after church. Before you even eat. We'll all be waiting.*

it read in Jacie's neat, calligraphy-like printing.

He folded it and put it slowly into his Bible, then looked up at the worship team and heaved a sigh. He had a hunch he wasn't going to enjoy seeing the girls this afternoon.

● ● ●

When he entered Alyeria an hour and a half later, the thing that surprised him most was that Jacie, Becca, and Solana weren't the only ones there. Sitting a little apart from the other three, looking out of place and uncomfortable, perched on a piece of log, was Hannah.

"Uh—hi, Hannah. I, uh—" Why was she here? This was Alyeria— no one had ever been here but Tyler and the three Brio girls, Becca, Solana, and Jacie. And how did Tyler raise the question of why Hannah was there without hurting her feelings and making her think he didn't want her there? Actually, at the moment, he *didn't* want her there.

Her eyes drilling into him, Becca explained. "I thought she should be here to talk about this with us, since she was there when you lied to us."

"*Lied* to you! I never lied . . . okay. I know what you mean. All right. I let you believe something that wasn't true. I could have—"

"I think it goes a little beyond that, Tyler," Becca said coldly. "You made me think you were spending time with J.P. because you were concerned about his spiritual condition, and all the time—"

"I *was*—I *am*—concerned about his spiritual condition. And we *did* talk about that last night. Or at least I tried. He wasn't—"

"Tyler, you're not going to weasel out of this. You already said you weren't truthful with us. And you weren't. You didn't go out with J.P. because you wanted to witness to him. You went out with J.P. because you needed somebody to go to a dirty movie with."

Tyler shifted uncomfortably on his feet. "It's one of the best-made movies of the year. I've seen it, you haven't, so I think I know better than you what kind of movie it is. It may not win best picture, but it'll probably get nominations for—"

"It's a dirty movie," Becca said.

"Tyler," Jacie said, her voice quiet, "it isn't just that you went to the movie. Why did you have to sneak around to do it? And last night when you could have been spending time with us, and with Nate, you were parading up and down Main Street with Jessica on your lap. The whole thing is just so . . . so not you."

"Geez, what is this? Has my whole life been broadcast when I wasn't looking, like *The Truman Show* or something? And besides, this didn't have anything to do with Jessica. We ran into her when we got back into town. And the only reason she was sitting on my lap is that we were all crowded into J.P.'s car."

"I'm sure it must have been miserable for you," Solana said icily.

"Why are *you* upset about this?" Tyler asked her, puzzled. "Do you really care if I went to see *The River Runs Downhill?*"

"Why would I care what you see?" she replied. "I'll probably see it myself." Solana was the only one of the group who wasn't a Christian—at least not yet. "But I don't like being lied to. And you did lie, Tyler, don't try to deny it. But you know what gets me even more? Just a few weeks ago you were all *over* Becca's rear end because she was trying to find out some things about Wicca, and now holy Tyler Jennings goes to see a raunchy movie about the occult."

"It *wasn't* about the occult!" Tyler said. "Stop telling me what the movie was about."

"I've seen the previews on TV, Tyler," Hannah spoke up for the first time. "It has seances and—"

"That was all just in one tiny little part," Tyler said. "The whole thing is about this guy's search for meaning in life, and at one point he even looks into Christianity and enrolls in religious studies at a university, but then he gets seduced ..." He wished he hadn't brought that up.

"He gets what?" Jacie asked.

"Well, he gets seduced by one of the professors. And then he finds out that the professor is involved in the occult ... well, it's pretty involved."

"Wow, must be some university," Becca said.

"It was a lousy university! That was the whole thing," Tyler said. "It was obvious that the people who made the movie didn't have any answers. Nada. None. So they decided there must not be any, so they made a movie that didn't have any answers. Which was a total shame, and I wish we could be having a reasonable conversation about the movie and what it all meant instead of having you jump down my—"

"You're changing the subject, Tyler," Solana said. "You big hypocrite! You say you—"

"Solana ..." Jacie cautioned. Then she turned to Tyler and said, "Tyler, we're hurt and obviously we're a little angry. But mostly we're concerned about you. It's just not like you. You're an up-front kind of person. You don't sneak. You don't lie. And now this. How did you get your mom to agree to let you go, anyway?"

Tyler froze. The four of them watched him for a couple of seconds, and then he watched a mixture of grief and anger wash across their faces. "Oh, Tyler, you didn't," Becca said.

"You lied to your mother too?" Solana squeaked. "Your *mother?*"

"No, I didn't," Tyler said coldly. He was getting tired of this. "I didn't tell her anything. She doesn't always ask where I'm going. She trusts me. She . . ." His voice trailed off as he thought about that last sentence.

Obviously, the girls had caught it too. "She trusts you," Hannah said. "So the way you repay that trust is by going to a movie you know she would be appalled by? *Because* she trusts you, you should have discussed this with her beforehand. And if you had, you know she'd have talked you out of it."

"Okay, maybe so. But you can't convince me that you haven't all done things that you didn't want your parents to know about. Even you, Hannah. Maybe it wasn't exactly my finest moment, but it wasn't anything any teenager hasn't done at one time or another."

He could tell by the looks on their faces that he was losing ground fast. The problem was, they all loved his mom nearly as much as he did. She worked for *Brio* Magazine, which Jacie, Becca, Hannah, and even Solana read, and she often called them to help out with the magazine for photo shoots, interviews or surveys, that kind of thing. Tyler loved his mom. She *was* cool, it was true. But he wasn't her; he was Tyler. And Tyler had to make his own decisions about some things. "Besides, I think this discussion is missing the point," he said.

"Of course," Solana said. "And what might that be?"

Tyler stopped for a minute to gather his thoughts. This was something he'd been thinking about a lot lately, and he wanted to present his thoughts well, so that the girls wouldn't automatically react against them. "I think, sometimes," he started cautiously, "we Christians are too restrictive when it comes to the arts. We see or hear something that doesn't seem biblical or moral to us, and we react against it without thinking. But if we want to reach our unsaved friends, why is it wrong to watch a movie that presents the same view of the world that most of them have? Because one thing I found out last night, in our conversation after the movie, is that J.P. *does* have a pretty similar view of the meaning of life—which is that life has no meaning. So watching a movie like that is kind of like research—"

"Totally different thing," Becca said.

"Why?"

"Because if J.P. were sitting right here, right now, talking about the meaning of life, we'd be having a *dialogue*—it would go two ways. I would not only be hearing him, I would also be letting him know how I see it. You can't do that in a movie, Tyler. Or a book, or a music CD. The artist's point of view gets poured all over you, but you can't talk back."

"You know why that doesn't bother me? Because a movie like *The River Runs Downhill* is an *exploration* of morality. The writer and director are exploring life, trying to figure out answers. Now, personally, I believe I have some of those answers, but how can it hurt to watch someone else try to wrestle with these tough questions?"

"G-I-G-O," Hannah said.

"What?"

"That's what my dad always says—garbage in, garbage out. You watch a movie filled with garbage, and the next thing you know, that's how you're thinking yourself. You can't pour garbage into your mind and expect wisdom to come out."

Tyler paused. He always had to be careful not to sound like he was criticizing or arguing with Hannah's parents; that just made her defensive. "Well, I don't think I would classify a serious movie as garbage just because I don't agree with it."

Solana laughed. "Oh, yeah? I think Hannah's got a point, gringo. I don't know how 'serious' or how 'good' the movie was, but why do you think guys like J.P. have been flocking to see the movie, Tyler? Because of the great statement it makes about morality and the meaning of life, or because it's got a bunch of naked women in it? What did J.P. *really* want to talk about after the movie last night, Tyler?"

He opened his mouth to reply, then stopped and shut it again. Solana won that point.

"The reason I don't plan to see the movie, Tyler," Jacie said, "and that I don't go to others like that, is that I don't want my mind influenced by that kind of thinking. And I don't want to be a stumbling block to others who might see me at the movie, or even coming out of it."

"If we lived our whole lives that way," Tyler said, "we'd never do anything, because no matter what you do or say, there's always someone who'll be offended by it. Besides, what's that verse in 1 Corinthians— 'Everything is permissible for me—' "

"Oh!" Becca said, exasperated. "You are *so* taking that verse out of context!"

"No, I'm not," Tyler protested. "It says—"

"What would Allen say about last night, Tyler?" Jacie asked.

A cold chill set in around Tyler's heart. "What?"

"Allen Olson. Did you ask him about going to see that movie?"

"No."

"And you know why not? For the same reason you didn't ask your mother. You knew that neither of them would have liked the idea, and would have tried to talk you out of it. And they'd have been right."

Tyler didn't feel like arguing the point with the girls right then, but inside, he was saying, *Would they? Would they have been right? They're a different generation. And neither one of them has my particular set of interests and strengths. They have their gifts, and I have mine. They've made choices in their lives that I wouldn't have made, and undoubtedly I'll make choices in mine that they wouldn't. Maybe last night is an example of that. But does that mean my choices are wrong? I don't think so.*

"Would you want Tyra going to that movie?" Jacie asked.

"Would I—*no*, of course not."

"If it's okay for you, why not for her?"

"That's the stupidest thing I've ever heard. She's in middle school, for pete's sake! She's just a kid! There's all kinds of stuff in there she wouldn't understand yet. And shouldn't be exposed to. It's an adult movie for very good reasons."

"A lot of people would say you're too young to see it yourself. And that you're too young to understand a lot of the stuff in the movie."

"Yeah, well, whoever makes up the ratings says I'm old enough."

"What if Tyra finds out you've seen it?"

Tyler hadn't thought about that. His heart lurched at the idea. "She won't."

"She follows you, Tyler. She watches you. She does the things you do and thinks the same things you do. You have an incredible influence on her life."

He snorted. "Influence! Yeah, right. She's likely to do the exact *opposite* of anything I do or say. She does nothing but argue with me."

Becca and Jacie laughed. "She does argue with you, yeah," Jacie said. "Because you're brother and sister. But she also copies you."

"It's the truth," Becca added. "Maybe you don't see it, but we sure do."

Well, even if that were true, she wasn't going to copy him in this, because she'd never know. "Listen, uh—I told my mom I'd meet her and Tyra for lunch. They're probably waiting. Sorry I wasn't more up-front with you guys about what I was doing, okay? Let's just leave it at that."

Becca shook her head. "Tyler—we're asking ourselves what's going on inside your head that could make you think what you did last night was a good idea. And nothing you've said here today helps us figure that out."

"You need to talk to your mom about this, Tyler," Hannah said.

He rolled his eyes. "I think that's something I need to decide for myself, Hannah. I don't think any of you can decide that for me."

"We just did," Becca said. "You're leaving for California what time tomorrow?"

"Morning. We're leaving for the airport around 9:30."

"Good, so you've got the rest of today and then tomorrow morning to find some way of telling her what you were up to last night."

"Yeah, like I'm going to drop that on her just before I head off to California for two weeks."

"Better that than not tell her at all," Becca said. "To go off without telling her something like this—that's like a lie, Tyler. This is a matter of honesty."

And those words were running through Tyler's head as he jogged back to his bike.

AllenOlson: Hey, if it isn't my old buddy Tyler! What are you up to tonight online?

ColoradoTy: just logged on for a few minutes to check weather out in cali. i'm right in the middle of packin for my summer surfin trip.

AllenOlson: Oh, yeah, I almost forgot. You're leaving when—tomorrow?

ColoradoTy: bright and early.

AllenOlson: Hey, you have a great time. By the way— everything okay lately?

ColoradoTy: of course. why?

AllenOlson: No reason. I just had you on my mind the past couple of days, and felt like praying for you. So I did. Several times, really. You haven't had any big tests or anything?

ColoradoTy: it's summer.

AllenOlson: Oh, yeah. Well, I thought God might be prompting me to pray for you for some reason. Maybe it was just because you're flying tomorrow.

ColoradoTy: yup. that must be it.

AllenOlson: Okay. Anything you want to talk about before you head out there?

ColoradoTy: like what?

AllenOlson: Like—I don't know. Like anything. How to meet surfer chicks on the beach, how to find God's will for your life—easy stuff like that.

ColoradoTy: nope. hey, i gotta go. packin to do.

AllenOlson: Okay, I hear you. Take care. And remember, if you need to talk while you're out there, you got my number, and I'm only as far away as the nearest cyber-café.

ColoradoTy: gotta go. signing off.

AllenOlson: Love you, buddy.

chapter

"I *have* everything, Mom!" Tyler said, exasperated.

He was loading his suitcases, two of them, into the back of the mini-van in the garage, and he'd heard enough of his mom's *Did you pack . . . Did you remember . . . Maybe you should take . . .* over the past couple of hours to last a lifetime. Then he looked up, saw the worry in her eyes, and softened his tone. "And if there's anything I forgot, I'll either borrow it or buy it once I get out there. I mean, it's not like I'm going to Bangladesh. I'll be with family. Kissin' cousins. They'll make sure I've got diapers and formula."

She touched his cheek. "I know. It's just—well—let's get started."

"Finally," Tyra grumbled from the backseat. "Can we dump him off and do something useful with the rest of the day?"

"Actually," Tyler said, sliding into the passenger seat, "I have a full slate of yardwork for you to do while I'm gone. Dad said he'd check on you to make sure it was getting done. There's a set of instructions on the kitchen counter, but basically, I want you to start by reseeding the front yard . . ."

"Ha, ha. Aren't you going to miss this, Mom? What are we going to do for two weeks? We'll go into insanity deprivation."

"Well, in that case," Mom said, backing out of the driveway, "lucky for me I still have you to keep me insane."

Tyler licked his finger and chalked up an imaginary point in the air.

"Oh!" Mom said. "Tyler, did you think to—"

"Ah-ah-ah—didn't we just discuss this?"

She nodded. "Sorry. I won't remind you to check to make sure you have your tickets."

"Don't need to. Checked before we left the house."

She patted his knee. "Won't you be glad to get on the plane and leave all these fussy females behind?"

"Yup and double yup."

There was a burst of laughter from the backseat. "What!" Tyler said. Something patted his head. He reached up and grabbed it—something flat, some papers—and found himself holding his airline tickets. He spun and looked angrily back at Tyra. "Where'd you get these?"

"I knew you'd be all proud of how efficient you were. So I just borrowed those out of your backpack after you put them in."

"Tyra!" Mom scolded. "That was *not* a good thing to do. What if you'd forgotten to give them back to him before he got on the plane?"

"He couldn't get *on* the plane without tickets, Mom," she said. "He needed a little jab through the armor."

"I'll give you a jab through the armor," Tyler grumbled, shoving his tickets back into the pocket of his backpack. Disgusted and annoyed, he tossed the backpack on the floor between his feet and looked out the window.

He'd been on edge all morning. It wasn't because of the trip—he was excited about the trip and had been looking forward to it for weeks. Months. His one big opportunity all year to do something he dearly loved—surfing. No, he'd been on edge because of his talk with the girls yesterday afternoon. *It's a matter of honesty*, Becca had said. Ouch. Tyler hated to come down on the wrong side of that issue—or even to have the girls *think* he was on the wrong side. If there was some easy way to tell his mom about it, he would—well, maybe he would. It's just—it would be so messy. Mom would be so upset. And he couldn't say it with Tyra around, so he'd have to think of some way to get her out of the way for a few minutes. Fat chance of that.

Well, with luck, maybe by the time he got back the whole thing would have resolved itself—somehow.

● ● ●

"Oh, gee, that's a surprise," Tyra said as their car pulled up in front of the passenger drop-off area at the airport. There, lined up like soldiers, shoulders back, at attention, each with one hand up to her forehead in a salute, were Becca, Jacie, Solana, and Hannah.

"Oh, how sweet," Mom said. "They had to come down for one last good-bye."

Yeah, right, Tyler thought. *More likely they've come down to check up on me. We said our good-byes yesterday.*

Solana tugged his door open and bowed. "Waylcome to Colorahdo Spreengs Eenternational Airport, señor," she said in a heavy Spanish accent. "Our redcaps weell take your bags, por favor."

"Don't expect a tip," he said, stepping onto the sidewalk. Tyra jumped out beside him.

"Don't worry, girls—I'll make sure you're well rewarded," his mom called from the car. Then, when they'd closed all the doors, she yelled, "I'm going to park! I'll be right back!" The car pulled away from the curb.

"I'm honored," Tyler said. "Especially since, last time I saw the four of you, you were trying to decide whether to roast me on a spit or just eat me raw."

"Oooh, sounds interesting," Tyra said. "Somebody want to fill me in?"

"It's nothin'," Tyler said. "They just finally told me how they really feel about you, and I leaped to your defense."

"Something like that," Becca said.

"Yeah, right," Tyra said. "C'mon. Gimme. What's up?"

Becca threw an arm around Tyra's shoulder. "Tyra, sweetheart," she said. "Can't your brother have any secrets from you? If not, then how about if I tell him about that time down at the shopping mall when I saw you and what's-his—"

"No!" Tyra shouted. "No, that's okay—let him have his pathetic little secrets."

"Wait," Tyler said. "I want to hear about what's-his—"

"Now, Tyler," Becca said. "You do have your secrets too. Don't you?"

Tyler looked at her hard.

"Or is it still a secret?" Becca asked. "Perhaps in the past day or so, a certain conversation has taken place . . ."

Tyler looked at her without speaking, then looked at Jacie. The expression on Jacie's face was very different. "I know it's hard," she said quietly. She looked at Becca. "Maybe he should wait until—"

"No," Solana said forcefully, "it's never good to wait about these things. This is something that doesn't age well."

"What doesn't age well? Will someone please tell me—"

Becca wagged a finger at Tyra. "Remember the mall," she said.

They lugged Tyler's suitcases to the ticket counter and he checked in. By that time, his mom had returned from parking the car. They stood by as he zipped his tickets and boarding passes back into his pack, then Becca said, "You want some coffee, Mrs. Jennings? There's a Starbucks over there."

"Oh—no, really—"

"We're going to have some," Solana said, "so it's no trouble. Tyler?"

"Uh, yeah—café mocha."

"Well," his mom said, "just a regular latte then."

"Come on," Becca said, grabbing Tyra by the arm, "and I'll get you one of those little candy sticks dipped in chocolate. All the kiddies like them."

The five of them disappeared around the corner of the concourse.

Tyler pointed toward some seats. "Let's sit over here while we wait." He knew that the girls had dragged Tyra away for only one reason, and it had nothing to do with coffee.

"Tyler," his mom said suddenly, "is there—well, there seems to be some tension between you and the girls. Or am I just imagining it?"

How to respond? He shrugged. "Oh, it's no big deal. It's, uh—a matter of tastes. We'll work through it after I get back."

She smiled at him. "A matter of tastes."

"Yeah."

His hand loosely gripped the chair arm between them, and she poked it a couple of times slowly with her finger, absent-mindedly, as if thinking. "Well," she said at last, "maybe that's not such a bad argument to have with your friends just before you go to California."

"Why's that?"

She hesitated, then said, "I talked on the phone last night with my sister. She was very glad you were coming out there. She's worried about Chaz."

Chaz, the cousin Tyler was closest to, was a year older than him. The two of them were much alike—similar tastes, similar interests, similar personalities. "What's wrong with Chaz?"

"Well, according to Evelyn, Chaz is changing. He's distancing himself from his family—"

"Isn't that what parents always say when kids get out of high school and start to have a life of their own?"

His mom laughed. "I suppose so. But I asked her the same thing last night. She said no, that this is different. He has new habits, new friends . . ."

"That might be good."

Tyler's mom shook her head. "I don't think so. Not in this case. I really do trust Evelyn's judgment about things like this, Tyler. She's pretty fair-minded. Of course, she's also right in the middle, so it's not like she can just step back and get some perspective on it all. She feels like some of the directions he's moving in now are the wrong directions. So maybe it's good that you and the girls have been wrestling with 'matters of taste.' You might have to make some decisions of your own about matters of taste in the next few days."

"What do you mean—decisions to make?"

"Decisions about—oh, whether to go with Chaz everyplace he goes, and whether to do all the things he does." She put her hand over his on the arm of the chair between them. "I trust your judgment, Tyler. I trust you."

Now where had he just been discussing that—her trust of him?

"And I know that you're not just going to let Chaz influence you in any way you don't think is right. What I'm hoping, in fact, is just the opposite—that you'll be a positive influence on him."

Tyler shifted uneasily in his seat. "Well—we don't even know for sure that he needs a positive influence. He may be just fine. I won't know what's going on until I get out there. I mean—did she say *what* exactly he was doing that she didn't like?"

Tyler's mom shrugged. "Oh, she doesn't like the music he's been listening to, that sort of thing. But unfortunately, she couldn't remember the names of any of the groups, or I could have checked them out down at the office. Have you talked to Chaz in the past few months?"

Tyler had called, but each time, Chaz had been gone. "No. I haven't."

"Oh. Too bad. I thought he might have mentioned something about his new group of friends, or the music they listen to."

Tyler shook his head. "I can't really picture Chaz with a new group of friends. I mean, his surf pack is tight—they've been together for years, since elementary school—it's like me and the Brio squad. And they surf the same beaches, they're together a few times a week—I just can't see it. Maybe she's misunderstanding what's going on."

His mom nodded. "Maybe. You'll soon find out."

Well, this was a new wrinkle. Chaz had always seemed to have a pretty close relationship with Aunt Evelyn—a lot like Tyler and his own mom. The two sisters were much alike, so that wasn't surprising. But what Tyler was hearing now *was* surprising.

He tried to remember what Chaz had said the last time they'd talked. Anything about music? Friends? Atmosphere at home, arguments with Mom? But Tyler couldn't really remember the last time they'd talked. It had been a while. And there hadn't been any danger signs that he could remember, no surprises, no question marks after he'd hung up, nothing like that. So whatever it was, maybe it was more recent. Or maybe it was nothing. Just the general nervousness and over-protectiveness of parents.

Not that Aunt Evelyn had ever seemed particularly nervous. Or over-protective.

"Okay," Becca's voice said. "One latte for the lady. One cup of grass-hopper spit for the gentleman."

"I take cinnamon in my grasshopper spit," Tyler said, reaching out for his cup. "Could you go bring me some, please?"

"Depends," Solana said, "on how cooperative you're being. Are you being cooperative?"

"Tyler!" his mom said. "Did you hear that? They just called your flight! You'd better get through security. You can take your coffee on the plane."

"It's grasshopper spit," Becca said. "Did you think I was kidding?"

"That was just the first call, Mrs. Jennings," Jacie said. "He's got a few minutes yet."

"I know," his mom answered, "but with all the security these days—especially with young men. They're checking shoes, going through carry-ons . . ."

"They just called for children and people who need help boarding," Tyra said. "Better hurry."

Tyler shouldered his pack. "I gotta go. Wouldn't want to make Tyra miss her cartoons."

Becca gave him a look, then shook her head. Surprisingly, though, she was the first to step up, arms wide, and gather him into a hug. "You turkey," she whispered into his ear. "But I'll be praying for you. And call, for pete's sake."

Solana was next, then Jacie. To Tyler's amazement, even Hannah stepped awkwardly up and offered a stiff hug. "Good-bye," she said shyly, looking at the ground. "I'll miss you."

Tyler looked at her for a moment, then turned to Tyra and held his arms wide. "Sis," he said. "C'mere. Gimme a hug. You know you want one."

"Better do it," Solana said. "His plane could go down—"

"Oh! Solana, don't!" his mom said, pressing her fingertips to her temples. "Just before he gets on the plane—please, don't."

Tyra grinned. "Well, with that in mind . . ." She wrapped her arms around him and made loud kissing noises in the air beside his ear.

"Hey!" he yelled. "Don't . . ." He pushed her away.

Tyler's mom took his shoulder, turned him toward her, and hugged him. Then she held him at arm's length and looked at him. "And speaking of Chaz—I'll be praying about that. Listen hard to him, think about what's going on, and I'll be interested to hear about it when you get back."

Tyler nodded. "I'll try."

She leaned forward, kissed his cheek, and said, "Now go. They just called your flight again."

Tyler looked around the group, grinned, and turned to head for the security check. He *would* miss them. Each one.

A few minutes later, he settled into his seat, popped a Van Morrison CD into his portable, adjusted the headphones, and closed his eyes. Most years, the only time he flew was for this summer trip to California. And he loved flying. Loved the sensation and loved the scenery, which is why he always chose a window seat. And it was a clear day, too, so he'd have a great view of the Rockies and the desert—and of the ocean and the beaches as they banked for their approach into John Wayne/ Orange County Airport.

He tried to concentrate on the music, but something kept intruding. A thought. What was up with Chaz? What was Aunt Evelyn so uptight about? Was there something to it?

Nah. Probably not. It was probably nothing.

A quick thought: Chaz's best friend, Terry. A maniac surfer, and a solid Christian, one of the leaders of the youth group he and Chaz both went to. Tyler would try to get Terry aside at the beach and ask him what was up with Chaz. He would know.

chapter 5

"Hey, guy," Chaz said, grinning lazily, as Tyler stepped off the escalator near the baggage claim in John Wayne Airport. He stuck out his hand and Tyler shook it. "Long time, all that."

"Good to see you, man," Tyler said.

"You got luggage?"

"Nah, it's all here in this backpack. Everything I'll need for two weeks."

Chaz laughed. "Could be. Only things you'll need for the next two weeks are your trunks, suntan lotion, and sunglasses."

"Yeah," Tyler said, "but just on the off-chance we want to go shopping or to church, I brought a few other things." He wandered toward the baggage claim.

"Don't you remember? In California, they close churches when the surf's up on Sundays."

He seemed like the same old Chaz to Tyler. Just a year older and with a slightly different look—but hey, it was California. Here, new looks came and went every month. Chaz was taller than Tyler by about three inches, and built like a basketball player, which made him look even taller. But Chaz didn't play sports much. Other than surfing, of course, which he did every available minute and had since he was an elementary-school surf-rat. Chaz's black hair refused to sun-bleach, something he had hated in middle school, when he had been vocally envious of Tyler's long, blond hair. Chaz was wearing that black hair now cut very short, in a kind of buzz cut, and he had a goatee about the same length, no moustache. Something else seemed a little different about him, but Tyler couldn't pin it down. It certainly wasn't his clothes—standard California summer attire: nylon cargo shorts, Birken-stock sandals, and a T-shirt. Wait—the T-shirt logo was different. Usually Chaz wore a surf-shop T-shirt; this one had the summer tour schedule for some band Tyler had never heard of.

Tyler hefted his first suitcase off the carousel, then saw the second one right behind it.

"That it?" Chaz asked.

Tyler nodded. "Let's get out of here."

A few minutes later they were pulling onto MacArthur Blvd., all the windows in Chaz's old BMW—his dad had passed it along to Chaz two years before when he'd gotten a new one—rolled down. Tyler scanned the buildings in the heavily built-up area near the airport as they passed: restaurants, tall office buildings, hotels . . . "Hey," he said. "Is that a new—you guys built a new Thompson Inn right here by the airport!"

Chaz's dad, James—no one ever called him Jim—was a Thompson, of the Thompson Inn Thompsons. He'd gone into the family business right out of college, and was now a senior V.P. Which was why Chaz's family had money.

"Yeah, actually the construction had already started last summer when you were here. It's been up and running for about six months now. We launched three new ones last year, which brings us up to 21. This is the flagship, now, though—the biggest and the fanciest. You should see it. I'll take you through it later." Chaz laughed softly. "It's kind of ridiculous, to tell you the truth. I mean, the kind of luxury businessmen think they need when they travel. We could probably cut the prices of a night's stay in half if we didn't throw in all that stuff. I don't think we should have done it, actually. I think it's stupid."

Well, that was a first. Tyler didn't think he'd ever heard Chaz criticize his dad or the Thompson Inn company before—he'd been raised to think it was the greatest business in the world. But he didn't sound like that now. Was this part of what his mom had been talking about?

In a very few miles, they were past the worst of the airport development and into relatively open country; hills stretched away to the southeast, where Tyler knew the University of California at Irvine campus sat. He poked his head out the window, closed his eyes, and let the warm, sweet air rush past him. Ah, California. Ignoring the smell of car exhaust, Tyler could pick out floral scents—was that jasmine, from the plantings alongside the road?—and a faint hint of sage. And the cool, clean smell of ocean.

"You got it in the car?" he said.

Chaz laughed. "Every time you get here, that's all you want. Yeah, I brought it."

"Stick it in the stereo, man."

Chaz popped out the CD that had been playing—some band Tyler didn't recognize—and stuck in a different one, pushed a couple of buttons—and then it began: Randy Newman's "I Love L.A."

"Sing it, cousin!" Tyler yelled, and sang along:

Rollin' down Imperial Highway . . .

Chaz joined in, laughing, his arm out the window, patting the side of the car to keep the beat, and both of them got louder as Newman began calling out their favorite Hollywood streets:

Sunset Boulevard
Santa Monica Boulevard . . .

And launched into the Beachboys-style background vocals.

"All right!" Tyler said, as the song faded out. "Yes. California."

"We got to get you some new music, cousin," Chaz chuckled. He ejected the Randy Newman CD and put another one in. "There's more to California music than 'I Love L.A.' He's so eighties."

"Okay," Tyler said, pointing toward the CD player. "So who's this?"

Chaz tapped one hand against the band insignia on his chest. "Spider. Great new band. Hey—speaking of bands, Bong's going to be in concert at the Staples Center just before you leave. I think we can still get tickets."

"Wow. How much?"

"Cheapest seats are $55."

"*Fifty-five bucks!* I only brought a couple hundred, and that's gotta cover me for everything for two weeks. I don't know. I'll have to think about this."

Chaz tapped the front of the CD player. "Tyler, my friend, we will introduce you to a whole new world in the next two weeks. Things you've never heard before." He grinned. "You'll never be the same. You'll be the most well-educated musician in the Rockies. Don't cheap out on me and miss the opportunity."

Tyler nodded, not sure what to say. Fifty-five bucks? He'd never paid that much for a concert before.

"So," Chaz went on. "What you been up to?"

Tyler tried to think of something Chaz would be interested in hearing. To his surprise, what he said was, "I went to see *The River Runs Downhill* the other day." As soon as he said it, he wished he could take it back. Not the way he wanted his time with Chaz to start.

Chaz turned in the seat and looked at him. "Really? Hmm. Your mom didn't mind?"

"Didn't tell her."

Chaz nodded appreciatively. "Wow. A new Tyler. I'm impressed. So—what did you think?"

"Well—I mean, it was a great movie. One of the best-made movies I'd seen in a long time."

"Exactly."

Tyler waited. "Exactly what?"

"Exactly it was a well-made movie. That's what I didn't like about it. It was so self-conscious. As if he knew all the things he needed to do to win an Oscar, and he wanted to be so careful to do all of them he forgot that it takes more than that to make a *great* movie. It lacked honesty. It lacked insight. It was like a musical performance in which every note is played exactly right—but without any emotion behind it. No spontaneity."

Tyler paused. "Wow," he said. "I mean—I guess I didn't see any of that in it. I still think it was good."

"Oh, it *was* good. Especially for Hollywood," Chaz said, pulling off MacArthur onto Coast Highway, heading south through Newport. "I'm sure it'll get Academy Award nominations. Might even win some. But so what? Hollywood is just a big meat market anymore. Everybody knows all the good films are coming from independent filmmakers these days. Or from foreign filmmakers, who still think the point of making a movie is to have something to say, instead of to make a bundle of money for some corporation that happens to own your studio."

Tyler looked out the window. "We don't even *get* foreign films in Copper Ridge. In fact, I had to go to Colorado Springs just to see *River Runs Downhill.*"

Chaz laughed. "Ah, yes. The Bible Belt."

Well, technically, Colorado wasn't in the Bible Belt. But Tyler decided not to argue the point. It definitely wasn't California, either.

"Well, tell you what," Chaz said. "Besides taking you to hear some *good* music, we'll see if we can take you to see some good movies, too.

Things that *definitely* won't be coming to a theater near you."

Tyler wasn't sure what that meant, and wasn't sure he wanted to know. "You keep saying 'we,'" he said. "You mean the regular guys, your surf buddies, Terry and Carlos and all them?"

Chaz shrugged. "Yeah, some of the old surf crowd, like Zack. And some new ones, although I think you've met most of them on the beach at one time or another. Good people. People that like ideas, like to talk, who know something about art and music."

Tyler looked at Chaz. "Not Terry? He's been your best friend for like forty years. I was looking forward to seeing him."

"Terry kind of dropped out of everything," Chaz said. "He didn't like the new crowd, didn't like the new music. He's leaving for college in a couple of weeks anyway. You might see him on the beach. He still surfs."

"What college?"

"Some religious college; I don't know."

He didn't know? His best friend was leaving for college and he didn't know which one? "So," Tyler said, "are the two of you still active in—you know—the youth group?"

Chaz grinned, not looking at Tyler as he made his turn away from the beach, up into Laguna Niguel, where the Thompsons lived. "Tyler, I'm not in high school anymore. What do I need with a youth group?"

"Well, I figured they probably have a college-age group, too, don't they? Where—"

"So listen," Chaz said, obviously changing the subject. "What do you want to do first?"

Tyler smiled. "Are you kidding? Let's hit the surf, man."

"Alas," Chaz said, "the surf is way down this afternoon. Not worth putting a board in the water. But early tomorrow promises to be bodacious. We can still hit the beach now, though. You can say hi to everybody. Let's go get into our suits."

chapter

They parked on the street a half block from the beach, and the closer they got to the sand, the faster Tyler walked. The sun was as gentle and inviting as only a Southern California sun can be, with the slight breeze from out over the water taking the bite out of the rays. Hurrying along, Tyler watched the gulls wheeling over the beach, heard their cries.

"Hey, man—it'll still be there in five minutes. What's the rush?" Chaz laughed. But Tyler hardly heard him. As soon as he felt sand beneath his sandals, he kicked them off, scooped them up, and began to jog across the beach. A few yards shy of the high-water mark, he tossed down his towel and his sandals, closed his eyes, and took in a huge breath, unable to keep the silly grin off his face.

Chaz jogged up behind him. "All my friends are down in front of Jackie's. Let's go down there and see who—"

"Not yet, man. Yeah, I want to see everybody, but right now . . ."

He stripped off his shirt—an old T-shirt he'd ripped the sleeves off—and the nylon cargo shorts he'd pulled over his swimsuit. "Right now I want to feel the water. Come on!" Still wearing his goofy grin, Tyler charged down the beach, dodging a couple of kindergarten-age boys, and ran as fast as he could straight into the water. It was cold! As always. Which was why he always entered the water this way, running straight into the surf, breaking through one cold wave after another, first just up to his shins, the next one to his knees; then the level of the sand dipped and the next wave hit him waist-high and hard, and he took two more slogging steps and tripped over the water, falling headlong into the shockingly cold surf. He dove, scraped along just an inch or two above the sand, kicking and stroking, forcing himself to stay down as long as he could, then leaping up out of the water—now chest-deep—with a shouted "Whooo! That's *cold*!"

Something splashed nearby, and a few seconds later Chaz emerged near Tyler, grinning, shaking the water out of his eyes. Tyler held a double handful of ocean up to his face and smelled it. "This," he said rapturously, "is *not* Colorado!"

"Not the last time I checked," Chaz said. "Let's move out about twenty, thirty yards and pick up a wave."

They swam out, diving twice under incoming breakers, then turned and treaded water, waiting for the right moment, waiting, waiting . . . And then as the swell approached, as Tyler felt himself being borne up by the water, before he could slide too far up the face of the wave, he broke toward shore, swimming as quickly, as energetically as he could, aware of Chaz swimming just a couple of yards to his left. And as he sensed the wave beginning to break at its crest, he reached his arms straight in front of him, stiffened his body—and felt the wave take him, felt his body propelled forward without any effort on his part, felt the power of the ocean, the speed, the roar—and then the wave broke over him, tumbled him head over heels against gritty sand, and he pushed his head above water, spluttering, laughing.

"Waves are pretty wimpy today," Chaz said somewhere close behind him. "Two, three feet maybe. Not worth taking a board out on."

Tyler turned, spotted him, and nodded. "Yeah, you're right, not a day for boards. But puny or not, at least they're waves! And considering how long I've waited for this, I've gotta catch me a few more of those!" He charged out through the surf again, swimming after the water got up past his waist, and found the right place to wait for the next wave.

Forty-five minutes later Tyler was still riding the small waves, and Chaz finally grabbed Tyler's foot and began pulling him toward the shore while Tyler struggled to hop behind him, spending most of the time with his face under the water. "Come on!" Chaz said. "We'll surf tomorrow! Let's go see who's here today."

"Hey!" Tyler said. "I can't breathe!"

"You can now," Chaz said, dragging Tyler up out of the surf and depositing him on the sand near the surf line, as a wave rushed up around him, scattering foam, sucking the sand from under his body as if trying to bury him. "Come on. I saw Miller walk by a few minutes ago, heading down toward Jackie's."

"Miller? I ever meet him before?"

"Don't think so. He's been around here for a few years, part of the beach crowd, but I never really hung out with him till a few months ago."

The two of them picked up their towels and began to dry off. Tyler held his arm up to his face, smelled the salt water on his skin, and smiled. "Ah, salt water," he said.

"You know what that arm ought to smell like?"

"What?"

"Coppertone. Remember last year? You got burned to a crisp the first day and couldn't surf for a week." Chaz reached down and grabbed a bottle of suntan lotion out of the pocket of the shorts he'd worn over his suit. He tossed it to Tyler. "Lotion up, white man."

Tyler obeyed.

When Tyler tossed the suntan lotion back to him, Chaz said, "Okay, let's go."

"Ten minutes first, just to sit here. Okay?"

"Man . . ."

"Humor me. I'm your out-of-town cousin and you're supposed to show me a good time."

"This is your idea of a good time? Just sitting?"

"At this particular moment, this is exactly my idea of a good time." He spread out his towel and sat on it, facing the waves. Tiny kids played in the surf from as far as he could see to the left to as far as he could see to the right. From the jetty, not far away, came the cries of a few sea lions.

"Is it my imagination," Tyler said, "or are girls' suits a little skimpier even than last year—if such a thing be possible?"

"It's not your imagination," Chaz answered. "Isn't that some kind of law? I, for one, am not complaining."

Tyler wasn't complaining either, although he felt like he should. That would be the 'good Christian boy' response. But for the moment, he felt like anything but the 'good Christian boy.'

Thinking of girls made Tyler think of his Brio squad, to whom he had said good-bye so awkwardly just that morning. The girls had never been out to California with him; he'd gone swimming with them in rivers, lakes, and swimming pools, but never the ocean. He grinned just thinking about it. Becca would take to surfing like—well, like a duck to water. She'd be better than him before the week was out. Hannah . . . hmmm. Would she even come to a beach like this—considering the bathing suits, the couples making out on the sand? And what kind of bathing suit would *she* wear? He could predict—a very modest one-piece, covered by an oversized T-shirt that she never took off, even when swimming.

Just then three girls walked past in swimsuits that definitely weren't modest. Chaz tapped Tyler's arm. "Must be an omen. They're heading our direction."

Chaz and Tyler tossed their towels and outer clothes over their shoulders and began to follow the three girls up the beach, at the surf line, stepping over and around the constant scramble of kids screaming and playing. Jackie's, where they were apparently headed, was a beach landmark—a combination snack bar and equipment rental where you could get a belly board for the day or a Coke and an order of a Southern California beach favorite called "strips"—something like nachos, but longer and softer, as if the tortillas had just been fried in oil long enough to heat them up but not long enough to make them completely crisp, and served with shredded cheese and a heavy salsa. Tyler looked forward to strips almost as much as he looked forward to the surf.

Chaz waved at someone. Tyler followed his gaze and saw a man nod back. He looked to be at least ten years older than Tyler—in his late twenties. He wore his hair and goatee exactly the same as Chaz did. In fact, he was similar in height and build to Chaz—the main difference between them being that Chaz tanned well, but the man they were walking toward seemed to freckle.

The man stood. "So this must be Tyler." He put out his hand. Tyler shook it.

"Pleased to meet you," Tyler said.

"Tyler, this is Miller. Miller, this is Tyler."

"Hey, somebody grab a camera and record this momentous occasion!" came a familiar voice, deep and gravelly, and Tyler looked up.

"Hey, Zack," he said, and shook his hand too. Zack was—well, Zack was different. He was the most musical of the group; in fact, he'd been playing bass in a decent local rock band the previous summer, and Tyler had been jealous. He was a decent rock vocalist, too, although in last summer's band he'd been restricted to backup vocals. But he wasn't the friendliest guy. He was quiet, with a tendency to be sullen, and outside of his band and his little group of friends, it was hard to find anyone or anything that he didn't view with quiet contempt. But he seemed to like Tyler okay—or at least to give him the benefit of the doubt because he was Chaz's cousin, and Zack and Chaz had been tight for years.

"Tyler, I've been looking forward to this," Miller said. "The rest of these yahoos have been talking about you for weeks, eagerly anticipating your arrival."

"Mainly we tried to get all the girls off the beach, for their own protection," Chaz said. "But as you can see, it didn't work."

"Thank goodness for that," Tyler said.

"And in the spirit of celebration," Miller went on, "I'm going to spring for strips and drinks for everybody. Tyler, what's your pleasure?"

"Dr Pepper for me."

"Okay, I already know what everybody else wants. But they'll have to settle for Cokes. Zack, come on and give me hand carrying everything."

"Don't forget Angel," Chaz called at them as they slogged away through the soft sand.

Who was Angel? Tyler wondered. But what he said was, "So—Miller. First name or last name?"

"First, believe it or not," Chaz said. "Miller Andrews. I tell him he's destined to be the president of either a university or a bank, because to be either of those things you've got to have a first name that works as a last name and a last name that works as a first name. Like Barclay Jamison, who's president over at UCI. Miller Andrews or Andrews Miller."

"How'd he get included in your group?"

Chaz laughed. "I think we got included in his. Anyway, I don't know—no special way. We just started talking with him every now and then here on the beach in front of Jackie's, and gradually—I don't know. We just had a new group, and he was in it."

"But not Terry."

Chaz shrugged. "Terry could have, if he wanted. Like I said, he just kind of dropped out. Listen, Miller's a good guy. He knows pretty much everything there is to know about music and movies and literature. And he's got a lot of friends. The other day a friend of his came down here to hang out with us, and he was one of the writers for 'Will and Grace.' Which, let me guess, is a show you don't like a whole lot. But it's a smart show, and funny, and you got to respect the people who write it. Anyway, he knows people like that."

"I thought Hollywood was just a meat market."

Chaz gestured impatiently. "It is. But some of the stuff they produce there is better than the rest. So they've got some good people trying to do a good job. Anyway, look—sit here and talk to Miller when we're not surfin' over the next couple of days, and you'll see what I mean. You'll be in for some of the most interesting discussions you've had in a long time."

Maybe. Something seemed wrong to Tyler about the whole thing. Why was this guy in his late twenties still a student, anyway? And why was he hanging around with teenagers?

Chaz spread out his towel and lay down. Tyler stood looking out over the surf. It was, by now, late afternoon, and the sun was low enough in the sky to be in his eyes, and to be reflecting almost blindingly bright off the ocean, diamonds flashing on the constantly moving water. One thing Tyler loved about the beach was the simplicity of the landscape. You had the sky. You had the sand. And you had the water. The shore was a relatively straight line, the horizon was another. Everything existed within that simple and bright geometric pattern.

Hundreds of people were in the water, spread across the width of the beach. Of the dozens directly before him, one stood out for some reason—a head, far enough out in the water to be submerged to her neck. There was no doubt that it was a girl, and a pretty one, too; Tyler's eyes were good enough to make that out. And it occurred to Tyler that the reason he had noticed her out of all the others was not just that she was pretty, but that she was looking back at him, with a level, steady gaze.

Her shoulders emerged slowly, and Tyler realized that she was walking back up toward the beach, still fixing him with that steady gaze and a tiny smile. Then he could see that her bathing suit was different—a one-piece. It looked foreign or something. Against the bright water, she was almost in silhouette and he could tell this girl had one of the best figures he'd ever seen anywhere. Water dripped from her shoulder-length hair. And still she looked at him. Did he know her? Who *was* this girl? He remembered hearing the myth of the appearance of Venus from the ocean borne up on a giant seashell, and he felt as if he were witnessing the same kind of thing.

Up out of the water she stepped and across the damp sand.

Tyler was aware suddenly of Chaz standing beside him. "Now that's a sight," he said. Tyler didn't answer. She was walking right up to him! What would he say? *Excuse me, but are you a goddess or something? Because you sure look like one.* Right.

Tyler was aware suddenly that his mouth was hanging open. He closed it. He still had no idea what to say, and she was almost here! She—

Wait. She wasn't walking up to him. She was walking up to *Chaz*, smiling at *him*. In fact, she didn't even look at Tyler as she approached them, then walked right between him and Chaz, placing a hand on Chaz's shoulder as she passed so close she almost brushed Tyler with her wet skin.

"Okay, we got strips! Tyler, here's your DP," came Miller's voice behind him.

Tyler turned and watched her walk into the circle of towels. She took a Coke cup from Zack and sipped some through the straw. Then she turned and smiled at Tyler. Something strange was happening to his skin, all over his body.

"Tyler," Chaz said, "meet Angel."

I'm in love, thought Tyler.

51

chapter 7

Late morning the next day, Tyler in his short wetsuit straddled his board a hundred yards out, facing the shore, enjoying the cold ocean water against his legs. It was Chaz's board, actually, a spare he let Tyler borrow. As much as he loved surfing, Tyler had never owned a surfboard of his own, and probably never would, or at least not while he lived in Colorado. Wouldn't make much sense to pay that much money for something you used only two weeks out of the year. Or at least that was what Tyler's dad said.

Despite Chaz's assurances, the waves weren't that great today, which was undoubtedly why there were only a dozen or so people out on their boards. And the wait between waves was long. Plenty of time to think.

The tension between Chaz and his mom had already showed up. Over a great breakfast of strawberry waffles that morning, there had been plenty of tension and eloquent wordless looks between mother and son when she'd asked what they had planned for the day. Then Tyler and Chaz had loaded the boards onto a carrier on top of Chaz's BMW and headed for the beach. To Tyler's surprise, Chaz had said as he pulled onto Highway 1, "Listen, Tyler—I saw that look my mom gave you when she was moaning about Miller. Let me guess. Your mom and my mom talked. Right? And my mom told your mom I was going off the deep end or something, and she wanted you to try to straighten me out. Am I close?"

Tyler had grinned wryly, embarrassed, but glad it was out in the open. "Uh—yeah. Real close."

Chaz shook his head. "Okay, listen, cousin. There's nothing wrong with me, nothing wrong with my friends. Look at it this way. Do you really think that the way your parents think, or the way your church thinks, is perfect? I mean, not about theology in particular, but about music, about literature, language, politics, all that stuff?"

"No, of course not. I mean, I disagree with them about a lot of that stuff myself."

"Okay, well, that's all we're talking about here. My mom probably said something like, 'Chaz isn't the same guy he was a year ago.' Well, I hope not. I hope I've grown, gotten a little smarter, and become more my own person, not just a younger version of my parents. You know what I've been doing this year?"

"What?"

"I've been testing everything I've been told. For instance—there were books my Sunday school teacher told me I should never read, because they would 'corrupt' me. Last year I read a bunch of 'em—checked 'em out of the library. And you know what? Some of them *weren't* worth reading. Others were great. To *her*, they were horrible books because they had bad words or sex scenes or something. Well—so what? Am I going to hell because I read a book where one of the characters uses four-letter words? I learned a lot about life from reading those books, because they were written by people who were smart and honest. Maybe they weren't Christians—but they were still smart and honest. So I tested what my Sunday school teacher said, and I found out—she was wrong. Gee, what a concept! She could actually be wrong about something."

"Okay, but Chaz, I'm not arguing with any of that. I don't think my parents, or my pastor, or anybody else is infallible and could never be just flat-out wrong about something. So don't feel like you have to defend yourself to me. Okay? I'm not spying for your mom, and I haven't been sent here on some secret mission to sign you up as a missionary to the Congo. I just came out to enjoy the surf and spend some time with my cousin. All right?"

And Chaz had laughed and nodded.

"But . . ." Tyler said tentatively.

Chaz sighed. "What"

"Well, what about your youth group? And Terry? Last summer, and the summer before, we did a lot of stuff with your youth group, and Terry was with us the whole time. This year, nada. What's up with that?"

"I told you, man. They call 'em *youth* groups for a reason. 'When I became a man, I put away childish things.' Isn't that what the Bible says? You know what a youth group is for? It's to keep kids out of trouble. So they spend all their time telling you what not to do. And there just comes a time when you don't need that any more. I want my life to be based on possibilities, not taboos. Positive, not negative. Besides, I'm startin' college in the fall—why do I need a youth group?"

Tyler hadn't responded, not sure what to say. And ever since, and even now as he sat enjoying the calling of the gulls that swooped and wheeled over the beach and the surf, he'd felt an odd uneasiness, as if he had betrayed something. Or someone. As if he had taken the easy way out.

"We could pack it up and try further south," Chaz said.

Tyler shook off his thoughts and looked at his cousin, floating next to him on the new board he'd gotten just a few weeks before.

"Still early," Chaz went on. "San Clemente, Del Mar ... waves might be better."

Tyler considered it, then shook his head. "Tomorrow," he said. "For today, this is fine. First day back on a board, all that. Good refresher course."

Chaz laughed. "A refresher course is something you don't need, Tyler. You're a natural."

Tyler glanced back over his shoulder. "Here comes one."

"You take it," Chaz said. "I'll get the second one."

Tyler flopped quickly onto his belly, vaguely aware of the grit embedded in the wax on the board against his knees and cheek, and began to paddle, easily at first, then more rapidly as the wave approached. When he felt the front edge of the swell lift and tilt his board, he lifted his head to see better, gave a couple more powerful paddles with both arms, and then pushed upward sharply with his arms, drawing his legs up in the same motion and slipping his feet under him, then carefully standing as the wave pushed his board forward. The wax he had applied thickly to the board that morning kept his feet steady, and he deftly guided the board to the right, following the way the wave would break. These little waves didn't provide a dramatic ride, but he worked the wave as well as he could on the short ride toward shore, then cut out of the wave and dropped into waist-deep water. His board tried to follow the wave toward shore, but Tyler just grabbed the cord attached to his ankle on one end and the board on the other and pulled it back toward him. Then he climbed back on and knelt. Unlike Chaz, who surfed year-round, Tyler didn't really have a set of "surfer's knots" on his knees and the top of his feet. He watched Chaz leap to his feet as he caught his wave.

Chaz's ride was no more dramatic than Tyler's had been, and in fact the wave wasn't quite as big as Tyler's. Chaz turned out of his wave near where Tyler waited, swerved his board till it pointed back out to sea, and stayed on his feet for a few seconds after his board had stopped, practicing his balance. Then he lightly hopped off.

Chaz looked at Tyler, laughed, and shrugged. "Hey, it's a wave," he said.

Tyler nodded. "Beats anything I could be doing in Colorado right now. Let's head back out."

Both paddled unhurriedly away from the shore, guiding their boards without much trouble over the small breakers heading shoreward, and soon reached the zone where they'd been picking up waves all morning. And when they arrived there and turned their boards to face the shore, they realized that they weren't alone.

Paddling out right behind them, grinning at Chaz in obvious friendship, was a huge guy with bushy long black hair and a heavy full beard, out of which his white teeth smiled brightly. "Hey hey!" he yelled, even though he was close to them by that time. Like Chaz and Tyler, he wore a wetsuit with short sleeves and legs that ended mid-thigh. The exposed parts of his thick arms and legs were covered with black hair, almost like fur. "Chaz! And let me guess: Cousin Tyler."

"Wolfman!" Chaz called.

Wolfman. The name fit.

He paddled out on the other side of Chaz, turned his board, and said, still in the same loud voice, "Well, hey—sorry about the waves, man. You come all the way from Colorado and we give you the kind of waves you could have gotten in your own bathtub back home. We got to make some sacrifices to the wave god tonight, buddy, get you some waves tomorrow worth ridin'." He got up onto his knees, lifted his arms and face toward the sky, and began to chant, swaying rhythmically from side to side.

Tyler cocked his head and looked at Chaz. Was this guy for real?

Chaz shook his head. "He's kind of seriously messed up, Wolfman is. Try to ignore him if you can. But it won't do you any good."

"You got some cigarettes?" Wolfman yelled. "A new cake of board wax? Maybe a copy of *Endless Summer* on DVD? The wave god kind of likes that stuff. Toss it over here and I'll offer it up. Oh Great Maliboo-hoo!" he yelled at the sky. "Please accept our humble offerings and give Tyler here a decent wave or two before he has to head back to the desert of surflessness. Anything between eight feet and tsunami-size will do. Nothin' less than six, or we'll defile your surf with belly boards. We'll come out here on rubber rafts. We'll throw our candy wrappers in the water. You hear me? And keep it up for at least a couple weeks. Okay, Wolfman over and out. You got any answers for me, just call my number and leave a message." Wolfman gripped his board, one hand on each side, threw his body in the air into a handstand—a wondrous thing to see, considering his size—and flipped off his board into the water.

Tyler watched the water where he'd disappeared. He didn't come up.

Chaz chuckled. "So now you've met Wolfman. You think that was crazy? I'll tell you what—that was Wolfman at his most subdued."

"Can't say we have anybody like that in Copper Ridge," Tyler said.

"Well," Chaz grinned, "you got to have the rough to balance the sweet." He nodded back toward the shore.

And there, paddling out toward them on her board, came Angel. Her blond hair hung wet and close to her head and neck, reminding Tyler of the first time he'd seen her, rising from the surf the afternoon before. She was, if anything, more beautiful today. She looked up, saw them watching her, and smiled back. She was wearing a short wetsuit like theirs, but patterned in swirls of red and purple and, somehow, more supple and form-fitting, as if it were made of spandex, like a bathing suit, except of course that made no sense, because the whole point of the rubbery wetsuits was to be thicker, to provide some insulation.

Tyler wasn't really aware of how he must look, drinking in the sight of her approach with such concentration and frank admiration, until he heard Chaz clear his throat, and then turned to see both Chaz and Wolfman grinning at him.

He could feel his face growing warm. "Is, uh—is she—are you—"

They both laughed at him. "I wish," Chaz said. "I tried to get something going with her."

"Everybody up and down this beach has, one time or another," Wolfman added. "Even me."

"You should see how she handles it," Chaz said. "She's good. She's really good. She manages to make you feel okay about the fact that she's not interested in you romantically. Quite a feat. Anyway, we're friends. That's all. But go ahead, take your shot. Don't let the fact that she's a year older stop you."

Wolfman laughed and swore. "She's a whole bunch younger than me, and that didn't stop me!" He laughed again. Tyler wondered just how old Wolfman was. Hard to tell behind all that hair.

Tyler looked at them for a few seconds, then turned his eyes back to Angel, who was much closer now and smiling at him.

"Hoo, look at that smile," Chaz said quietly. "I don't know. Maybe you've got a shot."

Tyler expected her to ask what they'd been talking about when she reached them. Most of the girls he knew, seeing a bunch of guys looking at her and laughing, would assume that they were talking about her and want to know what was being said. But Angel just turned her board and took her place beside Tyler and said, "Looks pretty flat out here. Been this way all morning?"

"Long as we've been here," Chaz answered.

Tyler got the impression that Angel knew they'd been talking about her—but either didn't care what they'd been saying, or already knew.

"Too bad. I'd like to get in at least a few good surf days before I leave. Might have to run down to Mexico if I want decent surf."

"You're leaving?" Tyler asked, then immediately thought his voice had sounded too plaintive.

"I have an aunt who's just a few years older than me," Angel started to explain.

"She's pretty cool," Chaz cut in.

"We usually go to Europe for a few weeks every summer," Angel continued.

"That sounds fun," Tyler said, trying to keep his voice natural. "When do you leave?"

"Not for a couple of weeks," she said. "Probably not till after you leave."

"Oh. Cool." He nodded and smiled. She smiled back.

"Here comes your wave, Angel," Wolfman yelled. He didn't seem to know any other way to speak. Tyler wondered if he talked that loud indoors.

Angel looked back over her shoulder. She slipped down into a prone position on her board and began to paddle. Tyler watched in amazement, wishing he had a camera. A magazine cover—definitely a magazine cover. But not for *Brio*.

He watched her stand and work the wave, which actually was one of the better waves of the morning. She was pretty good. Fair or better. Not as good as Chaz, or even Tyler. But she was confident and she knew how to read a wave. No beginner. All in all, Tyler was impressed with her ability—but more impressed with how she looked standing on her board in that form-fitting wetsuit. What *was* that thing made out of?

● ● ●

Using Chaz's computer, Tyler logged on that night for the first time since he'd arrived, and had just started reading his e-mail—one from Allen Olsen, one from Jacie, and a whole slew of others he hadn't looked at yet—when a tone sounded and an IM box popped up:

Artgirl: Hey, ColoradoTy! What luck! I'm here with Hannah and we're e-mailing all the kids from the Missions Trip! How's California? Ride any good waves? Fall in love with some surfer girl?

It was Jacie. Rats. The problem was that he didn't really know what he wanted to tell the Brio squad yet. About Angel, Chaz—everything.

ColoradoTy: hey, brio chicks. no great waves yet. ocean pretty quiet. and yes, of course i've fallen in love with a surfer chick—several of them, as i do every summer. this time i've already gotten engaged!

Artgirl: Wow, what great news! Now Solana can give up on trying to trap you into marrying her. How's your cousin—what's his name—Clarence? Percy?

ColoradoTy: chaz. he's fine. last summer before college. gettin ready to become a man.

Artgirl: Hi, Tyler. This is Hannah. Your mom told us she was a little concerned about Chaz. I hope you'll be able to help him get back on the right path. We'll be praying for you.

Great. The last thing he needed was to have to give a full accounting of his summer with Chaz to the Brio bunch when he got back so they could decide how effective a witness he'd been.

ColoradoTy: thanks, hannah. prayers always appreciated. i think, though, that a lot of the concern about chaz you can just chalk up to a parental hyper-nervousness.

Artgirl: Hannah still. So his friends are all right, then? Your mom said her sister had some concerns about his group of friends.

Arrgh! Why had his mom talked about this with them? Well, then again, why wouldn't she? It's not as if his mom would have expected Tyler to have any secrets from the Brios. Even if he tried, they always found out somehow. But this was—well, this was different. And it bugged him.

ColoradoTy: well, they're from california, which means

they would be considered extremely weird by colorado standards. but yeah, i think they're fine. they don't involve chaz in their illegal activities, and they all swear that if they get arrested, they won't mention either chaz or me. and besides, i think the colombian drug cartels get a bad rap—sure they deal drugs, but they do a lot of good, too.

Artgirl: Ha ha. Jacie again. Hannah couldn't even bring herself to reply to that one. Okay, I'll assume from your bantering tone that you don't see a lot of problems there. That's good news. We'll still be praying, though.

Chaz popped his head in. "I'm about to stick in *Vertical Limit*. Want to watch? Sounds like your kind of flick—all cheap Hollywood action."

Tyler grinned. So for all of his newfound sophistication, Chaz still liked to watch Hollywood action movies. Especially those with a strong outdoors connection. "Seen it twice. But yeah, I'll be there in a minute. Stick some popcorn in the microwave and I'll be there by the time it's done."

ColoradoTy: woops, got to run. the keg just arrived and the party's about to start. hugh hefner and crew just showed up, so the joint's jumpin. better sin—er, sign—off. but thanks for the prayers. will read your e-mails in the morning, if i'm conscious. hugs and kisses to all—bye bye.

He closed the program and turned off the computer, feeling relieved and at the same time uneasy that he'd managed to avoid saying anything of substance to the ones who, of all his friends, knew him best and supported him the most.

chapter

"WHERE'D MILLER SAY THESE GUYS WERE FROM?"
Tyler yelled.

"THE BLACK GUYS ARE FROM NORTHERN AFRICA—
MOROCCO, I THINK," Chaz yelled back, his mouth only a couple
of inches from Tyler's ear, and still Tyler had to strain to pick out the
words. And suddenly the band kicked it up a notch, as if they'd all
turned up their amps at once, and the tempo raced. "THE OTHER
STAR . . . SUNBEAR . . . EASTER SYRUP," Chaz screamed.

What?

Tyler looked at Chaz and shrugged. Chaz laughed—Tyler couldn't
hear the laughter, but he saw Chaz's mouth move and his eyes twinkle—
and then Chaz pointed toward the band and settled back into his chair
to listen.

The six of them—Tyler, Chaz, Angel, Miller, Zack, and Wolfman—
were crowded around a tiny round table in The Whelk, a jam-packed

music club in San Clemente. From where he sat, Tyler could have touched any of the six without shifting his position. He couldn't imagine how the waitresses were maneuvering among the crowd to bring people their orders, since there was barely room to take a breath. Although that had one definite advantage. Chaz sat on Tyler's right, Angel on his left, their legs pressed tightly together. And Tyler didn't think it was just the pressure of the crowd; it seemed to him that Angel was leaning into him.

It would have been hard for any red-blooded teenage male to *not* be aware of her. He'd been aware all evening how her clothes fit her just right. When she'd walked up to them in front of The Whelk, Tyler had been almost unable to speak—again.

He had been surprised and excited to sense, over the past couple of days, that Angel seemed to be attracted to him—if not as much as he was to her, then at least enough to notice. Chaz had mentioned it too. "I don't know," Chaz had said thoughtfully as they drove home from the beach that afternoon to change for the concert. "I've never seen Angel quite this way before. You have quite the effect on her. She seems ... more girlish, somehow. In the past it's like she dates not because it's what she wants, but more like she's doing you a favor. But with you, it's like she wants your attention."

"You really think so?" Tyler had said.

"Oh, yeah. She's given you more smiles in two days than she's given me in two years. *Real* smiles. Like a real girl gives a real guy. Usually she's—aloof. Or something. She smiles the way a schoolteacher would smile at a second-grader's stupid joke. But not with you. Which of course makes no sense, because she's about to leave for Europe and you're about to go back home to Colorado."

"She can come visit me in her private jet."

Chaz laughed. "Her parents are pretty well set, all right. They're both college professors, which doesn't necessarily pay a lot, except that her mom's a physicist and her dad's head of the math department. Plus her mom's got a few patents on things that bring in some pretty good money. Anyway, when they want to do something, they don't have to worry about how much it costs."

As if you do, Tyler thought.

"That's how she met Miller—through her parents, at university parties and stuff."

Tyler felt an odd sinking sensation. "She know Miller pretty well?"

Chaz looked at him oddly, as if gauging how much to say. "They had a thing," he said finally. "It was a while back. Just friends now. It was when she was, like, fifteen."

"Fifteen? And she was dating a college guy in his—what—must have been mid-twenties then?"

Chaz just shrugged. "You'd have to know her parents. They let her do what she wants. They don't believe in making decisions for her." He raised an eyebrow. "She can make *all* her own decisions."

Tyler had stared at him.

Chaz had looked at him and winked. "So play your cards right, Cuz."

Play his cards right? And what?

The waitress brought their drinks. They didn't have anything as mundane—or as cheap—as Dr Pepper here, so Tyler had ordered something called a Grenadine—pomegranate juice, Chaz had said—for which he now had to cough up five bucks.

Wolfman and Zack had ordered beer; Miller got a glass of something that looked like wine.

A sudden moist warmth at his left ear, and Angel said, "SO WHAT DO YOU THINK OF GIBRALTAR?"

Funny. She wasn't talking nearly as loudly as Chaz had, but somehow Tyler could understand her above the wall of sound that blasted across the room, loudly enough to make his ears hurt. He could actually feel the pressure from the speakers against his chest and thought that the beat was reprogramming his heart to beat in time.

She turned her ear toward him, and he spoke into it, so close his lips touched: "I CAN'T DECIDE. THEY'RE DIFFERENT, AND I LIKE THAT. THEY HAVE ALL THESE INFLUENCES THEY'RE TRYING TO BRING TOGETHER, AND I THINK THAT'S COOL. BUT TO TELL YOU THE TRUTH, I CAN'T REALLY SAY I LIKE THEIR MUSIC. IT'S—UH—IT'S KIND OF MONOTONOUS. EVERYTHING SOUNDS THE SAME."

She smiled at him, her tongue pressing against the back of her slightly parted teeth. She pressed her face alongside his and shouted, "I HEARD ABOUT HALF OF WHAT YOU SAID." She put her soft hand on his forearm. "WE'LL TALK MORE LATER." She pulled her face back just until they were looking into each other's eyes from a distance of about three inches. Her smile involved her whole face; it wasn't just a smile, it was more like she was offering herself to him. Tyler felt an almost uncontrollable urge to kiss her. She held her face there for a few seconds, then raised her eyebrows just a touch, as if to say, *What next? You decide.* And then she turned back toward the music.

Tyler barely noticed the music after that.

● ● ●

Two hours later, the six of them arranged themselves on rocks just a few feet above the water on the breakwater that lined the channel at the end of the Balboa Peninsula. Even though his hearing seemed dull after the onslaught on his senses in The Whelk, Tyler could hear waves rhythmically pounding the shore and the rocks on the other side of the breakwater. But they were sitting on the channel side, and the water was still.

Miller had picked up a couple of six-packs of Heineken at a liquor store as they'd walked out here, and now he begin to pull the green bottles out and pass them around. "Tyler?" he said.

Tyler shook his head and held up a can of Coke he'd bought at the same liquor store when he saw what Miller was getting. "I'm set," he said.

Miller nodded. "Change your mind, we got plenty." He tossed the bottle to Chaz, who somewhat to Tyler's surprise twisted the top off and took a drink.

It was a typical Southern California summer night—so much smog and reflected light that only a few of the brightest stars were visible. Warm, but with just enough cool breeze coming off the water to make Tyler glad he had a long-sleeved shirt. There was a concrete walkway just a few yards behind them, and every minute or so someone would stroll leisurely past—young couples with their arms around each other, elderly people with dogs on leashes.

"Well, I must say," Miller said, when everyone was settled and quiet, "I thought Gibraltar was a little disappointing."

Angel laughed. "You would."

Miller looked at her and smiled. "You liked them?"

She shook her head. "No, not particularly. I agree with Tyler—I thought their sound was too monotonous. Not enough variety, not enough dynamic range. And music should be emotionally engaging—I thought their music was emotionally flat. Like an academic exercise."

Wow. She'd taken his one comment and given it all kinds of new meaning.

"Sounds like you're judging music that arises from a totally different culture by the standards of our culture," Miller responded. "By pop music standards, even."

"No," Angel said. "You asked me whether I liked them. I told you why I didn't. I'm not judging anything. Now tell us why you didn't like them either."

"I didn't like them for almost the exact opposite reason. I didn't think they were being true to the principles of their own musical heritage, either North African or Romany."

Tyler covered his smile with his hand. It was almost funny, comparing what these people were saying with the conversations about music he had with his friends back home.

You like Alice in Chains?

I don't know. Not too much. You like 'em?

Yeah, they're cool. Lots of guitar. I like Bad Whiskey even better though.

You just like to watch their lead singer.

What's wrong with that? She's hot.

Miller went on: "I thought they simply took the window dressing of those musical styles and applied it to North American pop formulas. They were the Cowboy Junkies with African rhythm and gypsy violins."

Compared to this, Tyler and all his friends back home were a bunch of morons.

"Hold it," Zack said. "That's not fair. I kind of liked them. And sure, you could hear the North American influences. But so what? Is there any musician anywhere who hasn't heard American popular music? It's not a matter of applying their musical heritage to American patterns. It's just that American patterns have infiltrated the music of every culture that exists. Listen to Ali Farka Toure. Grew up in Mali but sounds like he's playing blues guitar. He says that's because the roots of American blues are in Africa. But the truth is, he's heard and been influenced by people like John Lee Hooker and Son House. Or take jazz—American jazz is everywhere."

"What I heard tonight wasn't jazz," Miller said in a condescending tone. "I know jazz, and that wasn't it."

Zack had an answer for that, but as interesting as Tyler thought this was, he found himself tuning out and just listening to the rhythms of their speech. How bizarre this whole thing was! How many things had he done in the past week that were completely out of his normal range of experiences? Going with J.P. to see *The River Runs Downhill*. Riding around with Jessica sitting on his lap. The argument he'd had with Jacie and the rest the next day—well, maybe it wasn't such an unusual thing to find himself on the opposite side of an argument from the Brios, but this time it had felt different. Real different. He still felt odd and guilty, remembering it. And now this—sitting out here with a bunch of people who were guzzling beer and talking music. *Really* talking music, as if they knew what they were talking about.

And Angel. Tyler stole a look at her, just a few feet away. A huge boat was slowly chugging back up the channel with its running lights on, people sitting in chairs out on the deck and laughing, and the glow from the lights played across her face. She was so intense, so completely engaged in the conversation. He felt a twinge of discomfort when she absent-mindedly took a drink from the beer bottle in her hand.

"Hey, Tyler," Chaz said. "Shoot. I just remembered. Jacie called while you were in the shower before we left tonight. You were supposed to call her back."

"Jacie," Zack said, his voice slightly teasing. "Hmm. Sounds familiar. Isn't that the chick who was always calling you last year?"

A short pause, then, "Girlfriend, Tyler?" Angel asked. He couldn't tell what the expression on her face meant. She looked amused.

"No. I mean—well, she's a girl and she's my friend, but she's not my girlfriend."

"Sure," Wolfman said. "One in every state."

"No, really," Tyler said, embarrassed. "She's, like—we've known each other since we were little. She's—well, it's just like me and Chaz. I can—"

"Chaz!" Wolfman yelled, laughing. "Whoa, you've got to prepare us for things like this, man! I mean, I never even suspected. When did all this start, man? I don't think I want you sittin' next to me anymore. Is that even legal? You guys are cousins!"

"Yeah, Wolfman, keep it up," Chaz grinned. "I'm gonna have Tyler beat you to a pulp. He protects me."

Angel stood and brushed off the seat of her jeans. Tyler couldn't help following the movement with his eyes. "You guys are too funny," she said in a voice that made it clear that, this time, she didn't really mean it. "I want to walk up the beach." She turned her back on the others. "Tyler, want to come?"

He froze a moment, then said, "Uh—yeah. Sure." He stood.

She turned back and smiled at the others, who all looked at her, speechless. "We'll be back in a little while." She smiled at Tyler and pointed up the beach. "This way." Tyler followed dumbly, still holding his Coke, even though he noticed that Angel's hands were empty; she'd lost her beer bottle somewhere.

They were thirty yards down the beach when she swirled back toward the group and called, "If you have to leave before we get back, Chaz, go ahead—I'll drop him off at your place." Tyler didn't think any of them had said a word since he and Angel had walked away.

Play your cards right, Cuz.

● ● ●

The first thing Angel did was slip off her sandals so that she could walk barefoot. It seemed so natural for her, strolling along barefoot on the night beach, her tiny sandals dangling casually from one finger. But Tyler, of course, already had a Coke can in one hand. He felt like an idiot for having worn his hiking boots. He had to sit in the sand, pull them off, then stuff his socks down into them and tie the laces together. Then he rolled his pants up to his knees, stood, and slung his boots over his shoulder. He had a sudden and unattractive image: taking Angel into his arms and having her bump her face against his sandy hiking boots.

She didn't seem inclined to talk at first, so he finished off his Coke as they walked. Then he had the empty can. Now what? He didn't see any trash cans around anywhere. He held it upside down till he was confident that it was empty, then tried to crush it flat in the sand. He stuffed it into his back pocket, aware that Angel was watching him, amused.

"Don't want to litter," he said awkwardly.

"I like that in a man," she said.

"Right," he said. "I know you Californians. You live to litter. You do it for the thrill."

"Surely we Californians can find something more thrilling than littering to do. Speaking of which—you're on your own out here."

"What?"

She pointed behind him.

He turned. "What? I don't see . . ."

"The sign," she said. "On the lifeguard station."

He could just make it out in the dim light: *No Lifeguard on Duty.* He turned back.

"You're taking your life in your own hands," she said. She raised an eyebrow. "Anything can happen."

A sudden shiver. Everything this girl said sent a thrill through him. She was—

Suddenly he noticed something. He looked toward the waves, then back behind him.

"What?" she said.

"The waves are—some light from somewhere must be reflecting off them or something. They're glowing."

She laughed a lovely laugh. It occurred to him that he didn't think he'd actually heard her laugh before. He wanted to hear it again. And again. "They *are* glowing. They're phosphorescent."

He looked from her to the waves and back again. "No way," he said.

He got his wish. She laughed again. "Yes."

He looked at them. "No way."

"You know what it is? It's some kind of plankton or algae that glows when disturbed. So when the water churns at the top of the waves, that disturbs them and sets off the glow. It's one of my favorite things, actually. Like raindrops on roses."

He nodded. Those waves were about the coolest thing he'd ever seen, breaking toward the beach capped with a ghostly greenish-white, wave after wave. "And dewdrops on kittens."

This must be his lucky night; she laughed again. "Something like that. When the dog bites . . ."

"When the bee stings . . ."

She held up her arms, and—remembering the mental image he'd gotten a minute or two before—he dumped his hiking boots on the sand, took her into his arms, and waltzed her through the damp sand just at the edge of the waterline. And they sang together "My Favorite Things" from *The Sound of Music*, stumbling just a little over the words, laughing over their mistakes.

They stopped dancing when they stopped singing. Her bright face looked up into his eyes. Behind her, he could see the waves, glowing. He didn't care what was causing it; the scientific explanation was completely irrelevant. It was magic. He looked back into her eyes. She seemed to be waiting. Was this the moment?

But with a quick flash of an even brighter smile, she pulled away and began to stroll down the sand again. He watched her for a moment, not sure which was lovelier, the movement of her body as she walked or the magic of the waves. Then he grabbed his boots and caught up with her.

"Last summer I went sailing with my parents up in the San Juan Islands," she said.

He nodded, even though he wasn't sure where the San Juan Islands were.

"The water was phosphorescent then, too. After my parents were asleep I would come out every night and go swimming, diving off the boat into that water that glowed with every movement of my body. I would swim around the boat in a backstroke with my head raised, watching the glowing trail I made through the water. It was *so cool*. Moments like that make me—I don't know. Make me think life is a lot cleaner and sweeter and more simple and fun than it really is."

He didn't know how to answer. His brain was stuck somewhere between the visual image she had just created for him, and his sense that she had just revealed something important about herself to him. But he wasn't sure what it was.

"Look at this," she said brightly. "Watch." She swiped her bare foot gracefully through the damp sand—and the mark her toe left in the sand glowed momentarily.

"No way," Tyler said.

She laughed again—exactly the result he'd been hoping for. "Yes."

He swiped his own toe through the sand. The path it left glowed.

"There's enough of the microorganism in the damp sand that the sand glows, too, when it's disturbed."

"Just like a firefly."

"Just like a firefly."

Tyler bent at the waist and spelled her name in the sand—A-N-G-E-L. Each letter glowed only for about the amount of time it took to make it, but still, it was incredible.

She smiled, then bent and spelled his: T-Y-L-E-R. When she stood again, she was very close. She looked at him. He smiled at her, unsure what to say. She looked back at the waves for a moment, then turned back to him and said, "I like you, Tyler Jennings." She touched his hand, then gently slipped her fingers through his. A glowing wave washed in around their feet, wetting their legs up to mid-calf and wiping out their names in the sand.

"I like you too," he said, his voice husky.

She laughed. "I don't suppose Jacie will like that much."

"Jacie's not my girlfriend!" he protested.

She shrugged prettily, her bare shoulders gleaming and graceful in the moonlight. "Even if she were . . . it wouldn't matter. Things change. People change."

Tyler nodded. Yes. He guessed they did. Chaz had changed. *I hope I've grown,* Chaz had said, *gotten a little smarter, and become more my own person, not just a younger version of my parents. You know what I've been doing this year? I've been testing everything I've been told.*

And now Tyler felt himself changing too. Testing. Definitely testing. And then he kissed her. And oh, it was sweet.

chapter

Tyler wasn't surprised, not long after he'd crawled into bed that night, to hear the door creak open and someone come in. He grinned into the darkness. Someone sat on the foot of the bed. Tyler pretended to snore, but Chaz whapped him on the foot. "Knock it off," Chaz said quietly. "I heard you come in, and you haven't had time to get to sleep."

"Doesn't take long after a night like I've had," Tyler replied. "Hoo, baby. I'm exhausted, man. I just dropped right off."

Chaz snorted. "Yeah, right. Okay, fess up."

"What?"

"Tell me."

"Tell you what?"

"You know. Did you do it?"

"What? Do what?"

"You know. Did you?"

"*No.* We talked. That's all we did. We walked along the beach—hey!

Did you notice the waves were glowing?"

"Oh, yeah. I was going to walk over and take a look, but we really got into some deep stuff last night and I forgot. So what'd you think?"

"It was about the coolest thing I'd ever seen. Angel had this whole explanation about microorganisms in the water that—"

"Not the waves, idiot! Angel! You guys officially got something going now or what?"

"Chaz—gimme a break. It wasn't like that. We talked. We talked about everything. She is the coolest girl. Okay, we held hands. I kissed her one time."

"Hey, you can tell me the truth. It's cool. I'm not jealous; I realized a long time ago it wasn't going to happen for me and Angel. So if the two of you—"

"I'm tellin' you the truth, man! That was it. We held hands. We kissed one time. And we talked. It was great. I mean, it was great."

Chaz waited. "That's it?" he asked finally.

"Chaz—yeah. That's it. Isn't that enough? I mean, you already told me that Angel doesn't exactly go out of her way to establish connections with guys—that she just allows them to show her some attention from time to time. Well—this was different! She asked *me!* So isn't that a big deal? Seems like it to me."

Chaz chuckled. "Yeah, I'd say that's a big deal. The rest of us spent about the next five minutes after you guys walked away just staring at each other and scratching our heads. I mean—I know she's had boyfriends occasionally since Miller. It's just that it's never been anybody any of us knew—always somebody she met in Europe or something, never somebody who hung around the beach."

"So I guess I fit the profile, huh? I'm from some exotic locale."

"Yeah, right. I mean, it would be different if you were from Aspen or Vail, but Tinhorn Gulch?"

"Copper Ridge."

"Whatever. And you're a year younger than she is. And you're not rich." He yawned and stretched. "Well, I just had to get the body count. Sounds like Angel 1, Tyler zip at this point. But hope springs eternal. You can sleep in tomorrow, night owl. Supposed to be a heavy fog in the morning. It'll burn off before noon; we'll surf then." He laughed quietly as he stood and walked toward the door. "Bet I know what you're going to dream about."

Actually, Tyler didn't even have to fall asleep to dream about Angel. As tired as he was, he lay in bed with his mind racing—going over everything they'd talked about, the look of her face watching the glowing waves, how their names had looked as they'd written them in the glowing sand. What she had told him about her life—he had felt as if she had really opened up to him, as if she had learned to trust him enough to tell him things she didn't tell to just anybody. Maybe not even to Chaz. Or Miller.

And the last image in his mind, as he drifted off to sleep, was of her swimming around her parents' boat in the San Juan Islands—he still had no idea where the San Juan Islands were, and he imagined palm trees on the nearby shore, and a huge tropical moon—as she looked behind her at the glowing path she made through the water.

● ● ●

From: ColoradoTy
To: AllenOlson
Subject: Surfin Safari

hey, old man. bet you wish you were out here havin fun in the warm california sun too. although who knows, maybe old codgers have lost any memory of what it's like to have fun. and anyway, the sun forgot to come out today—already ten o'clock and nothin but fog.

surf's been mediocre ever since i got here. we're thinkin of headin down to mexico for a day or two next week if things don't pick up.

the people i'm hangin around with here, my cousin

chaz and company, are into music big time. i mean these are people who actually *know* what they're talkin about. zack, a year older than me, plays bass in a good local band. and get this—he asked me yesterday if i wanted to sit in on their practice this afternoon. really—me sittin in with a good rock band, on guitar.

i hate to admit it, but i chickened out. i kept rememberin the fiasco with the band practice in my garage last fall. so i told zack i'd come just to listen, not play. now i'm kickin myself, but not enough to change my mind.

i think this trip is really good for me, allen. you know how sometimes you just need to get a different perspective on things? i'm hangin with people out here who don't see the world the same way you do, or the way my brio girls do, or the way i always have. that's a challenge. stretches me. i think i'll be stronger for it. probably changed by it, too. chaz says there's a point where you just have to test things for yourself and decide what YOU believe. not your parents, but you.

these people sit around testin stuff all day long, allen, and it's great. they'll explore any idea. it's exciting. and it all ties in to music for them. for me, too, i guess, if i'm honest. these people listen to music people in colorado haven't even heard about yet. they respect a musician for what he's trying to do, and how well he does it, not for whether they agree with his message or not. i don't think they even CARE what the musician's message is—they just want to be challenged and stretched by it. same goes for movies, books.

hey, i see shadows, and that means sunshine. better go grab my wetsuit. adios till next time, senior citizen.

ty

● ● ●

That afternoon, Tyler wandered into a house behind Zack, walking slowly, feeling excited and a little strange. Three of the guys in Zack's band lived here, and it looked a lot more like a recording studio than a home. It was up in Seal Beach, north of Huntington Beach, an old, semi-rundown beach house that served as joint rehearsal hall and recording studio. Tyler followed Zack into a big room that contained wall-to-wall amps, microphone stands, and at one end a big digital recording console attached to an Imac. Zack's band was Maldonado, named after a town in one of their favorite books. They were putting together an album of some of their best original stuff, to serve both as a demo in trying to find a recording label and also a self-produced CD to sell at their gigs.

Three other guys—band members, Tyler assumed—were already in there, two of them adjusting equipment and tuning up, and one sitting off to one side, listlessly nursing a beer. The two active ones looked up and nodded at Zack and Tyler.

Zack hauled his bass out of a closet, plugged it into an amp, and began to tune it up. Left to his own devices, Tyler watched for a while, then drifted into the kitchen, where he found some Cokes in the refrigerator. It occurred to him that some of the others might be thirsty, too, so he poked his head back into the family room and said, "Anybody want anything to drink?" He immediately wished he hadn't, because the answer he got was:

"Yeah, bring me a beer."

"Me, too."

Grabbing the beers out of the refrigerator, Tyler wondered whether handing someone a beer was a sin. They were going to drink it regardless of whether he got them one or not, he rationalized; this way, they just got it a little quicker. Still, he felt very odd and not very good as he passed out the brown bottles to the three musicians. Then he found a comfortable place to sit and watch.

The guitarist was outstanding. Tyler could tell that much just from watching him warm up, before he really even played anything. He played an old Stratocaster, and his fingers flew over the frets. But every note was clean and true. He knew runs Tyler had never even heard on records before. It made Tyler glad he hadn't offered to play along. He'd have made a fool of himself.

A tired-looking, very thin girl in baggy, shapeless clothes walked in, nodded vaguely to Tyler, and turned on the recording console. She, apparently, was their recording engineer.

To Tyler's surprise, just a couple of minutes after the girl entered, Miller walked in carrying a black case. "*Buenos tardes, mis amigos,*" he said.

It seemed to Tyler that they greeted him with real enthusiasm, as if they were genuinely happy to see him. And so was Tyler—not just because there was now one more person here that he knew, but because he would now actually get to hear the great Miller Andrews play.

Miller unpacked his sax, inserted the mouthpiece, blew a couple of notes, then set it aside and began to chat with the girl behind the console.

Tyler went back to the kitchen for another Coke, and Zack walked in behind him.

"I didn't know Miller was going to be here," Tyler said.

"Yeah," Zack said, washing his hands at the sink. "We need some sax on a few of the cuts we want to put on our album."

"Wow—so he's good enough you want him on your album," Tyler said, slumping into a chair at the dirty kitchen table. The whole house had a funny feel to it—dirty, with stuff thrown everywhere, but at the same time it felt unlived in.

Zack looked back at Tyler with a bit of a sneer. "Miller's probably the best musician here. He's done a lot of studio work, been in on a lot of sessions. How did you think he earned his money?"

"Somebody say money? I'm in, whatever it is," Miller said, wandering in.

"Hey," Tyler said. "I guess maybe I'm dense, but I had no idea you'd been in some recording sessions."

Miller shrugged. "No big deal."

"So what have you been on that I would know?"

Miller laughed. "Well, that's hard to say. I don't know what music makes its way back to Colorado."

"Well, what are some of the most popular albums you've been on?"

Miller looked at the ceiling, thought a minute. "I played on a few cuts of the James Taylor album that won the Grammy a couple of years ago."

Tyler could feel his jaw drop. "Did you play on 'Wishing Well'? That great sax solo?"

Miller laughed. "I wish. No, the soloist was David Sanborn. But we used a trio of saxes behind him, two altos and a baritone. I played alto."

"What's James Taylor like to work with?" Tyler asked, fascinated.

Miller shook his head. "Never met him, believe it or not. I just worked with the producer and arranger. Hey—Zack's been in on a couple of sessions lately too."

Tyler looked at him. "No kidding? Who with?"

Zack looked uncomfortable and embarrassed. "It wasn't all that much. Just played on a couple of cuts on an album from a new group nobody's heard of yet. Album isn't even out yet."

"Well, maybe nobody's heard of them yet," Miller said, "but I saw 'em on David Letterman last week, so they're on their way."

"You guys done jawin' in there?" came a voice from the practice room. "We're ready to roll. We're gonna start with "Head First."

"What's that one about?" Tyler asked, as they all shuffled back through the door.

"One of Marcus's originals," Zack mumbled, nodding his head toward the keyboard player. "It's, uh—well, you'll see."

And Tyler did see. When the band cranked up—and he had to admit, they were very, very good—and launched into their first verse, Tyler thought he had never heard so much profanity in one place in a short period of time before in his life. He tried to think of any profane language they *weren't* using in this song, and offhand he couldn't think of any. And after they'd sung it once, they sang it again, and again, and again, with Miller and the guitarist and Marcus on keyboards trading solos.

Why would they even learn a song like this, let alone write one? Tyler wondered. *They could never actually play it anywhere. Could they?*

Or maybe they could. This wasn't Colorado.

● ● ●

From: AllenOlson
To: ColoradoTy
Subject: Re: Surfin Safari

Ty, Ty, my much-beloved good buddy. Thanks for the long newsy e-mail. I read it with great joy and stuff like that. Sounds like you're having the time of your life, all right. I think it's great that you get to go out there and do that every summer. And I can't think of anybody I'd trust more to go out there without Mommy and Daddy (or even J, B, S, and H, which would be even scarier, to tell you the truth) looking over your shoulder to keep you on the straight and narrow. You're a solid guy, thoughtful and sensitive, and I know you'll do fine.

Having said that, I've got to admit I got a few butterflies in my stomach reading some of the things in your letter. You're completely right about coming to a point in your life where you have to test some things so that you can begin to own your own faith. I guess the question is: what does that mean? You don't have to take drugs yourself, for instance, to know that that's not a value you want to adopt for your own—you just have to read up on what effect they have on people, or observe that effect in others. You don't have to get drunk to know that that's not something honoring to God—you just have to read Scripture.

And that, I guess, is the test I'd like you to keep in

mind as you have these deep, meaningful chats with your new group of California buddies. I'm going to guess that these new friends are not believers, since you didn't mention it. They may have some great things to say. Just remember that everything they say has to be weighed against what you know to be true from the Bible. Maybe the Bible doesn't have a lot to say about modern music. But it has a lot to say about life. You say your new friends don't care what the musician's message is. God does care what someone's message is. Do you remember what Jesus said to the crowds in Matthew 15:11 when He was talking about how to truly honor God? The people at that time, of course, had all kinds of regulations about what you could eat and what you shouldn't eat. But Jesus said, ``What goes into a man's mouth does not make him 'unclean,' but what comes out of his mouth, that is what makes him 'unclean.' '' And He wasn't talking about spit. He was talking about what we say—our words, our message. And God cares not only what we say—He cares about the effect of those words in people's lives. Jesus again, in the Sermon on the Mount: ``By their fruit you will recognize them . . . every good tree bears good fruit, but a bad tree bears bad fruit.'' When I hear about a song that makes people examine their own lives and turn back toward God, I know that that's a good song because it bears good fruit. When I hear about a song that makes people feel depressed, perhaps even pushes them toward suicide, or that gives young men violent thoughts against society or against women, then I know that's a bad song—even if it's better crafted than the other song.

Is any of this making sense? You're probably laughing at me, thinking, *I already know all this.* But humor me. I'd like to chat with you about it. When are you available for an IM discussion? Just shoot me back an e-mail, and I'll make time for it, I promise. Humor an old man, okay?

Have a great and good time! And my prayer is that this will be a time that will bear GOOD fruit in your life. I just sent up a quick prayer for God to send an angel to watch over you, buddy.

Allen

chapter

Tyler woke with a vague sense that something was wrong. It felt a
little like waking up knowing that you have a dentist's appointment that
day, but of course that wasn't it. This would be another day of surfing
and spending time with Angel—so what was the problem?

Oh. Yeah. The e-mail from Allen. Tyler had checked his e-mail last
night before crawling into bed, and had read Allen's e-mail but hadn't
responded. And that was the problem. Tyler was surprised at himself,
but the truth was, he didn't *want* to respond to Allen's e-mail. Allen
wanted to set up an IM chat, and Tyler didn't want to have one with
him right now. Because Allen would ask him about a bunch of things he
wasn't sure he knew how to answer.

Allen would ask him how Chaz had changed, and how Chaz's spiritual life was, and what Chaz's new friends were like, and what they were
all doing together, and what kind of spiritual influence Tyler felt he'd
been on Chaz since he'd been there, and just exactly what Tyler had

meant when he'd said that he might not be the same person when he came back. Why had Tyler even said that in his e-mail? What had he been thinking? Of course that would be a huge red flag for Allen. Would Tyler have said that to his mother?

Hi, Mom, I'm having a great time out here, doin' a lot of surfin', and by the way, I may be a very different guy when I get home, but don't worry about it. Love, Tyler.

Not likely. So why had he said it to Allen? Would have been a whole lot better to figure things out for himself and *then* say something about it to Allen, the Brios, and the rest. Or not.

That wasn't all of it, though. There was something else in Allen's e-mail that bothered him. A lot. It was that Bible verse. How did it go? *It isn't what goes into a man's mouth that makes him unclean. It's what comes out of his mouth that makes him unclean.* Or something like that. And as soon as Tyler had read that verse last night in Allen's e-mail, that song Zack's group had practiced last night had zoomed into his mind. What had been coming out of their mouths as they'd sung? They'd been polluting the air, sure. But they'd also been polluting themselves, making themselves unclean. And Tyler had just sat there and done nothing about it, said nothing about it.

Well—what was he talking about? Who said it was his job to do something about it? These were grown-up guys, old enough to take responsibility for themselves. He wasn't their mother.

Shoot. He was giving himself a headache thinking about this. Time to get up and get some breakfast. He was on vacation, for pete's sake. Time to relax.

● ● ●

"Chaz had to run down to his dad's office to clear up some kind of problem with the computer system he set up for them," Aunt Evelyn said. "Did you know he worked part-time for his dad this past school year doing computer programming? And he's been working off and on this summer, too."

Tyler shook his head. "I knew he'd been working for the hotel chain, but I didn't know what he'd been doing." Aunt Evelyn was sitting out on the back deck. Tyler stood in the French door—this house was much too fancy to just have a sliding glass door like everybody else.

"Don't worry, he won't be gone long," Aunt Evelyn said. She patted the chair next to hers. "Come out and enjoy the day."

A little uneasily, Tyler did. On one hand, he loved being out here. The view of the ocean from this deck was absolutely beautiful. Every time Tyler sat out here, he wondered why anybody would choose to live anywhere else. And then he remembered that you basically had to be a millionaire to live here.

On the other hand, he knew why she wanted him out here. He could feel it coming—the Talk.

Sure enough.

"Tyler, I've been hoping we'd get a chance to chat, and you've been here what—a week now? Did your mom get a chance to talk with you about Chaz?"

"Just a little," Tyler mumbled.

"Oh, don't worry," she said. "I know it's hard to talk about him with me. But—I just—well, I'm worried. Chaz is—he's—oh, I'm not saying this very well. It isn't just that he's growing into his own man and pulling away from James and me. We expected that. It's—Tyler, it's everything from the music they listen to, to the language they use when they talk, to what they drink—and who knows what else. It's all part of the same thing, Tyler. While you've been here, has he—oh, I told myself I wasn't going to try to get information out of you, and now here I go doing it." She sat back into her chair, clearly upset.

Tyler cleared his throat. "Uh—I really don't think Chaz is doing too bad. I think he's okay."

She looked at him carefully, studying his face. "Oh, I hope so, Tyler.

It's so hard here. I feel like we're caught between two worlds. As Christians, we try to be a light in the world and to raise our sons to do the same. But we're surrounded—James in the business world, and the boys in school and with their friends—by a very different world, with very different values. In that world, man is the center of everything instead of God, and everything is relative. It's whatever you want it to be. It's very different out here than back in Colorado, Tyler."

You can say that again, Tyler thought.

"Values are different. The pressures and temptations are different. And the opportunities are different. And I know Chaz is as much a part of that world now as he is part of the Christian world. Or maybe even more."

Definitely more.

"Up till now, he's had his feet pretty firmly planted. Now I sense that he's lost that foothold. He's adrift, I think, Tyler, just like so many other young people here in Southern California. Or maybe it's everywhere, not just here."

Tyler thought of J.P. Even Solana.

She took a sip of her tea, then cocked her head as if listening. "Garage door," she said finally. "Chaz is home." She smiled, but it was not a happy smile. "Sorry for going on like this. I know you didn't want to hear it. Just try to be a good influence on him, Tyler. Reflect the values that you know are right. Let him see something different in you than he sees in the rest of his friends out on the beach. Now go." She waved her hand in an attempt to look carefree. "Have fun."

He hadn't had much fun so far today, Tyler thought as he headed into the house to meet Chaz. And the way he felt right now, he wasn't sure the rest of the day would be much better.

● ● ●

"I think you're bad luck, Tyler," Chaz said good-naturedly as the two of them, along with Zack, Miller, and Wolfman toweled themselves off, all taking hits off the same bottle of water Angel handed them. "We've only lost three or four games all year. Now you show up—and boom, we lose to a bunch of out-of-towners."

It had been a tough beach volleyball game on a blisteringly hot afternoon. Angel had sat this one out, even though, Chaz assured Tyler, she was plenty good at volleyball and could have held her own. *Probably just didn't want to make me feel bad by showing me up,* Tyler thought.

"Aussies, no less," Miller said. "Our reputation is shot. We've always prided ourselves on being not just the best-looking and most-talented and smartest guys on the beach, but the best athletes too. Looks like we'd better find another claim to fame. Can anybody juggle?"

"I can make my eyes go in two different directions," Angel said.

"Wolfman's got a few unusual talents too, but I don't think they would help our reputation on the beach," Chaz said.

"Enough of this chest-beating," Tyler said. "I've only got a few days left, and right now I'm heading for the water." He jogged back to where his board stuck up from the sand like a monolith beside the boards of the rest of their group, pulled it out, slung it under his arm, and jogged down to the waves. He didn't look back, but he knew that Angel would not be far behind him.

He was right. He hadn't yet climbed onto his board and the water was still cold on his skin when Angel, today wearing a bright lime-green bikini, glided up beside him, prone on her board. She smiled, said nothing, and continued paddling on. He hopped onto his board and followed.

A few minutes later, the two of them sat waiting for waves, and the others hadn't yet joined them. "Bong's in concert Tuesday night at the Staples Center. You planning to go?"

"I don't know. I'm torn."

"Why wouldn't you want to go?"

"Well—let me ask you. You like Bong?"

"Oh, yeah. Don't you?"

"Well, what is it about them you like so much?"

"Everything. I mean, I like their music, I like their lyrics. I like the whole image of the band."

"Okay, but that's the thing I don't understand. The image of the band is pretty . . ."

"You're talking about that concert up in Seattle when Simon exposed himself on stage, right? And then they all got arrested?"

"Well, yeah. So what about that? Why is that different from someone out in the park exposing himself to a bunch of 15-year-old girls? Why is it different if it's in a concert?"

"Because then it's *art*, Tyler! And this is nothing new—Jim Morrison got arrested for the same thing back in the sixties. It's part of what Bong is trying to communicate as a band. All of their lyrics are about shedding pretense and avoiding hypocrisy. And by exposing himself, not only was he standing there with nothing hidden, but he was also forcing society to expose its own hypocrisy."

"What do you mean?"

"Okay, he got arrested because he exposed himself, right?"

"Right."

"Wrong. He got arrested because he was a young rock singer. Same reason Jim Morrison got arrested. Go down the street to the cathedral and you'll find people praying to St. Francis of Assisi, but did you know that St. Francis once pulled off all his clothes in public and went parading around naked to make a point? Why is that different from what Simon did to make a point? Our society is full of double standards and hypocrisy, Tyler—especially about anything having to do with the human body. You can go down to the university bookstore and buy medical texts with photos of naked people in them, but nobody gets arrested. Buy a *Playboy* at the convenience store, and suddenly it's pornography. What's the difference?"

"The difference is the same as the guy exposing himself in the park. If he pops out of the bushes and exposes himself to some girls, it's not because he's some struggling artist trying to make a point—it's because he's willing to frighten and maybe injure those girls just because he gets some kind of weird sexual kick out of it. And a pornographic magazine is just another—"

"I agree with you about the guy in the park, Tyler. Really, I do. That's wrong. I think people like that *ought* to be arrested, because that's about power—he's taking control over those girls, forcing himself on them. But most of the beaches in Europe are clothing optional. Hardly any women wear their tops over there. And that's just accepted. So Simon got arrested for doing what thousands of people do every day in France, or in Scandinavia or Germany."

"What do you thing about that?"

Angel shrugged. "It's a different culture. Remember, it's not like everybody's looking at the women and saying, 'Wow—she's topless,' like they would over here. There, people might point at a woman if she *did* wear her top. Without it, she's just one more woman on the beach."

Tyler shook his head. What a world he found himself in. This was *definitely* not Copper Ridge.

"Come to the concert, Tyler," she said. "I enjoy you. And in a few days, we're both off for points unknown."

"My points aren't so unknown," he said. "They're all too well known."

"Whatever. I want to spend time with you before you go. Besides, I really do think you'll like Bong. Yeah, you'll probably think they act crazy. They do and say things you would never do and say." She grinned. "But so did St. Francis. Come on. Give it a try."

And Tyler knew that he would. Even if it took most of the money he had left to spend while he was here. Even if it made him feel very strange. Even if it would be harder to explain to his friends—and his mom—than going to see *The River Runs Downhill*.

And he also knew that it wasn't just because of Angel. Something was happening in him. Something that frightened him and fascinated him at the same time. And he knew he had to follow it and see where it led—even though it meant exploring places he had never explored before.

chapter

"Yo! Hey, Tyler!" Chaz's voice called. Tyler stood on his tiptoes and craned his neck to see over the shouting, laughing, milling crowd near the entrance to the Staples Center. "Over here, man! Hey, try to keep up!" Chaz laughed.

Finally, Tyler spotted Chaz waving both arms. Leading with his shoulder, Tyler tried to make it through the tightly packed throng of people. "Excuse me ... sorry ... oops, sorry ... excuse me ..." He slipped through a group of Asians speaking a language Tyler didn't recognize, then squeezed between a shaggy, paunchy middle-aged couple dressed as if they were headed to Woodstock and a group of Goths in black with studded dog collars, silver metal dangling from multiple body piercings, and humongous black leather boots.

Angel reached out a hand for him, right between a Latino guy with a hairnet and his girlfriend who was dressed like a hooker. The Latino gave him a hard look as Angel pulled him through. "Sorry," Tyler muttered.

Angel pulled him closely against her. "Thought we lost you, man," Chaz said. "Where'd you go? Find another group that seemed more interesting?" The five of them—Miller, Chaz, Zack, Angel, and Tyler—squeezed after Wolfman, who seemed the most adept at forcing his way toward the gates through the crowd.

"No, I just—I guess I was paying more attention to everybody around me than I was to you guys. Man. I mean, you got to realize, where I live everybody looks pretty much the same. Here . . ."

"Here everybody's a freak!" Wolfman boomed back over his shoulder, his voice carrying far in every direction, even over the incredible noise level. "Like me! Right?" He seemed at least a head taller than anyone else in the crowd. He'd chosen a strange getup for the concert: odd off-white pants that looked like pajama bottoms, his usual sandals, and a fringed shirt that looked like something Daniel Boone would wear, except that it was bright green. His dark, tangled mat of hair hung over the collar and to his shoulders.

"Yeah, but the thing is," Tyler said, "do you guys even notice that anymore? It's so obvious to me, but when you live here . . ."

"Yeah, sure," Chaz said. "It's part of the fun. Part of the show. I mean, look around. It's like a carnival, except that all of us who came to the concert are the performers. Not all of these people dress up like this every day. These are their concert duds. They come to see and be seen. Like us."

But really, most of Chaz's group was dressed pretty much like always. Angel was stunning in coral-colored shorts and matching sleeveless top, bare legs, sandals. Around them, though, the crowd was—well, by Copper Ridge standards, it would seem bizarre.

A group of pimply-faced skinheads in camo stood sullenly off to their left. To their right, a few fiftyish couples in formal evening wear mingled with several people that Tyler at first thought was a group of unusually tall women and then immediately realized was really a bunch of guys in flamboyant drag, not one of them under about six-five. Maybe that was because of their high heels.

And the voices. He suspected that the decibel level here would be just about high enough to cause eardrum damage as everyone on all sides talked at once, many of them in languages Tyler couldn't even identify. *It's like the Tower of Babel,* Tyler thought. *Only louder.*

How would he feel if he saw this conglomeration of people at a school football game in Copper Ridge? Weird, for sure. They wouldn't fit in there. At all. But here—well, the truth was, here they *did* seem to fit. And he realized that he was actually enjoying being here and watching them. Yes, it did feel a little strange, and he did feel a little out of place. Well, maybe a lot out of place. But it helped—a lot—being here with his group. And having Angel holding onto his arm.

She tugged him a little closer and leaned up to him. "Just to make sure you don't get lost again," she whispered with a mischievous smile.

Finally they handed their tickets to the usher. "We have pretty decent seats, I think," Chaz said.

"We should," Tyler grumbled, "for what we paid."

They slipped through a dark passageway and came out in the arena—an immense enclosed stadium where about half the seats were already filled and a steady stream of people moved out of the passageways and into the aisles, looking for their seats.

Miller pointed. "We're down there." They followed him, slipped into a row and settled into their seats, with Tyler between Chaz and Angel.

"See? Not bad," Chaz said.

It seemed to Tyler that they were awfully far away from the stage, but when he turned around and looked back, he could see that actually they were much closer than halfway. "Yeah," he said. "I guess."

He faced the stage again, which sat in the middle of a wide flat floor, and tried to take it all in. "All those people standing down there on the floor, around the stage—who are they?" he asked.

"They bought tickets for standing room," Chaz said. "Upside—they get to be close to the stage. Downside—they have to stand through the whole concert."

Tyler thought about it. "You ever do that?" he asked.

Chaz nodded. "A couple times, when I was young and thought it would be cool. What I found out is, you do it for the experience. If you want to hear the music and watch the band, you buy a seat."

Tyler checked his watch. About twenty minutes. He scanned the crowd, wondering what the Brio crowd would make of this. Solana would love it, of course, and Becca would—"Hey," he said. "Isn't that—you know—what's his name? The actor?"

"Where?" Angel said.

Tyler pointed. "He was in some sitcom for a while a couple years ago, and he played that geeky next-door neighbor in *The River Runs Downhill*. What *is* his name? Look—it's got to be him. People are coming by and giving him things to sign."

"Yeah," Chaz said. "I think you're right. Listen, you want to see celebrities, we should get you up here for a Lakers game. The stars do come out."

He checked his watch again. Nineteen minutes.

"You keep that up," Angel said, smiling, "you'll jinx the whole thing. They'll *never* come onstage."

Tyler turned toward her. "Okay," he said. "In that case, keep me occupied before I cause a disaster and an enraged crowd tars and feathers us all." He held out his wrist with his watch on it. "Stop me before I do it again."

She took hold of his hand and covered his watch with her other hand. "All right. Forget about your watch. Tell me about Colorado Springs."

He shook his head. "Not Colorado Springs. Copper Ridge."

"Whatever. Tell me about it."

Tyler opened his mouth a couple of times to try to explain, but nothing came out. How do you explain Copper Ridge to someone who lives in a mansion and spends her summers in Europe? And how do you concentrate when she's holding your hand in both of her warm, soft ones? "There's not much to tell," he said finally. "I mean—there's *really* not much to tell. It's a small town up in the mountains. We ski, we go mountain biking, I have friends—"

"Okay, tell me about your friends," she said.

Ouch. The trouble was, all day, Tyler's feelings of being pulled in two directions, which he'd felt to some degree the whole time he'd been out here in California, had been intensifying. On one hand there was the Colorado Tyler, who was steady and pretty much knew what he believed, who he was, and where he fit into things. On the other was the California Tyler, who was experimenting, testing, and didn't yet know where he was going to come down on a lot of things. And the California Tyler had this very troubling sense that he was not being true to the Colorado Tyler—or to his close friends, whom Angel now wanted him to talk about.

"Well—okay, what's this now?" he asked, grateful for the diversion. He nodded his head down toward the far end of the arena. A tight crowd had gathered there, and something was happening in the middle of it; voices were being raised. Uniformed officers rushed toward the knot of people.

"Looks like a fight," Angel said. "Happens at every concert. Probably some gang-bangers in a turf war. They'll get tossed out, and they won't get their money back either."

Sure enough, the officers waded into the crowd and soon emerged again with a half-dozen or so tough-looking guys, a couple of whom struggled to get free. They hurried them into the hallways and out of sight. The crowd began to disperse.

And to Tyler's relief, when he and Angel picked up their conversation again, the topic shifted to music.

The opening act wasn't bad, but they seemed a little strung out to Tyler, as if they were on something so that they couldn't quite connect with their music or their audience.

The intermission was supposed to last fifteen minutes, but it was closer to a half hour when the lights began to dim and the crowd applauded. When it seemed that most people were back in their seats, the lights went out. Tyler could make out small moving lights down around the stage—the Bong band members being escorted onto the stage with flashlights, he guessed. He heard the instruments play a few random notes as the musicians checked tuning, volume, got the feel for the instrument they held.

And when it started, it started *boom*—no announcement, no build-up, just right into the first crashing guitar chords and kick-drum beats, and when they hit the first note of that killer guitar riff from *Who's My Baby?*, the lights came up and there they were, Bong. Everybody jumped up, Tyler included.

Simon leaped to the mike, tore it out of its stand, and screamed the unintelligible lyrics as he prowled from one side of the stage to the other. Tyler could see hands reaching up toward the singer from the crowd that had rushed the stage. Unlike the warm-up band, Bong, and especially Simon, seemed fully engaged with the crowd; Simon was clearly singing directly to those whose hands thrust up at his feet.

Angel tugged sharply on his arm, and the next thing he knew Tyler was out in the aisle, which was already crowded with dancers, but Angel carved them out a place—mostly because as soon as the guys around her saw her, they stepped back to get a better look and allow her to dance. And she did—beautifully. And sometimes she seemed totally into the movement and the experience, eyes closed or looking down at her feet. Other times, though, she looked up at Tyler, smiling that seductive little smile and looking deep within him.

And Tyler tried his best to dance, although he felt self-conscious, as if he were on display. Someone crowded behind him, and he turned to see—Chaz, followed by Wolfman and Zack. Wolfman and Zack danced with true abandon, flinging their arms and legs wildly and more than once whapping Tyler uncomfortably. But that was okay; he felt a little less conspicuous surrounded by his friends.

He was aware, though, that when Angel looked up in her dancing, it was still his eyes she sought. And held.

He caught a sweet smell, like incense. At first he couldn't figure out where it was coming from, and then he noticed someone seated nearby lighting what looked like a cigarette. *I thought people weren't allowed to smoke in public places in California,* Tyler thought first, and then realized that what he was smelling wasn't tobacco. He noticed someone else hand-rolling something in cigarette paper and lighting it up.

Right here in public, Tyler thought. *Man, I am definitely not in Colorado.*

He looked up at the stage. Simon so far still had his clothes on, but his movements onstage were pretty suggestive. No one seemed to care.

Did Tyler care? He couldn't decide. If you'd asked him while he'd still been in Colorado, he'd have come out pretty strongly against Simon's stage antics. But now, here . . He remembered what Angel had said about Simon and St. Francis. Was that story really true? Maybe she had it wrong. But he could see how, to her, it wouldn't make any difference whether one of the two of them was serving God and the other just doing what his fans wanted. It was all free speech to her.

And here, right now, dancing in the aisle with a beautiful girl while some great music—regardless of what you thought of their lyrics, which Tyler couldn't make out now anyway, they were great musicians—blasted through the air all around him, here in this carnival atmosphere with tens of thousands of people who asked only to be left alone to do what they wanted, and who had absolutely no objection to your doing what you wanted to—here it all kind of made sense to Tyler.

And he wasn't sure how he felt about that.

But for the moment—Angel looked up and locked eyes with him, and he danced and tried to relax into it.

chapter

Tyler pulled on his last clean pair of shorts. It was his last day in California, and at the beach that afternoon, Miller had said, "Hey, let's gather all the disciples tonight for the Last Supper." He was just pulling his shirt on when Aunt Evelyn called through the bedroom door: "Tyler! Phone's for you. I think it's one of your Colorado friends."

Great. Should he tell Aunt Evelyn just to say that he couldn't come to the phone? Nah. Couldn't do that to one of the Brio squad. "Okay, just a minute." He shrugged his shirt into place and opened the door. "Thanks," he said, as she handed him the cordless phone. "Hi."

"Hey, Tyler," Jacie's voice said. "My gosh, you're hard to get hold of. Didn't you get the message the other day that I'd called?"

"Hi, Jacie. Uh, yeah, I got it, but—you know. Hey, I'm on vacation. Hold my calls."

"Yeah, yeah. So—what's up? Just get home from a wild day of battling twenty-foot waves and great white sharks?"

"Oh, Jacie, bad joke. Chaz just got bitten by a shark yesterday."

Pause.

"Ha! Gotcha," he said.

"That was cruel."

"I specialize in cruel, my friend. Anyway, yeah, I just got showered and now I'm about to head out again. I was just walking out the door."

"Disneyland? Crosby, Stills, Nash, and Young reunion concert? Audition for a movie role opposite Jennifer Lopez?"

"Naw, I blew off the J-Lo thing. Just dinner and hanging out. That's what we specialize in here in California. Hanging out."

"Wow, I didn't know Californians were so similar to Coloradans."

"Yeah, well . . ."

"So you have a minute to talk before you go?"

"Not really. Everybody's ready to go."

"Oh." Another pause. "Well—do you think you'll be too late to call me back when you get home?"

"Well, yeah. I mean, we'll be late, and you're an hour later there . . . Tell you what. I'll be home tomorrow night, drat the luck. We can talk then. Okay?"

Another pause.

"Hello? You still there?" Tyler said. "Really, I've gotta—"

"Is everything okay, Tyler? You doin' okay? Really?"

"*Yes*. I'm fine. I just have to—"

"No, I know you have to go. I just—I don't know. I have this feeling."

"Jacie, everything's okay. All right? We'll talk about the whole trip when I get back, but right now—"

"For some reason I've just really been thinking a lot about you for the past few days. And praying for you, too. I've just had this urge to pray for you. And Becca said the same thing. And I don't know why that would be unless—"

"I don't know why that would be either, Jacie, because everything's fine. But hey, I appreciate the prayers, okay? We could all use more prayers. So please tell Becca thanks for me, and right now I don't think I'm gonna be a very good guest if I keep my host waiting any longer, all right? What kind of witness would that be? So hugs and kisses to all, and we'll talk when I get home. Okay? Bye."

And as he hopped into the BMW and Chaz shot off toward Laguna, Tyler's own words echoed in his mind, over and over:

What kind of witness would that be?

What kind of witness would that be?

What kind of witness would that be?

● ● ●

Angel pulled her Audi Quattro into the garage—a huge three-stall garage, which now held, besides her car, a black Lexus SUV—and pressed the button to close the garage door behind them.

"Man," Tyler said. "Your dad's got plenty of room in here for a workshop, if he wants."

Angel laughed. "My dad? A workshop? He'd cut his hand off. He's a mathematician, not a carpenter. He's the kind of guy who'd be dead if he had to rely on his own ability to do anything practical, like build a house or grow food. Come on." She popped out of the car, and Tyler followed.

And tonight, as at any other time, following Angel was a real pleasure. She was wearing a dress, which had surprised Tyler a bit when she'd first walked into the restaurant, if only because he'd never seen her in one before. But she looked right at home in it, with her hair pulled back in a way that looked very sophisticated, simple dangling earrings, and a little makeup. Her dress was a white sundress with little thin straps—he knew that Jacie or Tyra would probably be able to describe it very accurately, even the type of fabric, but all he knew was how Angel looked in it, which was incredible. It set off her tan beautifully. And it was fashionably short, ending about halfway between hips and knees. And it sort of clung to her, like it was a slip or something. And now, following her across the garage, Tyler found himself very aware of the parts of her it was clinging to.

Angel used a numerical keypad to unlock the door into the house, which led into a huge family room, with a great pool table, fireplace, and sound system. She used another keypad mounted on the wall inside to disarm the security system.

Their home was immense, beautiful—and very quiet. "Anybody home besides us?"

Angel turned to him and grinned. "My parents are in D.C. till Sunday, at a conference. They get home just in time to wave good-bye when I head out for Europe."

Tyler felt an odd sensation in his gut. "Do they mind if I'm here? If we're here . . . uh, you know—alone together while they're not . . ."

She laughed. "It would never even occur to them that that's anything to be concerned about, Tyler."

He could just imagine the parents of any of the girls he knew back in Colorado not caring if their daughters entertained boys alone while the parents weren't home. Like Hannah. Ha.

Trying to find something to do that felt normal, he skimmed through the CDs in a huge rack near the stereo. "Wow," he said. "These yours?"

"You kidding? I mean, there's some good stuff in there—but nothing after about 1960."

Tyler nodded. "Yeah. All jazz and classical." He followed the rows of jazz CDs with his finger. Louis Armstrong, Sonny Rollins, Charlie Parker, Duke Ellington . . . "So what do you think?" Tyler asked.

"About what?"

"Music after 1960."

"That's where *my* CD collection comes in."

"And where's that?" Tyler asked, and then realized that he probably shouldn't have.

She smiled. "I'll show you later. First let's get something to drink."

And what is she likely to have around here to drink? he wondered. *If all she offers me is a beer, should I take it?*

Fortunately, that was one thing he didn't have to worry about. She pulled a couple of Dr Peppers out of the refrigerator and handed him one. But looking past her, he could see that the refrigerator was well stocked with Guinness and Heineken, and wondered what she'd have grabbed if he hadn't been there.

They walked back into the family room. Angel sat on the couch and patted the place next to her; Tyler sat. *Leather,* he thought, running his hand over it. How much had something like this cost?

"This is actually my favorite place in the house," Angel said. "Except for my room." She picked up a remote from the glass-topped table next to the couch, and Tyler figured she was going to turn on some music. Instead, she pointed it toward the window and pushed the button; the drapes slowly retracted. When Angel turned out the lights—also with the remote—Tyler could see that the hillside fell away before them, revealing the lights along the coast. It was an even better view than from Aunt Evelyn's deck, and you didn't even have to go outside to see it.

"That is . . . absolutely incredible," Tyler said.

"Isn't it great?" Angel said. "We've got the same view from the living room, right above us, and then from all the bedrooms above that."

"Seriously? You've got three floors?"

Angel nodded. "That's nothing special in this neighborhood, though."

They sat in silence for a few minutes while Tyler absorbed the view—and thought about what it would be like to live in a neighborhood where three-story houses and incredible views of the ocean were "nothing special."

"You want to pick some jazz?" Angel asked.

"You pick," Tyler said, not wanting to reveal his ignorance of jazz by picking something stupid.

As she sorted through the CDs, looking for something, Tyler sipped his Dr Pepper. "You have this many CDs in your collection?" Tyler asked.

Angel shook her head. "No. I don't have that many, really. When I'm home, I mostly play piano if I want music."

Tyler looked at her. How many more things were there about this girl that he didn't know? "You play?"

She nodded. She chose a CD and put it on the changer; it sounded old, like something from the twenties.

"So," he said. "Are you like Zack and Miller; you play in a band or something?"

She chuckled and shook her head. "No. No way. I hate performing, actually. I play because it helps me cope."

Tyler waited for more explanation, but she didn't say anything else. He took the last sip of Dr Pepper. "Helps you cope?"

She nodded. "In my songs I can say the things I need to say so I don't flip out. The kind of things my parents don't want to hear. Just because my parents are brilliant, Tyler, doesn't mean they're wise. Or loving." She waved a hand toward the luxury that surrounded them. "You see all this and you probably think, 'What a cushy life.' Life in this house sucks big time, Tyler. That's one reason I go off to Europe every summer, for as long as I can. Not that things are much better there. My aunt's a lot better than my parents, and she's fun, but it's not like she's stable. Every year it's something different. Astrology. Rolfing."

"Rolfing?" Tyler asked.

"Don't ask. For a while it was astral projection. Organic food. Herbal food supplements. Then she became a vegan. We had to make an emergency stop in Switzerland last year so that she could have her aura adjusted." Angel laughed, but it wasn't a happy laugh. "She's fun. She really is. I enjoy her. But if any of those things really brought her any satisfaction, why would she be jumping from one thing to another all the time? This whole neighborhood is full of people who are good at making money and lousy at living, Tyler. Well, maybe except for Chaz's family." She laughed again. "Chaz tells me all about what a pain they are, getting involved in his life and trying to influence what he does and what he believes, and I think, 'Chaz—I'd *love* to have your family.' "

"You ever tell him that?" Tyler asked.

She nodded. "Actually, yeah, a couple of times. But I don't think he paid any attention. Mostly, Miller and Chaz and all the rest of them just want to talk about music and movies and books. It's so much easier than talking about why your life is such a horrible waste."

"A *waste?* Angel, your life isn't a waste!"

She looked at him blankly. "Tyler, don't tell me what my life is like. Don't you think I know more about it than you do?"

He sat back, waiting for her to say more, but she just sipped her soda and looked out at the lights, far below. Finally, he said, "And those are the kinds of things you write songs about?"

She nodded again. "I went to a counselor for a while—a shrink. But I didn't see the point. It didn't change anything. So I stopped going and started writing songs. Which may not change anything either, but at least I have a nice song when I'm done."

"You ever play any of these songs for Chaz and the rest?"

She gave him a strange look. "Tyler, those guys are my friends and everything, but which of them do you think would make a good listening ear? Chaz maybe, but lately Chaz has had problems of his own; he doesn't want to listen to mine."

I should ask her more about Chaz, Tyler thought, but he didn't want to break the mood. "Okay, but they could at least comment on the music."

She looked a little annoyed. "I don't want their critique of my music, Tyler. Or yours either. If I write a song that talks about the deepest longings of my heart, do you think I want to hear someone say, 'Not bad, but the melody's kind of monotonous and the lyrics seem a little too whiny'?"

Tyler looked at her and smiled. "Tell you what. I'd like another Dr Pepper, and then could you play me some of your songs? And I promise not to critique them."

"Solemn promise?"

"Cross my heart."

Won't somebody
Somebody tell me
Won't somebody
Somebody point . . . the . . . way
If I can't find
Some kind of hiding place
I don't want to
I don't want to
I don't want to
Open my eyes on one more day

Tyler sat perfectly still, watching Angel at the Yamaha baby grand piano in the "music room"—which had an even bigger, more elaborate stereo system, and lots more CDs, and several other instruments hanging on the walls.

Well, if he'd come to California looking for good new music, he'd just found it. Angel's voice and simple piano arrangements were perfect for the dark, unhappy songs she'd been playing—songs of longing, and disappointment, and lostness. Honest songs. He'd promised not to critique them, and he wouldn't. He'd be hard-pressed to find anything to criticize—the songs were imaginative, completely unique, and well-crafted. *Better than anything I could do,* Tyler admitted—not very happily.

He thought about his own songs—what he wrote about. Compared with what he'd been hearing, they seemed so—well, shallow. Jesus-loves-me-this-I-know kinds of songs. He hoped she wouldn't ask him to sing any of his.

Won't somebody
Somebody tell me
Won't somebody
Somebody point . . . the . . . way
Mmm-mmm
Some kind of hiding place
Some kind of hiding place
I just need
Some kind of hiding place . . .

Her voice trailed off, and she finished with a soft chord on the piano. After the sound died, the two of them sat without speaking. Angel's face was still down, looking at the piano keys, and Tyler thought that he'd never seen anything so lovely and so sad at the same time.

What would Hannah say to her if she were here? Tyler wondered. *Probably launch right into her testimony, and Angel would tune her right out, or tell her to shut up and stop offering easy answers.*

Tyler cleared his throat.

Angel looked up. "No critiques. You promised."

He raised his hands. "Hey, I wouldn't even know how. All I can say is, I understand what you were singing about. Believe me, every thought, every feeling, they were very clear."

"Really?"

Tyler nodded. "Made me wish I could reach in and heal all that pain."

She shook her head. "You can't, Tyler. Nobody can. There are some kinds of pain you're just stuck with." She got up, and Tyler was immediately aware again of her dress, and of her. He felt his heartbeat pick up.

"I loved it," he said. "The music. Not just the songs, but how you sang and played them."

She motioned toward the wall, where a beautiful guitar hung—a vintage Martin D–45. "I'd like to hear—"

"Oh, no," Tyler laughed. "Not a chance. Not after what I just heard." He could just imagine what she would think of the songs he'd written.

"But—"

"No, really. Okay, look at it this way. I enjoyed your music so much I don't want to muddy up the memory with anything else."

She smiled. "Okay. Next time."

"Next time," he nodded, wondering, *Will there be a 'next time'?*

There was a pause, as if she were trying to make up her mind about something, and then she said, "You want to see my room?"

His heart leaped; he was almost afraid to test his voice. "Sure," he said.

Smiling, she held out her hand. He took it. So warm, so soft. She clung to him almost as if she were a little afraid as she led him up the stairs.

Here we go, he thought.

A little fog had rolled in by the time Tyler found himself walking the mile or so from Angel's house to Chaz's house, sometime after midnight. The streetlights—and there were lots of them in this upscale neighborhood—were ghostly in the fog, and sound was strangely deadened. And the eerie atmosphere matched his mood perfectly.

What just happened back there? Tyler asked himself. And he had no answers. He replayed scenes from the evening at Angel's house in his mind, and whoever he had been there, it hadn't seemed like Tyler. It had been somebody he didn't even know.

He hurried along the sidewalk, as if by putting distance between himself and Angel, he could distance himself from the memory. But he knew it wouldn't be that simple. The look on her face, the pain in her voice—these would be things he would not forget. They would haunt him. He knew it.

And who would he tell? Who could he talk to about it? Nobody. This was one that Tyler would just have to keep to himself. How could he ever admit to anybody else what he'd just done? This was a shame far too deep to ever confess.

A car rolled slowly by in the fog. Tyler turned his face away and hunched his shoulders, as if trying to hide his identity.

He longed for home.

But would home ever be the same?

chapter

Tyler watched the curtains billow softly in the breeze from his open bedroom window. It was a fairly warm morning, by Colorado standards. He almost felt warm enough to kick his covers off, but not quite.

He was still in bed not just because he was sleepy, although he'd had a long day yesterday traveling, with a three-hour layover in Salt Lake City. He felt rested. No, he was still in bed because—he felt disoriented. It seemed odd to be back in Colorado. It was almost culture shock, even though he'd only been in California for a couple of weeks.

He felt as if he had a lot to think about, but actually he was trying to keep himself from thinking about much of anything. He needed—what was it scuba divers did when they came up from a deep dive? He needed decompression time. So he didn't get the bends.

But in trying not to think about California, he found that he didn't much want to think about Colorado, either. Normally, on the first day back after a trip, he would call his Brio squad and get together to catch up. He didn't much want to do that. He needed to spend this day alone, maybe a long bike ride, maybe—

Footsteps pounding up the stairs. Feminine giggling. Tyra? No, too many footsteps.

The door opened a few inches, and Solana's grinning face appeared. Then a hand swept in above her head, grabbed her forehead, and pulled it back out of sight. The door closed again.

"You're supposed to knock!" Becca's voice said.

"Oh, pardon me!" Solana laughed. "And anyway, he's still in the sack!"

Well, it looked like he wasn't going to be given a choice. He smiled in spite of himself.

"Tyler, are you decent?" Jacie's voice asked.

"Relatively speaking," Solana added.

Giggles.

"Interesting question—but yeah, I guess," he said.

The door burst open and Jacie, Becca, and Solana rushed in. Hannah was right behind them—but she stopped in the doorway, seeming uneasy.

"Look at this room!" Becca said. "What a mess!"

"Who are you to talk?" Jacie said. "We've seen your room! And besides, he just got back from a trip, he hasn't even unpacked."

Tyler's suitcase was sprawled open on the floor.

"Hey, I'm still asleep," he said, trying to sound groggy. "Go away."

"Fat chance," Solana said.

"I tried to keep them out," Tyler's mom called from downstairs, laughing.

"Yeah, I'm sure you tried real hard!" he yelled back.

"Come on, Sleeping Beauty," Solana said, grabbing his covers and beginning to tug.

"Hey!" he said, alarmed. He grabbed them and pulled them tight. "I'm not dressed."

"Big deal!" Solana said. "It's not like we've never seen a guy in boxers before!"

"I haven't," Hannah said quietly, looking embarrassed.

"Yeah, and just how is it you're watching guys walk around in their boxers, Solana?" Becca teased.

"I've got a brother," Solana answered. "Now get up, Jennings! We've got a basketball in the car and it's a beautiful day!"

"Is it actually pumped up this time?" Tyler asked. "The last time you guys wanted to play basketball, you had one we couldn't even dribble because it was too—"

"What's goin' on down here?" a sleepy-eyed Tyra said, stumbling into the doorway beside Hannah. "Sheesh. I'm tryin' to sleep." She was still wearing just her sleep T-shirt.

"We're just trying to wake up your miserable, no-good brother," Becca said.

"Try a hammer," Tyra yawned. "Works for me."

"That's the next step," Becca said, "if he doesn't get out of bed soon. Now trundle off back to bed," Becca said, turning Tyra around in the doorway and giving her a gentle push. "What happens next may get ugly, and I don't want to be responsible for scarring your little psyche forever." Tyra shuffled off down the hallway.

"Hey, new music!" Solana said, bending over Tyler's open suitcase and pulling out the new CDs he'd brought back from California—some he'd bought, a couple Chaz had given him, and one Angel had bought him after the concert Friday night. She flipped through them. "Who's this—Spider? What are they like?"

"Spider?" Becca asked. "Are you kidding? You've got a Spider CD? Let me see." Solana handed it to her. Becca looked it over, front and back. "Man, if my youth pastor knew you had this, he'd lecture you so bad. He was going on about Spider the other day—how they're anti-Christian, how some of their stuff is blasphemous and way too explicit—"

"Yeah, well, if you notice, it isn't even unwrapped yet," Tyler said, "so I can't exactly comment on the lyrics. But I can tell you this—my cousin Chaz thinks they're great. You suppose your youth pastor has ever actually listened to them, or does he just like dumping on groups that don't adhere to his personal standards?"

"Up! Now!" Solana yelled, grabbing his covers again. "Or so help me, I'm pulling!"

"Out!" Tyler said. "I have to get dressed, and you don't want to be here when I do." He noticed Hannah pulling back into the hallway. "Plus I haven't even eaten breakfast yet. So you'll have to wait until—"

"Not so, oh ravenous one," Jacie said. "We've pooled our extensive resources and we're going to spring for an Egg McMuffin to welcome you back." She grabbed Becca and Solana and herded them toward the door. "You have five minutes. And no excuses!"

When the door was closed—and when he actually heard their footsteps going down the stairs—Tyler pulled himself out of bed, stretched, scratched, and dug around in his suitcase for some shorts and a shirt that didn't look too wrinkled.

So. Home again.

Now he'd find out if he still fit.

● ● ●

"Okay, bring it in," Tyler said, panting, bouncing the ball toward Jacie. These Brio girls might be girls, but they still gave him a workout on the court. He and Jacie were trying to beat Becca, Solana, and Hannah, and frankly they were getting trounced. Jacie didn't have a clue when it came to sports. Becca was almost as good as he was. And both Solana and Hannah were okay players.

True to form, Jacie's pass inbounds was short, and Becca picked it off. Tyler managed to cut off her route to the basket, but she passed back out to Hannah, who nailed it from near the three-point line—or where the three-point line would be if this playground basketball court had a three-point line.

"Eighteen-ten!" Becca exulted, giving Hannah a high-five. "You guys are goin' down!"

Tyler retrieved the ball. "Okay, Hannah, listen—I've really got to know," he said. "Your ball-handling skills are okay but not great, so I assume you haven't actually played in games all that much. But you've got a great jump shot. So—how'd you become such a shooter?"

Hannah looked like she was blushing. "Back in Michigan I was home-schooled, remember? And my brothers were always too small to actually play until recently. And we had a basket, so I would just go out and practice my shots."

"Yeah, well, stop practicing," Tyler said. "Or else I'm not playing any more. I'm taking my ball and going home."

"Sorry, Charlie," Becca said. "It's my ball. So I guess you're just going to have to stay and play."

This time, when Jacie inbounded the ball, Tyler rushed the sideline so she could almost hand it to him. He faked Solana and dribbled in for a layup. Eighteen-twelve.

Becca made it past Jacie easily on their next possession to put them back up by eight again. Tyler inbounded to Jacie, who passed it back to Tyler, and he drove hard for the basket with Hannah guarding him. She moved her feet just a little too slowly, though, and he caught her in the side with his shoulder as he broke past her, putting her flat on her keister.

He put the ball up for an easy two, then trotted back to where Hannah still sat. "Whoops," he said, reaching down to help her up.

"Offensive foul!" Becca yelled.

"No way!" Tyler said. "She wasn't set; her feet were still moving!" He pulled Hannah to her feet; she brushed off her bottom. "Guess I got a little rough there," he told her. "Sorry 'bout that, Angel."

Hannah looked at him, eyes wide. There was about three seconds of silence, and then Becca said, "Angel? Where'd that come from?"

"You into terms of endearment now, Tyler?" Solana said. "You can call me Baby. And let's see, I think Jacie's more of a Sugar. But Angel fits Hannah okay."

"That didn't sound like any term of endearment to me," Becca said. "That was a name. Like of a person. Who's Angel? Somebody you met in California?"

"Summer romance!" Solana crowed.

Tyler shot a look at Jacie. She stood holding the ball and looking confused and—and something. He couldn't tell. "Yeah, she was part of Chaz's gang. It's no big deal—she just looked a lot like Hannah. I called her Hannah a couple of times too." *You liar,* he thought. *You never called her Hannah.*

"So she was one of Chaz's groupies?" Solana asked. "Let's have it— the whole story. You haven't said a thing yet about the whole trip. So come on. Give."

Tyler chuckled. "She wasn't one of anything. She was the only thing—the only girl in the whole outfit. All the rest were guys. So we had to share her. We took turns; we each got her for a day."

"Really?" Hannah said, shocked.

"Yeah, really," he answered, then watched her face. She believed it. "*No,* Hannah, that was a joke. Angel was nobody's girlfriend; Angel is a very independent girl."

"Would we like her?" Jacie asked quietly. Tyler knew that there was a lot going on behind that question.

"Well—that's hard to answer. Solana might like her. She would definitely not fit in here in Colorado. She spends each summer in Europe; in fact she's there now. She's as Southern California as they come, in every way. She lives in a mansion—all three floors have a view of the ocean."

"She's rich—and you think I would like her?" Solana said. "What planet are you from?"

"You were in her house?" Becca asked.

"Look—the trip wasn't about Angel. Can we just get back to the game?"

"He was," Solana said. "He was definitely in her house."

Becca held her hands up to Jacie and Jacie tossed her the ball. Becca shot; nothin' but net. "If we're gonna get a full report on your trip, I vote for stopping the game. I want to give you my full, undivided attention."

"I never said I was going to give you a report."

"Actually, yes you did," Jacie said. "When I talked to you on the phone on Saturday, you said we'd talk about your trip last night. But you didn't call. So this morning will work okay."

"And there you have it," Becca said. "Your solemn vow. Which we will now hold you to."

"Why didn't you call her last night if you said you were going to?" Hannah asked.

"I was *tired*, Hannah. Long day."

They all looked silently back at him.

"Okay," he sighed. "Sorry I didn't call, Jacie. I, uh—oh, never mind. Look, all right, you can have my trip report. On one condition."

"What's that?" Becca asked.

"That we keep playing. Your team takes it out; I just scored."

Ten seconds later Tyler was guarding Becca. She dribbled the basketball, walking back and forth behind the free-throw line. "Talk," she said.

"We surfed, we sat around talking music and movies and books when we weren't surfing, and when we weren't doing that we went to hear live music. There's my complete trip report."

"Just one question, Tyler," Becca said.

"What's—" he began, but as soon as he began to speak, Becca bounced a pass right between his feet to Solana, who put it up for the basket.

"No fair!" Tyler said. "You want the report or not?"

"Sure we want the report," Solana said, "but you're the one who insisted on playing while you talked. Keep your mind on the game while you talk. If you can't do two things at once, let's stop the game."

"No, let's play," Tyler grumbled.

He bounced the ball in to Jacie; she passed it to him as soon as he stepped inbounds, and Hannah stepped up to guard him. "Don't knock me down this time, Tyler," she said, half-smiling.

"It's a physical game," he said, faking left, then pulling back. "You got to be ready to take your lumps."

"Now," Becca said, "you were about to tell us about the concerts you went to. Who'd you hear?"

"I still want to hear about Angel," Solana said.

"I think Tyler's made it pretty clear he doesn't want to tell us about Angel for some reason," Becca said, and Tyler felt like wringing her neck. "So let's at least hear about the concerts."

Tyler squared up and shot a long-distance jumper over Hannah's outstretched arm. It bounced off the rim, but Tyler charged in and got his own rebound, putting in an easy layup. "What do you want to know?" he asked no one in particular as he retrieved the ball and bounced it to Hannah to take out.

"Who'd you hear? Spider?" Solana said.

"Nah. I don't think they were around. We did go hear Bong, though."

There was another of those silences that last a few seconds.

"*What?*" Tyler said. "I didn't say I joined the group. I just said we went to hear them."

"Yeah, but—why?" Jacie asked. "Everything they stand for is the exact opposite of everything you stand for."

"Oh, come on, Jacie," Solana said. "They're not that bad."

"But—Bong?" Jacie said. "In their concerts, they—"

"I know what they do in their concerts, Jacie," Tyler said. "But this time they didn't do that. They just put on a great show and sang their music. Which was pretty darn good, too, if you want to know the truth. Even if I don't agree with what they say in their lyrics. Hannah," he said, trying to change the subject, "come on. Bring the ball in. Let's play."

"Wait," Hannah said. "I want to concentrate on what we're saying here."

Tyler sighed. "Look—the five of us would never have gone to hear Bong together. But—"

"I would," Solana said. "I like them."

"But I was with a different group of friends who wanted to hear them. And all in all, it was a good night. Bong is rich and famous for a reason, you know—because they make good music. Period. I'd like to think that if I sing a Christian song, even people who don't agree with my theology might enjoy the music."

"Yeah, and I hope you also think that eventually the message of the music might sink in and make some sense to them," Becca said, getting upset. "Is that what's going to happen to you with Bong? Eventually their message is going to make sense to you?"

"Why not?" Solana said. "I don't think they're so bad."

"Look," Tyler said. "I don't see any point in arguing about this. I went out there, I did what I felt was best at the time, and I came back. Home. To my friends. So let's be friends, okay? Hannah, let's play."

Hannah opened her mouth as if she wanted to say something to him, then shook her head and stepped across the line to inbound the ball.

Just before she did, Tyler shot a look at Jacie. She was looking back at him, and Tyler knew exactly what the look on her face meant.

When it came to standards in morality and culture, Solana was not the member of their group that Tyler should be agreeing with.

chapter 14

"Hey, hey, so the rumor's true," J.P.'s voice said over the phone. "The fugitive has returned to serve out his sentence."

"Yeah, that's about what it feels like," Tyler admitted, falling back onto his bed. "Just think, I could still be sitting on a sunny beach, surrounded by surfers, girls, and beach bums—of which I could easily become one."

"Hey, look—speaking of beaches, which in turn reminds us of girls—what are you doin' in about an hour?"

Tyler didn't have any other plans. And Jacie and Becca had talked vaguely about getting together tonight, which Tyler found himself wanting to avoid; he had not enjoyed their conversation about music—or about Angel—that morning. If they called and he was already gone . . .

"What did you have in mind?" he said.

"Earth to Tyler," Jessica said. "Hello? Where are you? Still back in California?"

Tyler looked up, embarrassed. "I'm sorry. Guess maybe I didn't get enough sleep. Long day yesterday."

Jessica smiled, although Tyler could tell she was also losing patience. Jessica was not a girl who liked being ignored. "And maybe a few long nights out in California, too? Meet somebody out there?"

He looked out across the sloping hillside in front of him in the fading daylight. As it turned out, J.P.'s idea for the evening had been for the two of them and Doug to bring Jessica, Andrea, and some new girl Tyler had never met before up to the reservoir. J.P. was wandering with Andrea down near the water, his arm draped over her shoulder and hers wrapped around his waist, while he talked, gesturing with his free arm, a smarmy smile on his face. Probably talking about himself. He had no idea where Doug and the other girl were.

"Yeah, met a lot of people, all my cousin Chaz's friends. We all pretty much hung out together."

"You told me that much already. I've been trying to get you to open up about the rest of it—what you guys did, what people are wearing out there this year, what music they're listening to, all those things. So far I'm not getting much out of you. So you want to hear about my two weeks instead?"

Tyler nodded gratefully. "I do, actually. Tell you what. I'll finish my burger and soda while I listen to you, okay? Since you already finished anyway." All Jessica had ordered, when they'd swung through the drive-through on the way up here, had been an ice water and a small order of fries, which she'd long since finished.

So he sat, watching her and occasionally looking off across the water to the mountains on the other side, black and silhouetted now against the darkening sky—the first couple of stars had popped out—while she talked on and on about what she'd been doing for the past two weeks.

But mostly what she talked about was clothes she'd bought and who was dating who.

He remembered the conversations he'd had with Chaz and his friends out in California, talking about things that actually mattered: music, books, movies, plays—ideas. He remembered that last evening with Angel. She'd talked about life. About the ugly parts of it as well as the good parts. She'd found an art form that let her express her deepest feelings—and had learned to do so beautifully. He'd never known a girl who could talk about things like that—well, except Jacie, maybe. But Angel was a lot smarter than Jacie, or at least more sophisticated. And Jessica—well, did Jessica even *have* any deep feelings? What would Angel have made of Jessica, sitting here blathering on about clothes? Angel had no need to talk about clothes. She dressed beautifully, but she didn't feel the need to—

"Tyler Jennings!" Jessica hissed. "What's the matter with you? I asked you a question! Twice!"

Sheesh. Tyler shook his head. "Man, I'm just not much good tonight. Listen, I'm really—"

"Hey!" J.P. called from down near the water. "You two done eating yet? C'mon down here! I got an idea!" When Tyler looked up, he saw that Andrew and some girl Tyler recognized from school had appeared from somewhere.

"Great," Tyler chuckled. "When J.P. gets an idea, I get nervous."

Jessica stood up. "It beats sitting here talking to myself," she grumbled. "Let's go down. Maybe it'll wake you up."

J.P.'s idea, as it turned out, was to play capture the flag—two couples on each team. Tyler had little doubt that J.P.'s real goal was to be able to sneak off into the brush in the dark with Andrea, but at least the game was something to do. They played until well after dark—luckily, there was enough moonlight to keep them from falling into the reservoir—and finished two games, both of which Tyler's team won, probably because he and Jessica were the only two who seemed to really have their minds on the game.

"Okay, enough of that," Doug laughed, panting; he had just tried unsuccessfully to catch Tyler as he sprinted back across their line with Doug's team's flag. "I say we build a fire."

"A fire it is," J.P. agreed. "I've even got some marshmallows in the trunk."

Tyler and Jessica stood to one side, watching the rest of them gather wood. He couldn't imagine himself sitting with this group until late at night. Jessica or no Jessica, at the moment he just wanted to be far away from here. "Jessica, listen—I'm sorry I'm such a waste of time and effort tonight. Really, I'm just dead on my feet."

"Oh, poor Tyler," she said gently—apparently the game had helped her get over her impatience with him. "I'll tell you what. Let's help them build the fire, then we'll snuggle up near it and I'll toast you some marshmallows. Okay?" She smiled. She did have a nice smile.

Maybe the fire wouldn't be so bad. "All right—if you promise not to burn them."

She laughed. "Any man who eats what I fix him had better plan on eating it any way it comes, Tyler. It might not be pretty."

And it wasn't. Her marshmallows were black on one side and under-done on the other. He hadn't known you could mess up toasting a marshmallow. Live and learn.

Still, true to her word, she snuggled. When she wasn't crouched by the fire toasting marshmallows she was snuggled up under his arm, her warm face buried in his neck. And it felt good. It took his mind, for a little while, off the confusion he'd been feeling ever since that last night with Angel.

Am I being unfair to Jessica? he asked himself, pulling her a little closer, enjoying the feel of her cheek against his. *Leading her on? Making her think there's some potential here for a relationship that, right now, I just don't see?*

Nah. He knew Jessica too well for that. She was enjoying being with him tonight. She might be sitting around a fire with someone else tomorrow night, doing the same thing. This was just how she related to guys. It didn't mean any more to her than it meant to him.

Somehow, even *that* thought haunted him.

● ● ●

Late that night, Tyler slumped in front of his computer screen, remembering. "Write to me, Tyler," Angel had said, near the end of that last night, tears glistening on her face. "E-mail—remember, I can read it on my cell phone. And Europe is full of cyber-cafés, where I can shoot you back a reply. Okay? Please? I want to hear from you."

"I will," he'd said. And he'd meant it. But now—what to say? He'd thought about writing to her two or three times since he'd been back, but had never gotten started.

What to say?

He scratched, yawned, longed for his bed. But he had to do this, had to say something.

He got up, padded down to the kitchen, searched the refrigerator—nothing but Coke. He grabbed one and popped it open, then ambled back up the stairs, drinking, running over possible opening lines in his mind:

Hey, Angel. How you doin'? So where are you now . . .

Angel, look. About that last night before we left. I been thinking . . .

Angel, I haven't been able to get you off my mind since I got home. I can't figure out what . . .

Hi, Angel! It's Tyler! Having fun in Europe? Everything's pretty much the same here . . .

He plopped back down. Okay, enough of this. He would just send her a quick note, nothing deep or serious, just say hi, I'm thinking about you, more later, and then end it. He logged on, checked his own e-mailbox—nothing urgent—and was just addressing a mail document to

Angel when the little bell sounded and an IM box popped up:

AllenOlson: Hey, Tyler old buddy! You must be home now. Glad to see the old folks? Guess your plane must not have crashed, so my prayers were answered.

Of all the luck. About the last person Tyler wanted to talk to right now. Well, he couldn't just log off.

ColoradoTy: up pretty late aren't you old man? this can't be good for the alzheimer's. drink a cup of warm milk and have the nurse put you to bed.

AllenOlson: Seminary is a tough taskmaster, Ty my son. My nurse and helpmeet is already asleep beside me here in the marital bed while I sit up researching my next paper on my new laptop. (Not brand-new, but new enough. It's revolutionizing my life. More about that later.) I've got hours of work before I sleep, and hours of work before I sleep, to paraphrase Robert Frost. Now— we never had that IM chat before you left California about what kinds of changes you were talking about in your e-mail. Feel up to that now? For a few minutes, while we chat, I'll graciously set aside my research into the efforts of inner-city churches to fight drug and alcohol abuse. Okay?

ColoradoTy: kind of you. really. but i must beg off. the house is currently on fire, and i was just e-mailing the fire department to come put it out.

AllenOlson: Amazing—the things they use e-mail for these days. What's next—e-mail marriage proposals?

ColoradoTy: in truth, old fogey, i was just about to log off and hit the sack for some much-needed sleep myself after a long string of long days. can we do it later?

AllenOlson: Surely. Just reassure me that this is still Tyler

Jennings I'm talking to. You talked of change. Is the Tyler Jennings who went out to California the same guy who came back?

Was he? Good question. And one that Tyler didn't want to touch with a ten-foot pole, at least not tonight. Because somehow, after his trip—after Miller, after Bong, after all those long conversations about music and art, and especially after Angel—nothing in Colorado felt the same.

ColoradoTy: that's what it says on my driver's license: tyler jennings. but of course i'm actually an alien who just took over his body, like in men in black. hey, of course it's me. come on. but we all change. you aren't the same guy you were before you got your laptop, right? we all change in subtle ways.

AllenOlson: Sometimes people change in not-so-subtle ways. And there's a difference between, on the one hand, putting your life in God's hands and then changing and growing as He leads you, and on the other, letting the world shape you. In Bible terms, there's a difference between conforming to the world and being transformed by letting God renew our minds. Guess I'm just trying to figure out where your last e-mail fits on that scale. Because I love you, babe.

ColoradoTy: i'm touched. i'm also beat, so signing off now. hasty luegos, muchacho. tyler jennings over and out. kiss the wife for me.

Tyler logged off and shut his computer down. Rats. That was the problem with buddy lists. He couldn't write to Angel now because Allen would know if he stayed online.

Well. He was tired anyway.

He'd write to her soon.

Thursday evening, Tyler pulled his Escort into the driveway at a quarter after seven, cut the engine, and sighed. He'd be working at Fishburne's Sporting Goods part-time for the rest of the summer, and today had been his first day—heck of a way to start off, putting in a full eight-hour day, ten to seven with an hour off for lunch, but that was okay; he needed the money.

He dragged himself out of the car and started for the house. He was starved, but Mom had warned them that she'd be home late today; his dad was off on one of his trips and not due back till the next day.

He grabbed a Dr Pepper out of the refrigerator on his way through the kitchen. He'd been thinking all the way home about what Becca had said about the group Spider—anti-Christian, explicit lyrics, blasphemous . . . Time to listen to that Spider CD Chaz had given to him and see for himself. They'd listened to Spider in Chaz's car quite a bit, but Tyler had mostly been paying attention to Chaz or the others in the car and had just been vaguely aware that he liked the group's sound.

He grabbed his headset. He would sit out in the backyard and play it on his portable CD player. His suitcase still sat on the floor, exactly where he'd dropped it Sunday night. He kicked through the dirty clothes inside, but the CDs weren't there. Solana had pulled them out; where had she put them? He looked around his room. Dresser, bed, bookshelves, stereo cabinet—plenty of CD cases, but not the ones he was looking for, not the new ones.

He looked everyplace a second time, then stood in the middle of his room scratching his head.

Tyra's door was open a crack, but he could hear movement inside. He rapped on the door. "Tyra?" No answer. "Hey." Nothing. He pushed the door open. She was lying on her side on her bed, back to him, headphones over her ears, rocking to a beat Tyler could just make out.

He grinned. Great timing. He could probably get her to bounce all the way to the ceiling if he poked her ribs hard right about now. Still grinning, he tiptoed across the floor, trying not to shake the floor, leaned over the bed, reached for her ribs—and his grin disappeared as if it had never been there.

Spread out in front of Tyra on her bed were his California CDs. The case she held was the Bong CD, and the words exploded off the front cover as if he could see nothing else: "Parental Advisory: Explicit Lyrics."

He yanked the headset off her ears. "Hey!" she yelled. Her eyes blazed as she spun onto her back to face him. "Tyler, you . . ."

"Give me those. All of them." He reached over her to gather them up, and she tried to grab his hands. "Those are mine! I want them right now."

"Stop it! I was listening!"

Tyler grabbed the Bong case out of her hands. "Well, they aren't yours to listen to, are they?" His heart was beating hard in his chest, and Tyler was aware that it wasn't just anger. He felt fear—fear over what she was listening to. Things that he had brought into the house, that she had gotten out of *his* room. "I want every one of them. Right now."

She grabbed up the rest of the cases on her bed and threw them at him; a couple of them fell to the floor and clattered open. "All right! Here! Take them! Are you happy now? Just leave me the one I'm listening to so I can finish—"

"No," Tyler said. "You don't have any business listening to that band. They sing about—"

"Oh—*what?* I don't have any business listening to them? Is that what you said? Then why do you have the CD? If they're so horrible, then why are *you* listening to them?"

"Because I'm not in eighth grade anymore, that's why," Tyler said, with an unpleasant twinge of guilt. What was this? Why should he feel guilt? He'd gone all through this already in his own mind. Tyra was the problem here; she'd borrowed his stuff without asking, and now she'd gotten in over her head. She was a kid. She was way too young for this band. "You really think Mom would let you buy a CD like this? No way."

"You think she'd let *you* buy it, or even bring it into the house, if she knew what was on it? Listen to these words . . ." She flipped through the little booklet that had been in the CD case.

He grabbed it out of her hand. "Don't read those out loud! What's wrong with you? We don't talk like that in this house."

She laughed at him, the nasty kind of laugh that only an angry little sister can manage. "We don't talk like that in this house? But it's okay for you to have CDs that talk like that? You big hypocrite."

Well, that was about once too often for being called a hypocrite. He grabbed the CD player and popped the CD out of it. "Keep your hands off my stuff. And don't bother asking—the answer's no." He tried to gather the boxes and CDs into his arms, but it was an awkward stack.

"If I shouldn't be listening to it, then neither should you!" she yelled.

He snorted as he turned toward the door. "What a crock of—" He stopped dead.

Mom stood in the doorway, her face white.

● ● ●

Five minutes later, the three of them sat in the family room. Or at least Tyler sat. Tyra lay sprawled on the couch. His mom stood at the end of the couch holding up the CD cases, her face stony. And despite her defiant posture, there was no misunderstanding the panicked expression on Tyra's face: *Busted.*

"I want to hear it from the top," Mom said. "Tyra, where'd you get these CDs?"

"I knew Tyler had 'em," she said sullenly. "I wanted to hear 'em, so I took 'em out of his room."

Tyler wished he could be one of those characters in the movie, *Honey, I Shrunk the Kids*—so that he could just disappear behind a bread crumb or something.

"We'll talk later about invading Tyler's privacy and taking his stuff without permission. Right now we're talking about listening to unsuitable material, music that violates the standards I try to keep in my home. And—" She looked at Tyler. "Bringing that stuff into my home in the first place."

"I could have just checked 'em out of the library," Tyra said. "It's not like it's that hard to get."

"Don't get me started on libraries that check out to minors music CDs that have *Parental Advisory: Explicit Lyrics* stickers on them."

"*Mom,*" Tyra whined, "there's nothing wrong with listening to these CDs. It's not like I'm going to turn into a gangsta or put my hair up in dreadlocks just from listening to—"

"Tyra, I *know* what's on these CDs. We have people who review these things for us at the magazine. I know these groups. I've studied the lyric sheets. And this is *not*—I repeat, *not*—anything I want in my house. We have talked about this before, Tyler. I thought I made it clear." She held up the stack of CDs. "Do you have any more like this?"

"Mom," Tyler said, "it's not like—see, when I was out in California—"

"Do you have any more?"

He sighed. "No, that's pretty much it."

Mom looked deeply into his eyes, held it for a few seconds, and then looked down as if thinking. She was silent for a long time while neither Tyra nor Tyler moved—except to send nasty looks at each other.

"*What?*" Tyler said at last.

"Don't take that tone with me, Tyler," Mom said. "You're in no position, believe me." She was quiet for a moment longer, then said, "Okay, go on up to your room, change, and get yourself some dinner. There are leftovers in the refrigerator. We'll talk more about this later. And I mean later tonight, not next week, so don't run off anywhere."

He opened his mouth to defend himself, then couldn't think of anything to say.

"Go on," she said. "I need to talk to Tyra, and frankly you aren't helping."

And maybe that last thing was what hurt most of all.

● ● ●

Tyler was finishing up the plate of leftover spaghetti he'd microwaved for himself when he heard Tyra marching upstairs, apparently making as much noise as possible to let everyone know how abused she was. It was just a few minutes later, when Tyler was rinsing his dishes to put in the dishwasher, that Mom walked slowly into the kitchen, poured herself a cup of coffee, and sat at the counter. He glanced at her. She pointed to the stool next to her. "Have a seat," she said.

That was pretty much the last thing Tyler wanted to do, but he sat.

"Tyler." She took a sip. "It amazes me that we're having this conversation." She sipped in silence for a few minutes longer. Tyler knew her well enough to be able to tell how the wheels were grinding in her head, thinking things through, figuring out where to go from here. Finally: "I give you a lot of freedom. A *lot* of freedom, Tyler."

"Not so much," he protested weakly.

"Not so much in comparison to whom? Solana, whose mom doesn't hold the same values I do? J.P., whose parents don't seem to care what he does or where he is? In comparison with most other Christian kids whose parents care about them and about what they do, I give you a lot of freedom. And why? Because I've always been able to trust you. I trust who you are and I trust what you'll do when you're not right under my nose."

Several scenes flashed in front of his eyes from that summer: sitting in the theater with J.P. watching *The River Runs Downhill*, going to the Bong concert with Chaz and the rest, that last night in California with Angel . . .

"And that's why I've never given you a list of 'Thou Shalt Nots' about what you can listen to, or even what CDs you can have in your room. Do I have to change my beliefs about you, Tyler? I just have so many questions in my mind—questions that should have been in your mind before you bought those CDs."

"I didn't buy all of them," he mumbled. "Some of them, Chaz gave me." He didn't mention Angel.

"Yes, Chaz. Chaz whom I hoped, and Aunt Evelyn hoped, you would be a positive influence on, rather than the other way around."

Tyler rolled his eyes, then immediately regretted the obvious disrespect. But his mom, even though she clearly saw it, didn't respond to it.

"That wasn't fair to you, Tyler—I realize that. We shouldn't have placed on you the responsibility to influence Chaz, who's a year older than you anyway. That's his parents' responsibility, not yours. So please understand one thing: If you're feeling guilty about anything that happened between you and Chaz out in California, you can stop—I don't blame you for any of that."

That's not what I'm feeling guilty about, Tyler thought miserably.

"There are so many things you should have been asking yourself: Is this the kind of group I want to enrich by buying their CDs? Is there some danger in bringing these CDs into a house where a little sister lives whom I'd rather not expose to this kind of thing? What are the standards in my home, standards that might be violated by material like this? It shouldn't be the kids who set the standards in a home, Tyler—it should be the parents. And, yes—I know what you're thinking. But think—even though your dad might not always be the best example, do you really think he would support you about bringing material like this—" She held up the CDs. "Like this into his house? I don't think so."

Tyler thought about the lectures he'd so often gotten from his dad. No, his dad might not know much about music, but he would be sure to have nothing but contempt for groups like Spider and Bong. His motives might be entirely different from Mom's, but his stand on these CDs would be the same.

"I'm wondering, Tyler, if I haven't been making a huge mistake in giving you so much freedom without exercising a little more direct supervision and accountability."

Whoa, whoa. Tyler didn't like the sound of that. "Mom," he said, "using freedom wisely isn't about never making mistakes. *Everybody* makes mistakes. And sometimes you have to try things out. How would I really know what these groups are saying unless I listen? Sometimes you have to taste something before you know whether you like it."

His mom smiled. "I talked with my sister yesterday. She was telling me about a talk—well, an argument—she had with Chaz right after you left. You know what? He said the same thing you just said."

He'd said the same thing to Tyler, too—an echo of that conversation flitted through Tyler's mind. Is that where Tyler had gotten the idea?

"Anyway," he said, "these guys are exploring a lot of ideas that might sound pretty crazy to us, but this is real stuff. This happens. Maybe it's bad stuff, but it happens. Maybe society needs people who aren't afraid to explore the tough topics, even if it's not something people want to hear—"

His mom shook her head violently, angrily. "Have you read these lyrics?" she asked, holding up the Bong CD. "They're about violence against women."

"Mom—just because a song is *about* something doesn't mean it's saying it's all right."

"Tyler—I don't know any other way to interpret these lyrics than to say that they advocate violence against women. Listen to these—"

"No—no, that's okay," he said uneasily. "I remember the lyrics." The last thing he wanted was to hear his mom's voice reading obscene lyrics.

She looked up at him. "Well, then, I guess you can't argue, as some kids do, that you never listen to the lyrics anyway. Not if you've got them memorized."

Slowly, she put the CD cases down and sipped her coffee for a minute or two. "I guess you can tell, Tyler, that I'm very disappointed in you," she said at last.

He nodded, not sure what to say. This wasn't something he heard very often from his mom.

"You've always been a responsible young man, Tyler. I think this was a bad choice. But, as you say, it's not about never making mistakes. Still, I want to make sure you learn some things from this."

Was he about to get grounded?

"I want you to remember tonight. My anger. Tyra's bad choices—and by the way, I didn't let her get away with blaming you for what she'd done; she made her own choices and she'll pay the consequences. And I also want you to get rid of the CDs. Any that have *Parental Advisory* labels on them, and any that *should* have had those labels on them.

You know what I mean. Even if you don't agree with me about those CDs, Tyler, I want you to get rid of them because they offend me and I don't want them in my house."

Tyler looked away and said nothing. It wasn't the money so much. But this meant he'd have to get rid of the CD Angel had given him.

"Tyler?" his mom said.

He sighed. "All right," he grumbled.

"I want you to try to help undo the mess with Tyra by thinking of something you can say to her that will help straighten her out about this."

"Mom—"

"When you caught her with your CDs you 'had a cow,' to use her term. Right?"

He nodded.

"I know why you got upset, Tyler. And that's what I want you to remember when you talk to her—that you care about her and react strongly to the idea of any loss of innocence. Right?"

Well, that's not how he'd have said it, but . . . "Right."

She nodded. "Okay." She stood. "Tyler . . ." She stood quietly, thinking. "This was a surprise to me tonight. A real surprise. And not a good one at all." She looked right at him. "I hope there won't be any more surprises."

Four words ran through his mind: *The River Runs Downhill.*

"I hope so too," he said.

● ● ●

Hey, Angel. Listen, I been thinking a lot about that last . . .

Angel, I hope your European trip is going great, hope you're having a lot of fun. I wish . . .

Hi, Angel, it's Tyler. Say—

"Hey—Tyler. Phone's for you." Tyra's voice was icy. This was the first thing they'd said to each other since their big blowup earlier that night. The phone landed on his bed, and Tyler quickly closed the writing program on his computer so his numerous false starts on writing to Angel wouldn't show.

"Tyler Jennings at your service," he mumbled into the phone.

"Hi, Ty," Jacie's voice responded.

Hmmm. Tyler wasn't sure how he felt about talking to Jacie right now, considering how all of his conversations with her and the Brio squad had gone since he'd been back.

"Jacie's Construction Business calling."

"Construction?" Tyler flopped back onto the bed.

"Yeah—bridge building. I feel like we need it after the last few conversations. Tell me the truth—you weren't all that happy to hear my voice on the phone just now, were you?"

He laughed. "Sounds horrible when you put it that way, doesn't it?"

"Yep. It sure does. But I don't blame you—we've been riding you pretty hard since you got back. So I'm thinking, let's build some bridges and get back to being just Jacie and Tyler again. Okay?"

"Sounds good to me." And it did sound good. In fact, he found himself wishing he could tell her about the whole scene tonight with Tyra and Mom. But that would just be throwing gasoline on a fire. Jacie would be all over him for letting Tyra get her hands on those CDs. Yeah, Jacie would take Mom's side. Big time. "But can we do that without even talking about California at all?" he went on. "Because I've got this hunch that, if we do, it's just going to be the same stuff all over again."

Jacie laughed uneasily. "I don't know. Can we? It just seems to me like there's something there that needs to be talked about, Tyler, and I don't know what it is. I mean, I'm sorry we've been giving you such a hard time, but we're all sort of confused. You know us—we get emotional about things, we like to talk face-to-face and work things out. And that's been hard to do since you got back."

"Yeah, but why? Why should it be harder to talk now than before?"

"I don't know. Gee, I sound like a broken record. *I don't know, I don't know, I don't know.* But to me, you just don't seem like yourself. Did something happen out in California that you haven't told us about?"

"You see—that's why I didn't want to talk about California. You're starting with the conclusion that I've done something wrong. A *lot* of things happened out there, just like it does every year, and maybe I've grown up a bit because of that." Where had he heard that line before? Oh, yeah—Chaz. "But none of it is stuff you have to be concerned about. I went out there, I surfed, I had a good time, and I came home."

"*How* good a time? I just keep thinking—"

"Jacie—okay, look, here we go again. What happened to Jacie's Bridge Building Incorporated?"

She sighed. "Okay. You're right. I'm riding you again. Sorry. You're my bud and I love you. Okay?"

Tyler sat silently stewing.

"Hello? Still there?"

"I'm still here," he grumped.

"Tyler, you know—we all do stupid things sometimes. We feel bad, we ask forgiveness, we survive it and go on—"

"Where are you coming from with this, Jacie? And where are you going with it? Who says I did anything stupid? Why do you—"

"Have you talked to Allen Olson about it, Tyler?"

Silence.

"You haven't?" she asked.

"I—*yeah*, I talked with him."

"You talked with him about whatever it is you're not talking to me about?"

Tyler's brain scrambled for ways to answer, then realized that he was talking to Jacie. He couldn't get away with anything not really true. "Well—we talked. We, uh—we didn't get real specific."

She didn't answer.

"I was in a hurry. It was late," he said.

"You seem to be in a big hurry these days when anybody wants to talk to you. Seems like that's been true even before you went to California. Starting about the time you went to see *The River Runs Downhill*."

"Don't even start in on me about the movie. We covered all that."

"No, we didn't, Ty. And I guess that's one of the reasons I'm confused. We've always been able to talk about anything. We *have* talked about anything, stuff that would amaze anybody who heard us. And now I'm confused because I feel like you're throwing up this big barrier: *Private. Stay out. I will not talk about anything beyond this line.*"

"I—*no*, Jacie, I'm not—I haven't . . ."

When she finally spoke, he couldn't remember another time he'd heard her voice more vulnerable, more emotional: "Yes, Tyler, you have. And I'm afraid I'm losing you. Tyler, I—I want my Tyler back."

chapter 16

Tyler had just unpacked a shipment of carabiners and was rolling them out to the sales floor to re-stock the display of climbing gear when he spotted Becca and Jacie walking in. They were craning their necks, looking around, and it wasn't hard to figure out who they were looking for.

He felt a sudden odd contradiction—or at least it would have been odd three weeks before. Now he was getting used to it. On one hand, he wanted to turn around and disappear back into the stockroom, where he knew they couldn't follow (unless they wanted to disobey the huge "Employees Only" sign on the door), and on the other, he wanted just as badly to call out to them and wave them over.

He didn't do either. He didn't have to. Becca spotted him and, grabbing Jacie's elbow, pulled her toward Tyler, a warm smile on her face. "I told Jacie before we even got here that we'd find you in the climbing section," Becca said. "Sure, you claim to be working, but you're just getting psyched up for the fall climbing season."

"In that case, why wouldn't I be in the mountain biking section?" Tyler asked, sorting out a handful of carabiners and looking for the proper place on the rack. "Or backpacks, or sleeping bags?"

"Just call it woman's intuition," Becca said. "And don't knock it, since I happen to be right."

"Blind luck," Tyler said. "I didn't pick this aisle because I like it—I have a shipment of new stuff to stock."

"Umm-hmm," Jacie said. "And this entire new shipment consisted of climbing stuff?"

Tyler grinned. "Well, I did see a couple of pallets of women's sports-wear, soccer balls, and turkey calls," he said.

"We rest our case," Becca said. "And now we have a question for you. Are you working tomorrow morning?"

Actually, no. He had wanted the early shift tomorrow, since it was Saturday. But being the new guy on the rotation, he'd pulled the crummy hours—five to nine. Which would pretty much eliminate any idea of doing anything with anybody on a Saturday night. Tonight wasn't much better: he'd be working till seven, and then had promised Mom he'd rush home for dinner. No big nights out this weekend.

Even so, he found himself reluctant to tell them that he was free in the morning. At least until . . . "Hard to say," he hedged. Then he caught Mrs. Fishburne's eye—and she didn't look happy. Employees standing and talking to their friends when they were supposed to be working was one of her pet peeves. He held up his wrist and tapped his watch. "Can I go on a break?" he called to her politely. She nodded.

Behind the store, he and Jacie and Becca settled on a low cinder-block fence. "What you got in mind?" he asked. "For tomorrow."

"We promised Mrs. Peterson we'd come by and help with her Sat-urday sing-along," Jacie said. "Richard's gone—went to Salt Lake with his folks for the weekend. So she needs help with the refreshments and stuff. Okay, okay—" She held up her hands. "I see the expression on your face. And I know you don't like the music. So can you just think of it as a nursing home visit or something like that?"

Good question. Why couldn't he just think of it that way, instead of thinking about the music at all?

Because since he'd gotten home from California, he'd spent huge amounts of time thinking about music. Remembering the conversations he'd had with Chaz and Miller and Zack and Angel. Remembering hanging around with real working musicians, people who'd been in recording sessions, who had their names on CD credits. Remembering listening to sophisticated new music with people who knew how to listen to it and talk about it, who could tell what the musicians were doing right and what they were doing wrong.

A flash of music washed through his head—from that last Saturday he'd gone to Mrs. Peterson's Community Center sing-along: "Let Me Call You Sweetheart," played with some of the weirdest canned percussion he'd ever heard in his life. Could he go back to that? He didn't think so.

He looked at Becca and Jacie, waiting expectantly for an answer, and he also saw that they had already figured out what answer they were likely to get. Becca's face showed scorn and frustration. Jacie's showed— what? Hurt? Sorrow?

He hated to disappoint them. But things change. Maybe he had reached the point in his life where he didn't have to do every little thing just because it would be a nice thing to do. Maybe he'd reached the point where he had to identify his priorities and pursue them. And for Tyler, that meant music—in a major way.

● ● ●

"My gosh, Tyler," his dad grumbled at the dinner table that night. "Are you sure you got enough potatoes? Leave some for the rest of us, for Pete's sake."

Tyler sighed and put some of the mashed potatoes back into the bowl. He hadn't had much to eat that afternoon—he'd spent his break talking with Jacie and Becca. He'd forgotten that his dad was getting home today. When he'd walked in tonight and heard his voice, it had been an unpleasant surprise—as always. "Speaking of the rest of us," Tyler mumbled around a mouthful of Crock-Pot roast beef, "where's Tyra?"

Tyler's mom looked up. "She didn't tell you she was going to eat at Melissa's and then spend the night there?"

Tyler shrugged. "No, but that's no surprise. It's not like she says any more to me than she has to these past couple of days." Ever since the blowup about the CDs, that is.

"What're you two fighting about now?" Dad grumbled into his plate.

Tyler's mom flashed him a warning look, which meant that she hadn't discussed it with him yet and she wanted the chance to do it in her own way and her own time, so she didn't want Tyler to say any more about it now. "Kid stuff," she explained. "We handled it."

Dad let it drop—which meant that he'd had a long trip and he was tired. Ordinarily, he'd have sensed and resented any attempt to keep anything from him.

It had, in fact, been a pretty long trip for his dad. This was the first time he'd been home since Tyler got home from California. It might have been nice if his dad had shown a little interest in how things had gone out there. Instead, all his dad had said when he'd seen him was, "Start the new job yet?" No reference to California. Well, that was fine. A lot of things had happened out there that his dad was just not capable of understanding anyway.

Tyler didn't pay much attention to the rest of the dinner-table conversation. Mostly, Mom asked Dad questions about his trip, whom he'd seen, what kind of orders he'd gotten and meetings he'd attended, where he'd stayed, and so on, which his dad answered absent-mindedly with short, halfhearted answers.

And then the phone rang.

Tyler's mom hopped up to answer it.

"Just telesales," Dad said. "Don't bother."

Mom kept going. "I always answer the phone when one of my kids isn't here," she said. She grabbed the kitchen cordless. "Hello?" Pause. "Speaking." Another pause. "You're sure? That can't—that's not—just a minute."

She carried the phone into the guest bedroom down the hall and closed the door.

What was that all about? Tyler could hear, as he finished the last of his meal, the buzz of his mom's voice on the phone. Dad seemed at first to have put her out of his mind; he lowered his head tiredly over his plate and shoved in a few more mouthfuls of food. Then, as he chewed, he cocked his head toward the doorway and concentrated. Eventually he gave Tyler a thoughtful look, then rose and followed his wife down the hallway.

Well, whatever it was, Tyler thought, it didn't have anything to do with him. He was here, he'd been working all afternoon, keeping out of trouble, and the only thing he had to worry about was thinking of something fun to do with the rest of his evening—as soon as he had a shower.

Carrying his dishes across to the sink to rinse, Tyler noticed that now he could also hear his dad's unintelligible buzz—but many decibels louder than his mom's voice. He was ticked about something.

The guest bedroom doorway popped open again, and Tyler craned his neck to see his mom, obviously upset, come down the hallway and trot up the stairs. He could hear his dad's voice, apparently talking into the phone: "Listen, I don't care *what* your policy is on underage admissions or how rigorously it's followed. What I want to know is, what time is the blasted movie going to be over? And I want to know right now!"

Movie? Tyler's stomach sank.

His dad stormed back into the room and slammed the phone back into the cradle, then started toward the stairs, muttering to himself. But

Mom came hurrying down with her purse. They shared a look—anger on his dad's face, fear and disappointment on his mom's—and then both turned toward the door to the garage.

"Uh, what's up?" Tyler asked, not wanting to hear the answer.

"We'll talk about it when we get back," Mom said—then paused and swiveled toward him. "You were telling me the truth, Tyler? You didn't know anything about Tyra's plans for the night?"

"Mom," Tyler protested. "Of course I was telling the truth! I have no idea what she's up to."

Mom nodded and disappeared into the garage behind Dad. Tyler could hear Dad hollering as they piled into the car: "I've told you a hundred times—you trust those kids way too much! You have to check up on 'em! Why didn't you call over to what's-her-name's house to make sure Tyra was there? They'll tell you whatever they have to tell you to get out of the house, and then . . ."

Tyler popped open a Dr Pepper and sank onto the family room couch. He had a feeling it was going to be a long night.

chapter

The three of them stormed in forty-five minutes later, when Tyler was on his third soda. Tyra, in tears, swept dramatically into the family room, ignoring Tyler, and sobbed, "But you could have at least waited in the car! I'll be hearing about this at school for the rest of my life!"

What's she wearing? Tyler wondered. It was a tight, short baby T-shirt, and low-riding tight jeans that showed a good two inches of skin. Tyler felt embarrassed just looking at her. When had she gotten that outfit? No—it couldn't be hers. Mom would never let her buy that.

"Why'd you have to wait right there in the lobby?" Tyra wailed. "With the theater manager, no less! My friends will never speak to me again, because now they're going to get in trouble, too! And Jennifer will probably lose her job!"

"She *should* lose her job, if she's deliberately letting underage kids into adult movies," Mom said, her face red—not just from anger; her eyes were swollen. "And if you think *that* was an unpleasant experience, just see what happens *next* time you pull a stunt like this!"

"What movie did she see?" Tyler asked quietly. Everyone ignored him.

"There won't be a 'next time,'" Dad said coldly. "You won't get the chance for a 'next time.'"

Oh, wow, Tyler thought. *Suddenly he cares—when it embarrasses him, or reflects poorly on him, and when he gets a chance to throw his weight around, then suddenly he cares what we do. What a dad.*

"Tyra," Mom said, pain in her voice, "why would you even *want* to go to a movie like that? It's . . . it's . . . I just don't even know what to say. Or to think. And to *lie* to us about it! After the CDs the other day, and now this . . . and those clothes! I don't let you dress like that, so you just borrow them from your friends? How long has *this* been going on?"

"Come on, Mary," Dad said contemptuously. He didn't show any curiosity about the subject of the CDs, so Tyler assumed that Mom had brought him up to date on it in the car. Great. "These problems have been right there in front of you for years, just slowly developing. You kept thinking your kids were growing up so well, and I kept telling you—"

"Oh, honey, please," Mom said, swiping a tissue across her eyes. "Not right now."

"Hey!" he answered. "This is something you need to—"

"What movie did she see?" Tyler asked again, loudly. Everyone stopped talking and looked at him.

"*The River Runs Downhill,*" Mom said, nearly whispering.

The River Runs Downhill. Scenes from the movie played in Tyler's mind as he sank back against the cushions of the couch. No. No, no, no. Tyra was way too young. He felt sick to his stomach. The thought lodged firmly in his mind of his little sister sitting watching those scenes. And now it was done. She'd seen it, and he couldn't change that. "It's playing in Copper Ridge now?" he said weakly.

"Started last weekend," Mom said.

"Oh, come on, Tyler," Tyra said angrily. "*You're* the one who—"

"Oh, no you don't," Mom said. "Don't try to blame this one on Tyler. I told you the other day—Tyler's responsible for his mistakes, and you're responsible for yours. Tyler didn't buy you a ticket to that movie, and he didn't make you—"

"No, Tyler's way too cheap to buy me a ticket," Tyra said. "But he did buy his own."

There was a pause. Tyra and Tyler exchanged hostile glares. He wished she could read his mind: *You slimy little toad. I'll get you for this.* And he could clearly read her expression: *If I'm going down, you're going down with me.*

Mom sounded completely exhausted when she said, "Tyler—what's she talking about? Have you seen *The River Runs Downhill?* When? Out in California?"

His mind raced. Was there a way out of this?

He looked at Tyra. "What makes you think I've seen it?"

She gave the ugly laugh only desperately angry and frightened little sisters can give. "Oh, come on, Tyler—you big hypocrite! Everybody knows you saw it! Half the high school saw you and J.P. coming out of the movie in Colorado Springs a couple of weeks ago, and then cruising around town in the backseat of J.P.'s mom's P.T. Cruiser with Jessica on your lap, and then going drinking up to the reservoir—"

"Oh, Tyler!" Mom said. "Drinking?"

Dad nodded. "I knew it. And who knows what all you did out in California. Okay, from now on—"

"Wait, wait!" Tyler said. Damage control time. Right now. "Wait a minute. That's crazy! That's just crazy. Tyra, do you believe everything you hear? Just because somebody says it about me, you believe it?"

"Tyler, you're not going to get out of this," she said. "I talked to Michelle Geisler and she saw you and J.P. coming out of the movie herself. She was just going into another movie and she saw you coming out of *The River Runs Downhill.* And the two of you were talking about the movie, and she heard you. So don't try to deny it." She turned back toward Mom. "You can protect him all you want. I know you will anyway; you always let him do anything he wants and them jump all over me for the slightest thing. But that's why I went to see the movie. I wanted to see what was so special about it that Tyler would risk getting into trouble to go see it. So, okay, if I get in trouble, I get in trouble. But what happens to him?"

Ordinarily, Mom would have been quick to answer that what happened to Tyler was none of Tyra's business, and she would handle it with Tyler later. This time, she said nothing. She just looked at Tyler with red, weepy eyes, and an expression that told him how confused and disappointed she was. Dad loomed in the background, and a hard truth suddenly sank in—Mom spent a lot of time and energy running interference for the kids with their dad, and Tyler had just taken away a lot of her power to do that.

"Still—if that's what everybody's saying," Tyler said, "they're just wrong. Period. Yeah, J.P. and I went to see the movie—back just before I went out to California."

Mom sighed. "Oh, Tyler."

"And we rode around in his mom's cruiser after we got back to town, but what's the big deal about that? No, I didn't go up to the reservoir with him that night, if he even went—I checked out and came home. What they did after that, I have no idea. But when I was with them, there was no drinking, no reservoir, nothing we couldn't do in public on Main Street on a—"

"What I heard was you and Jessica were awfully cozy—" Tyra started.

"If you didn't see it," Tyler said to her, raising his voice, "then do us all a favor and keep it to yourself. Things are confused enough around here, thanks to you, without spreading lies and rumors from a bunch of middle schoolers."

"Not just middle schoolers!" Tyra said. "I heard it from—"

"Stop it!" Mom said. "Just stop it, you two! Tyler, I want to know what's going on. This is just—this is not like you. Can't I even trust you anymore? You bring music into my home that offends my standards, that you *know* goes against everything I stand for, and you go to movies—and influence your own sister to go to movies—that expose you to all the things I would rather not see you exposed to. I said just last night I don't want any more surprises, but, believe me, I'm plenty surprised tonight, and I don't like it. Not one bit. Now can you give me any idea what's going on inside your head?"

Tyler sat back and tried to calm himself down so he could think. *Could* he tell her what was going on inside him—the changes, the questions? He had a hard time explaining it even to himself. Oh, it seemed to make sense when he was with Chaz or J.P., and if he didn't think about it too deeply it all seemed to fit. But to actually explain it . . .

"The thing is . . . ," he started, then stopped.

"We're waiting," Dad said.

Tyler closed his eyes wearily. If only Dad weren't here. "Okay, you said it yourself, Mom. You said those CDs offended your standards. All right, I understand that, and I'm sorry if you were offended. But how do I know whether they offend *my* standards? How do I even know what my standards are about content in music unless I take a look at what's out there, think about it—"

"Tyler, I think that's a cop-out," Mom said. "You didn't have any trouble knowing what your standards were when you caught Tyra listening to your CDs. Immediately you knew that those CDs violated your standards for what you wanted your little sister to listen to. Right?"

Tyler nodded slowly. True. And *River* definitely violated his standards for what he wanted his little sister to see. Painfully so. He still felt like someone had kicked him in the gut every time he thought of her sitting watching that. Funny—when he'd watched it, he'd thought of it as a movie. When he thought of her watching it, he thought of it as garbage.

He took a deep breath. Okay, try another tack.

"Okay, it's like—I mean—I want to be a musician, right? A song-writer? So I have to study what other artists are doing—other songwrit-ers, moviemakers . . . I need to figure out how they do what they do, and why. Just like a painter might have to learn to paint nudes if he's ever going to learn—like in that book *My Name Is Asher Lev*, right? About the Jewish guy? You like that book," he said to his mom, plead-ingly. But she just stared back at him.

"Tyler," Dad said, "what a load of bull. You don't know what you're talking about. You're just making this up as you go to get yourself off the hook."

"No!" Tyler said. "Really. Miller said—"

"Miller!" Dad said. "Who's Miller?"

"One of Chaz's friends, out in California. He's a musician, too. He said—"

"Tyler, Miller doesn't live here," Mom said, "and neither does Chaz. They can listen to and watch what they want. But a home has certain standards. It isn't Miller's job to set those standards for our home—it's our job," and she motioned toward herself and Dad. "Miller isn't raising our daughter. We are. So leave Miller out of this."

Tyler raised his hands in mock desperation. "First you ask me why I did it, and then you won't even listen to the answer?"

"I've had enough of this," Dad growled. "I don't *care* what your rea-sons were, frankly, Tyler. You blew it and you got caught. You, too, Tyra. So you're both grounded for two weeks."

"What!" Tyra said.

"Wait—*two weeks!*" Tyler protested.

"That's right!" Dad yelled back. "Two weeks! And if you keep it up it'll be longer—like maybe till next year. I've had a long trip, I'm tired, and I come home expecting a little peace and quiet, and what do I get? I have to run all over town looking for my missing daughter who shows up dressed like a sleaze, and I have to pull her out of some R-rated flick which, it turns out, my son influenced her to see! Two weeks, and I don't want to hear another word about it. Now I'm going upstairs and I'm going to crawl into bed and go to sleep. I only got three hours of sleep last night and I'm beat, thank you very much, not that anybody bothered to ask. So if you're going to cry about it, cry quietly. Good night." He stomped off up the stairs.

Tyra sniffled and wiped her eyes. "Mom . . . two weeks is—"

"Tyra, don't complain to me," Mom answered. "It could have been longer. Maybe it should have been. How on earth are we ever going to trust you again?"

"All right," Tyler said, "I understand that. But it's not the same thing when you're . . . I mean, I start my senior year in a couple weeks. I'll be off to college somewhere this time next year and I'll be making all my own—"

"That's next year, Tyler," Mom said. "Right now you're in high school and living at home. You need to respect the house rules. Period. Now I'm going upstairs to talk to Dad for a few minutes before he goes to sleep." She started for the stairs.

"Well," Tyra said, "could you at least ask him—"

"No!" Mom barked. "I will not ask him to shorten your punishment. You deserve what you got. Now just live with it. And do *not* push the boundaries of what that means." Her face melted into sorrow. "Oh, Tyra . . ." Her voice broke, her eyes filled once again with tears, and she ran up the stairs.

There was silence in the room for a few seconds as both of them stared after her. Then: "Nice going, hotshot," Tyler said.

"Don't even start," Tyra said, and stormed toward the stairs herself.

"And change your clothes," Tyler said when she was halfway up. "Dad was right. You look—"

She froze him with a look, half bitter anger, half little-girl hurt. Then she flounced up the stairs.

Tyler leaned back, his heart still beating fast, his mind racing with snatches of conversation from the past few minutes.

Why would you even want to go to a movie like that? And to lie to us about it . . .

You kept thinking your kids were growing up so well, and I kept telling you . . .

Tyler—what's she talking about? Have you seen The River Runs Downhill? *. . .*

I talked to Michelle Geisler and she saw you and J.P. coming out of the movie . . .

Oh, Tyler . . . This is just—this is not like you. Can't I even trust you anymore? . . .

You don't know what you're talking about. You're just making this up as you go to get yourself off the hook . . .

And the one he'd heard way too often lately, and that now kept echoing in his mind, over and over again:

You big hypocrite . . .

You big hypocrite . . .

You big hypocrite . . .

The phone rang.

Wonder if I'm grounded from the telephone too. Tyler decided to pick it up anyway. "Hello?"

"Tyler, what's going on?" Becca said, her voice concerned. "Solana said she was just going into a movie tonight when she saw your mom and dad in a big scene in the lobby of the theater with Tyra and the theater manager and everybody talking at once and your mom crying—what happened?"

Tyler sighed. What a small town. "Long story."

"Well—are you okay? Is Tyra okay? When did your dad get back into town? What was all that about?"

"Tyra got busted. No, that's not right. We both got busted. The border guards are going to show up any minute to take me back to Mexico."

"She got busted doing what, Tyler? Solana said your dad looked like he was about to punch the theater manager."

"You're not going to like it."

No answer.

"Okay," he said. "She snuck into *The River Runs Downhill.*"

Tyler heard Becca gasp, then muffled talking as she held her hand over the phone while she told the others. Then he heard them all gasp. He smiled in spite of himself. Girls. He could just see it—the fingers going up over their lips as they sucked air. Not Solana, though. If somebody wanted to see her tonsils while she gasped, then let 'em.

"Did she know you'd seen it?" Becca asked.

"She knew."

"Oh, Tyler. You must feel . . ." She let the thought dangle. More muffled conversation on the other end of the line. "So what did your dad say? Are you grounded?"

"For two weeks. Me and Tyra both."

Pause, then: "You want us to come over?"

"Please."

They were there in five minutes, Solana still in some kind of shimmery outfit that she'd apparently been wearing for her night out at the movies. There'd undoubtedly been some guy involved, and Tyler smiled wondering who it might have been and how she'd managed to ditch him. He liked the thought that she wouldn't have even hesitated to abandon her date when her friends might need her. Hannah, Becca, and Jacie all wore their grubbies. He got them sodas from the refrigerator and they all wandered into the family room. Tyler sat in the middle of the couch, with Jacie on one side of him and Solana on the other. Hannah and Becca took overstuffed chairs and leaned toward the couch.

"I guess I don't need to ask how she knew you'd seen it," Jacie said. "I've heard about it from three different people myself."

Tyler rolled his eyes and shook his head.

The girls sat quietly for a moment, then Hannah said, "Tyler—don't you think non-Christians are just looking for any little mistake Christians make so they can call us hypocrites—"

That word again. Tyler raised his hand. "Please. No sermons. I feel really bad about Tyra already. I mean, if she wanted to go to the movie, she'd have gone anyway whether I gave her an excuse or not. But I feel like I *did* give her an excuse, and that bothers me. Why should I have to live my life as if I were an eighth-grader just so I won't do anything my eighth-grade sister shouldn't do? It's not fair."

"It doesn't have anything to do with fairness," Hannah answered. "It's all about what results from our decisions. When you—"

"No, really," Tyler said. "No lectures. The last thing I need right now is a guilt trip."

"The last thing *anybody* needs is a guilt trip," Solana agreed. "And that's not what we came to do—or at least that's not what *I* came to do." She shot Hannah a warning look.

"That's right," Jacie said. "We're here because we care about you and Tyra and we want to be an icepack on the bruise, that's all. But, Tyler, it would help if we could understand some of what you've been going through in the past few weeks, because we feel like you've shut us out of much of that. And we *do* care. We love you, Ty. So come on—open up."

He looked at her, deep into her, and knew she meant what she said. "No lectures?"

"No lectures," she said.

"No sermons?"

"No sermons," Hannah sighed.

"No questions?"

No one answered. After a moment of silence, everyone laughed.

"Well, I guess I can handle a question or two," Tyler said. He took a drink of his Dr Pepper and settled back onto the couch. He smiled when Jacie and Solana settled closer to him on either side. Girls. Guys would have leaned away to gain more separation.

"I went to see that movie with J.P. because I had to know. Not just whether it was any good, but whether a good moviemaker could actually use things like nudity and profanity to accomplish a good purpose. I guess I was asking myself—does an artist, in seeking the truth, have to hold to the same moral standards as the rest of us? Or are they granted more freedom—legitimately—because of what they're doing?"

"That's situational ethics," Hannah began, but the others silenced her with a look.

"And did you find out anything?" Becca asked.

Tyler shrugged. "I don't know. It's such a can of worms. I talked about it a lot with Chaz and his group out in California, too. I mean—well, okay, think of *The River Runs Downhill*. It's one thing to say the writer and director should have the freedom to shoot nude scenes. But the actors and actresses are getting *paid* for that. How is that different from prostitution? And what about the husbands and wives of the actors—how do they feel about it? What about the strain that puts on their marriages? The more you think about it—the more problems you come up with. But . . ."

After a pause, Solana said, "But what?"

"But I felt like I . . . like . . ." Why couldn't he say what he was feeling?

"Do you really think all of those filmmakers are seeking the truth, Tyler?" Hannah asked. "Aren't a lot of them just trying to get rich by making dirty movies, and they don't care whose lives they mess up in the process?"

Becca chuckled. "Good job of sticking with the question format, Hannah. Even if it was a thinly disguised lecture."

"Well . . ." Hannah began.

Tyler laughed. "No, that's okay, Hannah. Actually, you're right. We all know that. But does that mean that that's what *all* of them are doing? Okay, here's an example. At Chaz's church out in California, I once heard the pastor use some strong language—a word my mom won't let me use—in his sermon. Right in his sermon! And then he said, 'I use the word for emphasis.' Well—was that right or wrong? It was for a good purpose. But was it wrong anyway? So . . ." He was bogging down again. How could he make them understand?

"You keep coming back to Chaz and your California trip," Jacie said. "Why don't you talk about that?"

He nodded. "Okay. I'll try. But I can't even say I've made sense of all of that in my own mind yet." He hesitated.

"Are Chaz and his friends Christians?" Hannah asked.

"No. Chaz is the only Christian in the group, and right now he's in kind of a funny place. But I thought it was great that these people were exploring art and music in every possible way, and I could—"

There was a rustle at the top of the stairs. "I thought we heard voices down here," Mom said, and she and Tyra came down. Both of them appeared to have washed their faces, and the red was gone, but their eyes were still puffy. Tyra had changed clothes and looked more like herself.

"We're sorry, Mrs. Jennings," Becca said. "Are we making too much noise? Is Mr. Jennings upstairs?"

Mom laughed. "Yes, he's upstairs, but he's dead to the world. He's not exactly a light sleeper. You'd have to set off a bomb down here to wake him up now. It's good to see you girls."

Tyra seemed shy; she didn't look at any of the girls directly, Tyler noticed. Mom guided her over to the loveseat and they sat. "You must have heard that we had a bit of a crisis here tonight," Mom said.

"Mom . . ." Tyra protested weakly. Mom put a hand on her arm.

"I was at the theater," Solana said.

Mom nodded. "I saw you." Then she laughed and winked at Solana. "I thought your date was going to die when he tried to pull you away and you elbowed him in the stomach."

"You *what*?" Becca said.

"The jerk!" Solana laughed. "I kept telling him, 'Let go! I have to find out what's going on! These are my friends!' And he kept saying, 'Come on! The movie's about to start! And I want to get some popcorn.' So finally I stuffed my ticket back in his hand and said, 'Fine! You hungry? Eat this!'"

They all laughed, imagining Solana, fire in her eyes . . .

"You were telling us about Chaz's group," Jacie prompted when the laughter died down.

"Yeah," Tyler said. "Chaz's group." Hmmm. Things felt very different now with Mom and Tyra sitting here. "Well . . . I don't know how to say it without feeling like I'm dumping on Colorado. But people out there seem to know more about what's going on. They seem more . . . sophisticated. They've read more. Seen more movies. Been to more concerts. And when they hang out and talk, which they do a lot, they aren't talking about who's dating who or what's on sale down at Cadwallader and Finch. They talk about real stuff."

He hesitated. He could tell that this wasn't sitting very well with Hannah, Jacie, Becca, and Solana. He could hear the wheels grinding in their heads: *Don't we talk about "real stuff"?*

"Do you hear what I'm saying?" he pleaded. "I needed to talk with people who actually knew about the weird kinds of music I listen to sometimes, and could tell me things I didn't know about it. People who could . . ." His voice trailed off. He looked at his mom, and she looked back. A moment passed.

"Tell you what," she said at last, patting Tyra's leg and turning toward her. "Let's you and me head down to Dairy Freez and get some nonfat French fries and a Coke. They're open late."

"I thought I was grounded," Tyra grumbled.

"When you're with your mother, you have secret powers," Mom answered. "Come, princess." She took Tyra's hand and pulled her to her feet. "We'll be back," she said to the group.

Tyler sat silently for a couple of minutes after they heard the garage door close. Finally he said, "Maybe it all comes down to Angel."

"Angel?" Jacie asked uneasily.

Tyler nodded. "Angel."

chapter 19

"So you're finally going to tell us about Angel," Solana said.

"Now I'm not sure I want to hear it," Becca said, giggling uneasily.

Tyler took a deep breath. "Angel is Chaz's age—a year ahead of me. She starts at Stanford in the fall."

"Stanford?" Jacie said.

Tyler nodded. "I told you her parents were pretty well-off. Anyway, she's drop-dead gorgeous, a good surfer—want me to go on?"

"No," Jacie said quietly.

"So we hit it off pretty well, which surprised the rest of the group because usually she tends toward friendship, not romance," Tyler said. "It was just . . . well, it was really incredible. One thing just sort of led to another. We had long, quiet talks on the beach, we surfed . . . Anyway, the last night before I came home . . ."

"You want to see my room?"

His heart leaped; he was almost afraid to test his voice. "Sure," he said.

Smiling, she held out her hand. He took it. So warm, so soft. She clung to him almost as if she were a little afraid as she led him up the stairs.

Here we go, *he thought.*

Tyler shouldn't have been surprised by the size of Angel's room, not after seeing the rest of the house, but he was. It wasn't a room; it was a suite. Bedroom, bathroom, sitting room—and all of them large. The sitting room had a large TV, DVD player, great stereo system, computer, couch . . .

Angel went first to the stereo, picked a CD, and put it on. He was surprised by her choice of music at first—mellow, more like jazz, and he didn't recognize the artist. Then she turned to him, smiled, and moved toward him, raising her arms to his shoulders. At first he thought she was going to kiss him, but she put her head against his shoulder and began to dance. "Call me corny," she said, "but I love good old-fashioned ballroom dancing. Did it with my dad when I was little."

"No, I, uh—it's not corny at all," Tyler stuttered. "I just, uh, don't know if I remember all the steps from when we learned it in gym class, so if I—"

"You're doing fine," she said. "Just relax into it and don't worry about making mistakes."

And what they mainly did wasn't really ballroom dancing anyway, Tyler knew—it was just plain old slow dancing, standing holding each other and swaying slowly to the music. But Angel didn't seem to care. In fact, she seemed more peacefully happy than she'd been all evening.

And Tyler was in no hurry for the moment to end. Her hair brushed his cheek, and he nestled into it, breathing its clean, perfumed freshness. Whatever perfume she was wearing, it was wonderful. His heart beat so powerfully he was sure she must be able to feel it.

I'm in the bedroom of a beautiful girl, slow dancing, Tyler thought. *Is this bizarre or what?* He forced himself not to ask the obvious question: what next?

What came next he would remember all his life. She slowly stopped swaying after the third or fourth cut on the CD, and just stood for a moment, one hand on his shoulder, the other hand in his, looking deeply into his eyes. Then slowly, slowly, she raised on tiptoe and kissed him gently on the lips. Her eyes closed. She held the kiss, in no hurry for it to end, and then pulled back and opened her eyes again. Her expression changed, and she looked down.

"What?" he said. "Something wrong?"

"No. No, I—not really."

Tyler lifted her chin softly, so that she looked back into his face. "Something is. What?"

She sighed. "I'm sorry, Tyler. Really. I guess singing my songs just put me in a weird mood. Let's sit down." They sat on the couch, snuggling close, his arm around her shoulder and her hand up, holding his.

"You want to know something?" she said.

"Sure."

"The things we've talked about tonight?" She gave a sad, breathy little laugh that sent shivers down Tyler's spine. "I never talk this way with anybody. What is it about you, Tyler Jennings? What makes me open up to you this way? Do you have some strange power over women?"

Now it was Tyler's turn to laugh. "Yeah, right. No, believe me, that isn't it."

She shook her head. "But there is something—there is something in you, Tyler. And you know what? Whatever it is—I wish I had it."

If anyone acknowledges that Jesus is the Son of God, God lives in him and he in God.

Tyler started. Where had those words come from? He wasn't even sure he knew what verse that was—something in 1 John, he thought.

"I'm sorry," Angel said. "Did I say something wrong?"

"Uh—no. Why?"

"You just got the funniest look on your face."

"Oh. No, I'm just—surprised. I mean, you seem to have everything. Why would you want something I've got?"

She rested her head against his chest. "Tyler, I have absolutely nothing that means anything. All that stuff we talk about with Chaz and Miller and the rest—the music, the books, the philosophy—all of that? It's just a bunch of wind to fill up the loneliness and the emptiness. The biggest idiot of them all is Miller, Tyler, because as smart as he is, he hasn't even figured that out yet. He still thinks it all means something. He'll probably be old and wrinkled before he realizes that his whole life was a waste, and then he'll sit down one day and put a bullet through his head. But you, Tyler—" She turned her head up to him. Now her face was only a couple of inches from his; he felt her breath on his face, and almost couldn't breathe himself. "You have a genuineness and a—a truthfulness in you that the rest of those guys can't even pretend to have. What is it? What do you know that none of the rest of us know?"

Then you will know the truth, and the truth will set you free.

He shook his head sharply. Where were these things coming from? And did he know the truth? Weren't many of the things Miller and Chaz were saying truth too? And weren't they living much freer lives than he did?

"There it is again," she said, touching his cheek and looking deeply into his eyes. "What is it, Tyler? What are you thinking? Share it with me."

"No, really, I don't know what I can tell you."

"Yes. There's something in there right now, I know it. You're thinking something. And I need something, anything—I'm about to get on the plane to go to Europe with my kind but scatterbrained aunt, and she'll be yakking in my ear the whole way over there about our alien ancestors who landed in UFOs when the earth was just a ball of rock, or some stupid thing, and I need something solid to help me keep my sanity. So please, Tyler." She stroked his cheek; her lips were so close to his now they were almost touching. "Please give me something—a thought, a little bit of hope, some wisdom—anything. As long as it's something real, something that'll last, and not just hot air."

Heaven and earth will pass away, but my words will never pass away.

Tyler stroked her hair, looked into her eyes, then drew her head toward him and kissed her forehead. "I wish I could." *But if I tell you what I really believe—about the Bible, about Jesus, about God, then you'll think I'm just one of those crazy Christians and you won't want anything more to do with me. Sure, you say you want what I have. But when I tell you what it is, I can just imagine how the light of trust and friendship in your eyes will fade and die and you'll say you're tired and it's time to call it a night. I've seen it happen before. And I don't want it to happen with you, Angel.*

She pulled back again, looked deep into his eyes. "You can."

He shook his head. "I don't know what you mean."

She nodded. "You do. You have to. Tyler, everybody in the world I live in, the world of my parents' friends, the university, Miller, Zack, all of them—that world is dead. But there's something in you—" She tapped his chest gently but insistently with her fingertips. "Something in here—that's alive. And I desperately need something like that."

For God so loved the world . . .

He brushed back her hair from her forehead. "Hey. Come on. It's not so bad. How many people would be complaining about their life just before they get on a plane to go to Europe?"

. . . that he gave his one and only Son . . .

She cocked her head, tried to look happier. "It does sound dumb, doesn't it?" But her face fell again, and he watched her eyes fill with tears. "But it isn't dumb. I know what I feel, Tyler. It's something my shrink has never been able to touch. Something none of my friends have ever been able to touch, and that my parents have never even tried to. Music expresses it—but it can't heal it. And now if you're telling me you can't either . . ."

. . . that whoever believes in him . . .

Tyler nodded his head. Yes, he knew what she wanted. She couldn't have made it any clearer. But suppose he spoke—and she rejected it, as he was sure she would? What would happen when she told Miller and Chaz and the rest what he'd said? What would happen next summer when he came out? They'd want nothing to do with him.

. . . shall not perish . . .

She put her head against his chest again, and he felt the wetness of her tears soak through his shirt. "I'm dying, Tyler," she said. "Drying up inside." Her shoulders heaved once, twice, and then she was weeping against him. "I've tried everything," she gasped, "and nothing satisfies. Nothing! It's all—it's all meaningless. And if you can't help me . . ."

. . . but have eternal life.

Tyler held her closer, trying to calm her. But the uneasiness inside him was growing greater even as her sobs were beginning to subside. Who *was* he? This girl had asked him for help—help he'd have tried to provide a month ago, help he'd spent much of the summer trying to provide for people in Venezuela. Why was his tongue tied now? What did he really want?

But whoever disowns me before men, I will disown him before my Father in heaven.

The thought struck Tyler with such power that he jumped on the couch. Was that what he'd done? Surely not!

Angel, still red-eyed and hiccuping, looked up sharply. "What is it? Did I hurt you?"

"No, I—I just . . ." But he couldn't just blab out the plan of salvation here to this girl—could he? It would sound so simplistic, so foolish, compared with everything else they'd been discussing for the past two weeks. Just two days before, they'd been sitting on the beach discussing philosophers like Nietzsche and Kierkegaard. How would she react? No. No, he couldn't. But that didn't mean—

"Tyler, I'm sorry about all this. I really am." She stood up, then took his hands and pulled him to his feet. "I know I look really bad, too—probably my makeup's all smeared, my face all red." She began to move slowly backward, gently pulling him toward the door to her bedroom.

He looked over her shoulder, saw the outline of her canopy bed beyond the door. There was a soft, flickering light—a candle.

"I feel bad about how the night turned out," she whispered. "Let me show you—"

"Angel." He stopped his feet, tugged gently on her hands so that she would stop as well. He lifted her hands to his lips and kissed her fingertips. "I appreciate it. I really do. And the night hasn't been bad at all."

Her eyes welled up again. "You don't mean that."

He nodded vigorously. "I do. You are—you are the most beautiful girl I've ever known. And there's so much to you, inside and out. I just regret that we're both going in different directions tomorrow."

She stepped closer, touched his face. "Will I see you again?"

"Yes—sure, of course. Somehow. I want to."

"Write to me, Tyler. E-mail—remember, I can read it on my cell phone. And Europe is full of cyber-cafés, where I can shoot you back a reply. Okay? Please? I want to hear from you. I *need* to hear from you. There's so much you didn't say tonight—I know it. I just know it. I could see it in your eyes. And I want to know what it was. *Please* write."

"I will. I promise."

Her lips trembled, and she covered her mouth with her fingertips—then leaned quickly forward, kissed him gently on the mouth, and turned and fled into her room, closing the door behind her.

He nearly fell going down the stairs.

The streetlights were ghostly in the fog as he walked back to Chaz's house, and sound was strangely deadened. And the eerie atmosphere matched his mood perfectly.

What just happened back there? *Tyler asked himself. And he had no answers. Whoever he had been there, it hadn't seemed like Tyler. It had been somebody he didn't even know.*

He hurried along the sidewalk, but the look on her face, the pain in her voice—these would be things he would not forget. They would haunt him. He knew it . . .

chapter 20

No one spoke for five minutes after he finished. Tyler wiped his eyes and blew his nose on a tissue from the box Jacie had fetched from the bathroom. He looked up and grinned miserably. Each of the four girls was wiping her own tears. "This is embarrassing," he said.

"Not in front of us it isn't," Becca said, waving her tissue.

He shifted on the couch, causing Solana and Jacie to adjust their positions too, they sat so close to him. "So that's it," he said. "I had what she needed. What she was asking for. And I didn't say a word, because—because I'm a jerk. Because I was a whole lot more aware of her beautiful body in that little sundress than I was of the need in her soul. And because I was afraid of what she would think. And of what Chaz and Miller and Zack and the rest would think, too—just because they happen to know a lot about music and movies. What a ridiculous, stupid—"

"No, Tyler, stop," Becca said. "Don't be so hard on yourself. You know what I thought you were going to tell us? That you went to bed with her."

He nodded. "You know what? I probably could have. Of course it would have been wrong. But considering who I was that night, I'm not sure why I didn't. I could have. And anyway, what I did was worse, I think."

"That poor girl," Solana said. "You were right, Tyler—even though she's rich, I feel for her. I kind of thought she'd be like Jessica, but she's not. She's more like me." Solana was leaning against him now, and Jacie sat close on the other side, her arm through his.

"The thing is," he said, "I feel like an absolute spiritual failure. Like I'm a complete disappointment to God. Like I disowned Him."

"Tyler," Hannah began, then stopped. She waved her hands in frustration. "I'm afraid to say anything! I'm afraid you'll think I'm trying to—"

"No, go ahead," Tyler said. "I want to know what you think."

Now she looked unsure of herself. "I haven't thought it all through yet," she said, "but you know the verses in John that talk about being *in* the world, but not *of* the world? It sounds to me as if you've been getting awfully close to being *of* the world. You know? So without your Christian friends around you, and your Christian music, and Allen, and instead finding yourself surrounded by people who had completely different values—you didn't have anybody to hold you accountable, anybody to influence you in the *right* way. Tell me—do you really think the people you were spending time with out there were people who brought out the *best* Tyler?"

Tyler thought about the discussions he'd had with Chaz and Angel and the rest. They had stretched him, made him think, lifted him to a higher place intellectually and artistically. But did that make him a better person?

Jacie nodded. "I think you're right, Hannah. Tyler, Angel needed you to be at the very top level of who you can be. So you could resist the wrong and replace it with the right. And you're a good enough Christian that you *could* have done that for her—when you're at your best. But none of us is strong enough to stand up to that kind of temptation, that kind of confusion, on our own. That's why we need to stick together."

Tyler nodded. "You know what?" He looked around the room at each of the four of them and grinned crookedly. "I'm my best self when I'm with you."

They all sat silently for a moment, letting that sink in. Then Solana leaned forward, grabbed a tissue out of the box, and pressed it against her face. "That's the nicest thing anyone's ever said to me," she said, and no one laughed.

"So," Becca said. "What you were doing out there in California, all those discussions, all that—was that wrong?"

"I don't think it's a question of was it right or wrong, black or white," Tyler said. "It's like Hannah said—a matter of what it encouraged in me. The best? Or did it displace the best and replace it with something less? And I hate to admit it, but I think the answer's pretty obvious. And you know what else?"

Becca shook her head. "What?"

"Chaz," Tyler said. "He's been on the same path I was heading down. And he's been there a lot longer. And now that we're sitting here talking about this, I can see the result of all that, as plain as day. Last summer he was involved in a Christian youth group, hanging out with Christian friends, listening to Christian music, thinking like a Christian. This year all that's changed. All of it. It wasn't because he had non-Christian friends, and it wasn't because he was listening to some non-Christian music. It was that he made a shift in what influenced him; he started to let the world's culture influence him more than his Christian friends influenced him. Now he's pretty much turned his back on his faith. At least on the outside."

Jacie gripped his arm tighter. "You have to talk to him."

Tyler grimaced. "I don't think he'll listen. He's pretty—"

Jacie gave him a look. "Tyler. It's *his* responsibility what he *does* with it. It's your responsibility to *say* it."

Tyler nodded thoughtfully.

"And there's somebody else you have to talk to, too," Solana said.

Tyler looked at her blankly.

"*Angel!*" Solana insisted.

"Angel," Tyler repeated. "I've completely blown it with Angel. I mean, I had the perfect chance, and I blew it."

Solana shook her head. "Tyler. Is she *dead?* Is there something you haven't told us?"

Tyler chuckled. "Not that I know of. As far as I know, she's off in Europe somewhere."

"And able to retrieve your e-mail with her cell phone—hey!" Becca said. "Why don't you just call her? Call her right now! We'll help you know what to—"

Tyler waved the idea off. "No. I don't really trust myself to be able to handle that discussion well. I would need to think it through ahead of time to come up with the right words. Besides, it's the middle of the night over there."

"Okay, then, *e-mail* the poor girl!" Solana said. "Tomorrow morning at the very latest. Don't put it off, Tyler, you turkey, or you'll never do it."

"Solana," Hannah said, "I just can't believe . . ." Her voice trailed off.

"Can't believe *what?*" Solana said.

"I can't believe you're insisting that Tyler e-mail this girl immediately to tell her about Christ. I mean, I could see it if you were a believer. But why are *you* so insistent that Tyler—well—evangelize her?"

"Because the poor girl's crying out for help!" Solana said, exasperated. "If she were thirsty, I'd be telling him to give her some water, wouldn't I? Well, her thirst is in her soul."

The others all looked at each other. "Wow," Becca said finally. "Solana. Wow."

"But I agree with you completely, Solana," Hannah said. "He needs to e-mail her right away, and tell her everything she was asking him to tell her out in California. He needs to be light! And salt! That's what we're called to do. She's in a dark place in her life. Tyler can light it up—with the light of the world."

Tyler laughed.

"What?" Hannah said.

"I just think—well, it seems odd that you and Solana are the ones telling me to witness to Angel. Hannah, I would think that you would want me to keep away from Angel and everything she stands for, lest I be polluted by the world, or something like that."

She pointed at him. "You almost were. Right? And anyway, I learned a lot of things on the missions trip this summer. I learned that God has His own way of doing things. He's bigger than our circumstances—any circumstances. Even Angel's. He can still touch her and heal her. And He can even use you to do it, Tyler. Think of that."

"Even Tyler. Wow," Becca said.

"What a God we serve," Jacie said. "He can use the foolish things of the world to confound the wise—"

"Okay, okay," Tyler said. "I get the point."

The door from the garage into the kitchen opened, and Tyler heard footsteps and the rattle of grocery bags. Tyler hadn't even heard the garage door, he'd been so involved in the discussion. Quickly, he wiped his face to make sure there was no sign of tears left.

Mom and Tyra wandered in from the kitchen, their arms around each other. Tyler was glad to see that they'd worked through the feelings left over from their argument. "My, what a somber group," Mom said. "But I've got just the thing for you: How about a sundae party?"

Becca hopped up. "Perfect, Mrs. J! Hope you got bananas!"

"What would a sundae be without bananas?" Mom replied.

"And nuts," Tyra said.

"Marshmallow crème," Mom said, crooking a finger to beckon them into the kitchen.

"Caramel and strawberry and chocolate syrup," Tyra said.

"Three flavors of ice cream," Mom said.

"Don't forget the sauerkraut," Tyler said, following the others into the kitchen.

Ten minutes later, they all leaned over the kitchen counter, shoulder to shoulder, shoveling their gloopy, drippy sundaes into their mouths. Mom was on one side of Tyler, Jacie on the other.

"So," his mom probed. "You guys have a good chat? I couldn't tell when we got home whether it had gone well or you'd just heard that somebody's dog died."

"No, it was a good chat," Tyler said.

"Very good chat," Jacie nodded, squeezing his arm.

"Glad to hear it," she said. "I want a complete report from all of you, in writing, on my desk by ten o'clock tomorrow morning."

"Can't do it, Mrs. J," Becca said, her mouth full of ice cream. "We have to go help Mrs. Peterson with her senior citizen sing-along thing at the Community Center tomorrow."

"Oh, wonderful," Mom said. "I think it's great that she's doing that. Hey—Tyra. You want to go along?"

Tyra rolled her eyes.

"I think I can get a special dispensation for you to leave the house for that," Mom coaxed. "Otherwise, think about it—grounded, stuck in the house all day Saturday, your dad grumping around—"

"I'll go," Tyra said quickly.

Tyler dug in. He'd loaded his bowl up with chocolate ice cream and every topping on the table, with bananas sliced over the top. He relished every mouthful—until, halfway done, he suddenly realized that no one was talking. He looked up. Every pair of eyes around the table was focused on him.

"*What!*" he asked.

Becca cocked an eyebrow at him.

"No," he said, "Come on. Not that. Didn't we talk about that already?"

"I don't think we ever got a firm answer on that," Becca said. "Did we, Jacie?"

"You might have to forget it anyway, girls," Mom said quietly. "Remember—Tyler's grounded."

Tyler looked up sharply. "*I'm* grounded? What about her?" He poked his spoon toward Tyra, who stuck out her tongue at him. "She's going!"

"Well, I said I thought I could get a special dispensation for her. Not sure I can get one for you." Mom stuck a spoonful of ice cream in her mouth.

"What? Why her and not me?"

"Well . . ."

"That's not fair! If I have to stay home, she should have to stay home. And if she gets to go, then I should go too!"

Mom dropped her spoon back into the bowl with a clatter. "Very well, Tyler," she sighed dramatically. "You win. You can help Mrs. Peterson in the morning too."

"Darn tootin'," Tyler said. "If she—hey, wait."

Hannah stifled a giggle. Becca said, "Well, great, Tyler. Just be ready when I show up for Tyra in the morning and I'll escort you too. And hey—maybe you should bring your guitar."

"Bring my guitar? Are you kidding? I don't even know half those songs, and besides, I don't *want* to play along with the rumba queen. It's bad enough having to show up and sing "Red River Valley" and pour Kool-Aid. If I have to—"

"Tyler," Jacie said sweetly, pulling closer to him.

"No! Really! I don't want—"

"What a big, kind, strong boy you are," Mom said, sounding embarrassingly close to baby talk as she pulled him into a hug on the other side.

"Group hug!" Becca yelled, coming around the counter.

"No—wait! Listen—" Tyler protested.

"I'm not hugging him!" Tyra said.

"You can hug me," Hannah said, "and then we'll both hug the rest of them."

"Okay."

And suddenly he was completely engulfed in feminine arms, faces pressed against his chest and shoulders and back. Hmm. Maybe being ganged up on wasn't so bad, even though he continued halfheartedly to protest, "What is this? Let go of me."

Well, maybe I could manage to limp through a few of those songs on my guitar tomorrow, he admitted.

Guess I'm back home.

And it isn't a bad place to be.

chapter 21

You are my sunshine,
My only sunshine

Mrs. Peterson poked a button or two on the organ she played, and suddenly the tempo of the canned percussion jumped awkwardly. Grinning, Tyler adjusted the rhythm he strummed until he matched the new tempo. At least for now.

What would his friends think if someone videotaped this shameful performance and passed bootleg copies around school? He actually scanned the rows of happy-faced singers in front of him to make sure he didn't see any camcorders.

Then he laughed at himself. What was he talking about? His best friends were already here.

You make me happy
When skies are gray

There were Hannah and Becca, with Tyra between them. Jacie sat a row farther back, with Mr. Gallagher, who was too weak to hold up his own songbook. Becca looked up at him, and Tyler rolled his eyes at her. She smiled back and gave him a thumbs-up. That must be for his willingness to play, he decided; it certainly wasn't for the music.

You'll never know, dear,
How much I love you
Please don't take my sunshine away

Mrs. Peterson rushed immediately into a polka-like version of "This World Is Not My Home," and Tyler sat out a measure or two until he could understand her rhythm and tempo, then joined in.

"Why do you choose the particular songs you do?" Tyler had asked hesitantly that morning while he was tuning his guitar and she was telling him, in rapid-fire, nonstop fashion, which songs they'd be playing that morning for everyone to sing.

"Oh, I know you young ones don't like these songs much," Mrs. Peterson had laughed, waving a hand at him. "Some of these songs are older than I am! I guess you must think they're pretty old-fashioned."

"Well—no—"

"Oh yes you do!" she had laughed. "You don't have to mince words around me, Tyler Jennings. I saw you boys laughing at my songs a few weeks ago; don't think I didn't. But there's a method to my madness. For one thing, I want to get these old folks to have a good time singing silly old songs that they know and love and that remind them of when they were young. That relaxes them. Makes them open up just a little. So when we sing the spiritual songs at the end, they'll listen more, maybe actually allow God to speak to them.

"Now for you and your friends, 'Let Me Call You Sweetheart' wouldn't work that way. But it does for old Mr. Gallagher. Did you know he's been a committed *non*believer all of his life. A few years ago he wouldn't have been caught dead in a room where Christian songs were being sung. And now here he is, singing right along with us. Don't you think that's just amazing? I do."

Tyler had nodded. Yes, he could see that. Just like Christian rock groups used their sound to gain a hearing for the Gospel. "But—why do you choose the Christian songs you do? I know a lot of new ones that you might—"

She laughed. "Oh, bless you, Tyler. Yes, I know the new ones too. We sing them in church on Sunday mornings, and I sing right along with everybody else. And some of them are wonderful. But you know what? Some of the great old ones just don't get sung enough any more. And they have such beautiful meaning. Just listen, Tyler:

Turn your eyes upon Jesus, she sang in her quavery alto.
Look full in his wonderful face
And the things of earth will grow strangely dim
In the light of his glory and grace.

She sang it slowly, eyes closed, as if she had all the time in the world and wanted to savor every word. There were tears glistening in her eyes when she opened them again. "Oh, Tyler, how can I *not* sing a song like that? Do you hear how much truth is there, Tyler? Do you? Maybe it means more to me than it does to you because the things of earth are *already* growing dim to me, and it won't be long before I really and truly *will* turn my eyes upon Jesus. And for all the beautiful new songs we sing in church these days, Tyler, that's one that just doesn't get sung enough. So we sing it here, along with all the other beautiful old-timey songs all us old folks grew up singing. I can't resist. Now—stop getting me sidetracked and let's get ready to sing!"

The angels beckon me from heaven's open door
And I can't feel at home in this world anymore.

Tyler strummed a strong chord or two to give it a sense of finality because he sensed that Mrs. Peterson was drawing this session to a close. She gave an awkward run up the organ keys, missing about half the notes. *Her hands are tired*, Tyler realized. *She's playing even worse now than when we started.* Sure enough, when she lifted her fingers from the keys, she slowly brought her hands together and began to knead them as if they were sore. He noticed for the first time that her fingers were crooked, and that the knuckles appeared swollen. He leaned forward slightly to get a better look at her face; it seemed drawn and tense, as if she were fighting pain.

But that look disappeared as she called out to those sitting in the rows facing her. "That's all for today!" she cried merrily.

"How about 'Tumblin' Tumbleweeds'?" someone yelled.

Please, Tyler thought. *Not 'Tumblin' Tumbleweeds.'*

"Oh, now, Carl," Mrs. Peterson laughed. "You ask for that one every week! Besides, my fingers are tired. We'll sing it next week. Right now we have some lovely refreshments that the young people have fixed up for us, so let's haul our tired old bones over to the refreshment table and dig in!"

Tyler packed his guitar up while the old folks were getting stiffly to their feet and shuffling toward the table Hannah and Jacie and Tyra and Becca were now standing behind, ready to pass out cookies, coffee, and Kool-Aid.

"Tyler, I'm so glad you brought your guitar today," Mrs. Peterson's voice said right behind him.

He zipped up his gig bag and stood. "You bet, Mrs. Peterson. Glad to do it." Well, not exactly true. At least not when he'd pedaled grump-ily down here this morning. But the truth was, it hadn't been half bad.

"Oh, I know you had much better things to do this morning, you and your lovely young friends, so I appreciate it all the more."

"Oh, it really wasn't anything, Mrs. Peterson," Tyler said, wondering what he'd have been doing if he'd stayed home instead, grounded as he was. Watching Saturday morning cartoons? "Not like you. How long have you been doing this, anyway?"

She looked confused. "Doing this? You mean leading this group here at the Community Center?"

He shrugged. "Or any group. How long have you been leading people in worship music?"

"Oh, my." She looked thoughtful. "I started playing piano at our church when I was fifteen. I've done that for the churches I attended most of the time since. Plus I sang with a traveling evangelistic group for many years—oh, heavens, that was exciting! So many people came to know Him! When I married, my husband was a composer of Christian music—cantatas, choral music, and so on. I helped him by arranging much of his music, and we traveled around the country giving concerts, introducing his new compositions, conducting choirs. Oh, my, Tyler, I can't remember everything we did. But I guess I've been doing it for sixty years."

Tyler couldn't grasp it. "Sixty years."

"Yes, although of course it doesn't seem like that long—you'll understand what I mean when you get to my age. But I've been privileged, Tyler, to be allowed to serve Him in little ways like this for a long time now, and I'll keep on doing it as long as I live and breathe."

Sixty years.

Ruefully, Tyler remembered the things he'd said about Mrs. Peterson and her Saturday morning sing-alongs when they'd been here a few weeks before:

Is it her dynamite keyboard work, or those screamin' vocals? You know, the Spice Girls disbanded. Maybe she should—

When she launched into "The Old Rugged Cross" with that crazy beat, I was biting my tongue, and my lips, and my hand, and my toes—anything to keep from laughing!

Her music was—"out of it" doesn't even come close. It wasn't just that the songs were old—I like a lot of old songs. She was—they were—hopeless.

Oh, yeah, he'd been hilarious, all right. And she'd been serving God with her music for sixty years . . .

She reached up and patted his cheek with a dry, trembling hand. "Oh, Tyler," she said with joy. "You'll do great things for Him. I just know it." She stroked his hair away from his forehead. "I *know* it. I just have a feeling about you."

He took her two hands in his. "Thank you, Mrs. Peterson. Coming from you, that means a lot."

"Tyler!" Tyra yelled. "We need more Kool-Aid!"

"Oh, my," Mrs. Peterson said. "It's a privilege to serve people, and we don't want to sleep through our moments of opportunity. We'd better get moving!"

"I'm on it," Tyler said, giving Tyra a cold glance and wondering why she couldn't make more Kool-Aid herself. Then he realized that she'd probably seen him getting pats from Mrs. Peterson and thought he needed rescuing.

We don't want to sleep through our moments of opportunity—is that what she'd said? Well, that sounded like what he'd been doing, ever since he got back from the missions trip.

He slapped his cheek—hard. *Wake up, Tyler! You dropped the ball with Chaz, and with Angel and J.P. and Tyra. They needed you to serve them, and instead you served yourself. But it's not too late to change all that—now get on the stick, Bozo!*

He looked up as he marched toward the kitchen—and Hannah, Jacie, and Becca were all looking at him as if he'd lost his mind.

He shook his head, laughing. "I didn't lose it—I think I just *found* it!" he hollered, and trotted into the kitchen to make some Kool-Aid.

● ● ●

so there you have it, he concluded his e-mail to Angel that night.

i should have said all of this to you that night, but i was too confused and selfish and self-centered and—yeah, okay, you were beautiful and i was payin a lot more attention to how you looked than to what i should be sayin. plus—and this is a big one—i was afraid of what you would think of me after.

hate to admit it, but i'm still afraid of what you'll think. i'm on the verge of beggin you not to despise me now that you know that i'm one of those "christians." but you know what? i'm not gonna beg you. i'm just gonna tell you the truth. after that, whatever happens happens. if you hate me, you hate me.

reach out and take it, angel. he loves you more than anybody ever has. you want love? he's got it. you want a family? he's got one for you. you want purpose and direction, instead of the emptiness you see in miller and the rest? he's got that for you too. i know it doesn't make sense to you now—but please, please don't turn away. let the truth of what i'm sayin soak into you until you can begin to see the God behind it.

a very wise old woman said something to me today: *we don't want to sleep through our moments of opportunity.* this is yours, angel. you remember tellin me about all that pain you feel, and how nobody can do anything about it? don't let it all go to waste. this is your moment of opportunity. grab it. and if you do, you'll never look back.

that same wise old woman said something else to me today—and now i say it about you. *you'll do great things for him. i just have a feeling about you.* i really do.

will the angel who comes home from europe be the same angel who went there? here's what i'm prayin—that the one who comes home will be an angel filled with peace and with god's love.

and that's what i should have said.

tyler

Check Out Focus on the Family's

The Christy Miller Series

Teens across the country adore Christy Miller! She has a passion for life, but goes through a ton of heart-wrenching circumstances. Though the series takes you to a fictional world, it gives you plenty of "food for thought" on how to handle tough issues as they come up in your

The Nikki Sheridan Series

An adventurous spirit leads Nikki Sheridan, an attractive high school junior, into events and situations that will sweep you into her world and leave you begging for the next book in this captivating, six-book set!

Sierra Jensen Series

The best-selling author of The Christy Miller Series leads you through the adventures of Sierra Jensen as she faces the same issues that you do as a teen today. You'll devour every exciting story, and she'll inspire you to examine your own life and make a deeper commitment to Christ!

Mind Over Media: The Power of Making Sound Entertainment Choices

You can't escape the ideas and images that come from the media, but you *can* weed through the bad and grasp the good! This video uses an exciting, MTV-style production to dissolve the misconceptions people have about the media. The companion book uses humor, questions, facts and stories to help you take charge of what enters your mind and then directs your actions.

Life on the Edge—Live!

This award-winning national radio call-in show gives teens like you something positive to tune in to every Saturday night. You'll get a chance to talk about the hottest issues of your generation—no topic is off-limits! See if it airs in your area by visiting us on the Web at www.lifeontheedgelive.com.

Cool Stuff on Hot Topics!

My Truth, Your Truth, Whose Truth?

Who's to say what's right and wrong? This book shatters the myth that everything is relative and shows you the truth about absolute truth! It *does* matter . . . and is found only in Christ! Understand more about this hot topic in the unique video *My Truth, Your Truth, Whose Truth?*

No Apologies: The Truth About Life, Love and Sex

Read the truth about sex—the side of the story Hollywood doesn't want you to hear—in this incredible paperback featuring teens who've made decisions about premarital sex. You'll learn you're worth the wait. Discover more benefits of abstinence in the video *No Apologies: The Truth About Life, Love and Sex.*

Masquerade

In this hard-hitting, 30-minute video, popular youth speaker Milton Creagh uses unrehearsed footage of hurting teens to "blow the cover" off any illusions that even casual drug use is OK.

The Ultimate Baby-sitter's Survival Guide

Want to become everyone's favorite baby-sitter? This book is packed with practical information. It also features an entire section of safe, creative and downright crazy indoor and outdoor activities that will keep kids challenged, entertained and away from the television.

Dare 2 Dig Deeper Girl's Package

Have you been looking for info on the issues you deal with? Yeah, that's what we thought. So we put some together for you from our popular Dare 2 Dig Deeper booklets with topics that are for girls only, such as: friendship, sexual abuse, eating disorders and purity. Set includes: *Beyond Appearances, A Crime of Force, Fantasy World, Forever, Friends, Hold On to Your Heart* and *What's the Alternative?*

**Visit us on the Web at
www.family.org or www.fotf.ca in Canada.**

PREFER TO USE A CREDIT CARD?
1-800-A-FAMILY
1 - 8 0 0 - 2 3 2 - 6 4 5 9

IN CANADA
1-800-661-9800
CALL US TOLL-FREE

ARE YOU READY TO LIVE LIFE ON THE EDGE?

At Focus on the Family, we are committed to helping you learn more about Jesus Christ and preparing you to change your world for Him! We realize the struggles you face are different from your mom's or your little brother's, so Focus on the Family has developed a ton of stuff specifically for you! They'll get you ready to boldly live out your faith no matter what situation you find yourself in.

We don't want to tell you what to do. We want to encourage and equip you to be all God has called you to be in every aspect of life! That may involve strengthening your relationship with God, solidifying your values and perhaps making some serious change in your heart and mind.

We'd like to come alongside you as you consider God's role in your life, discover His plan for you in the lives of others and how you can impact your generation to change the world.

We have conferences, Web sites, magazines, palm-sized topical booklets, fiction books, a live call-in radio show . . . all dealing with the topics and issues that you deal with and care about. For a more detailed listing of what we have available for you, visit our Web site at www.family.org. Then click on "Resources," followed by either "Teen Girls" or "Teen Guys."

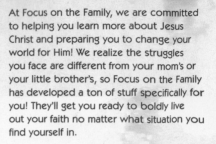

TRYING TO REACH US?

In the United States:
Focus on the Family
Colorado Springs, CO 80995

Call 1-800-A-FAMILY
(1-800-232-6459)

In Canada:
Focus on the Family
P.O. Box 9800
Stn. Terminal
Vancouver B.C. V6B 4G3

Call 1-800-661-9800

To find out if there is an associate office in your country, visit our Web site:

www.family.org

WE'D LOVE TO HEAR FROM YOU!

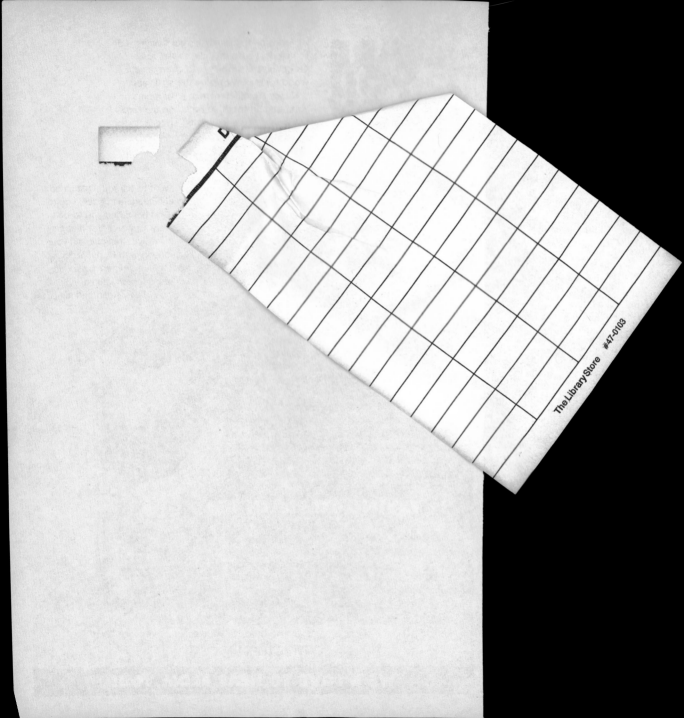